BRUTAL BEDTIME STORIES

HORROR STORIES

This is a work of fiction. Names, characters, businesses, places, events and incidents are either the products of the author's imagination or used in a fictitious manner. Any resemblance to actual persons, living or dead, or actual events is purely coincidental.

Brutal Bedtime Stories
Second Edition November 2018

READ MORE HORROR

Read more horror from Haunted House Publishing
and download a **FREE BOOK!**

TobiasWade.Com

CONTENTS

WELCOME TO HELL, PLEASE TAKE A NUMBER

WELCOME TO HELL, PLEASE TAKE A NUMBER

DAVID MALONEY

WHEN MOST PEOPLE THINK OF DEMON POSSESSION, THEY picture the classic projectile vomiting, head spinning around variety. While that does happen, it's mostly novice demons that cause that, the vomiting and abnormal behaviour being a result of the host's mind rejecting the possession. In reality, most demon possessions are a lot more subtle.

They're the little voice that tells you that you're fine to drive when you know you've had too much, or that you can cheat on your wife just this once and no one will ever find out. Or, if you've ever known someone with Alzheimer's who got really mean towards the end, you're like as not looking at the work of a demon.

Dementia demons are mostly inexperienced rookies though. They do it because old broken minds don't fight back, so it's pretty much impossible to screw up. And if you're in Hell you want good stats on your first possession, otherwise you'll get kicked right to the back of the line and you won't see another chance for thousands of years.

Oh yeah, the line. Everybody in hell gets a number in the line, and the more evil you do with each possession, the better your place in line. So if you're lucky enough to get a possession, you'd better wreak havoc and try not to get exorcised or killed. It used to be hell trying to keep track of the paperwork of who went where, but things are running a lot more smoothly with the new computer system. We're still way behind earth technology of course—we don't get a lot of computer engineers down here for some reason. We've got plenty of salespeople though.

But before you can even hop in the line, you've got to go through what basically amounts to demon college. They call it a college, but it's really more like those corporate training seminars they have in America. Satan wanted it to be soul crushing, after-all.

Most of the introductory stuff is boring, like how to take control of the mind of your victim. That really is the foundation for everything though, because if you can't do that your victim's mind will kick you right out and you'll be back in Hell, at the back of the line with a failure of possession charge on your record. And you definitely don't want that.

The advanced stuff is where it gets more interesting, and that's where you get to choose a specialty. Most people go into Addiction, because it's one of the easiest majors and you get a reasonable amount of time before your host OD's or just gets used up. Some people go into Mental Illness, but that can get you institutionalized, and you don't really get to have fun with your new body if you're stuck in a padded room all day. There's also a dictator class–Professor Hitler teaches that one. But not many people take it. Not only is it impractical, Hitler always ends up going on some tangential rant about Jews at the end of class. We get it Hitler, you don't like Jews.

Professor Bundy's class is pretty popular though. There are a lot of wannabe serial killers in Hell, and it gives amazing stats if you can pull it off on earth. Ten or more victims and you're allowed to jump the line and possess another body without going back to Hell first.

The last thing you should know about demon possession is how it happens. After all, you wanna avoid it if you can. The most common is Ouija board use. People will accidentally summon up a demon, and by letting it control their hands they allow their consciousness to overlap. The demon sneaks in through that window. If it's a particularly talented demon it can fragment its consciousness and possess everyone with their hands on the board. The same thing can happen with séances. Most demons will choose the weakest link, but some will be able to possess everyone in the room.

Anyway, I'm afraid this is where my story ends. My host body is dying and typing is getting pretty exhausting. But before I leave you there's one more thing I want to tell you. The most ancient and skilled demons only need a tiny overlap in consciousness to possess you. They may only need to converse with you for a moment, or even just trick you into reading something they've written. Maybe a story that distracts you just long enough for them to slip in unnoticed. You may feel uneasy or paranoid when it happens, or you may feel nothing at all.

How do you feel now?

HOW THE SCARECROW DIED

DAVID MALONEY

JOSH WAS ONE OF THOSE KIDS WHO WAS JUST BORN TO BE A bully. He was built more like a gorilla than a human teenager, and he had the disposition of a rabid Rottweiler.

There are a lot of different ways to bully someone, and Josh was an expert in all of them. He stole lunch money, shoved heads in toilets, beat kids up and even pinched girls asses in the hallways. But the thing that really made Josh born to be a bully was his dad.

The man looked like an even bigger, uglier version of Josh, and he basically owned the small town we all lived in. He seemed to think that he owned the people too.

If somebody pointed out that Josh shouldn't slap girls' asses in the hallway, you can bet a few phone calls later that person would be out of a job thanks to Josh's daddy dearest.

To this day I sometimes wonder if the horrible events that would forever besmirch our town's history could have been avoided if someone had just held him accountable. But nobody ever did, so I guess I'll never know.

The thing that started it was something simple: Josh took a special interest in making one particular kid's life miserable. Little Billy Johnston was just too easy of a target: he was skinny, pale, and kids called him "the scarecrow" because of the patches in his clothes.

Of course, it wasn't Billy's fault that his mom was poor and couldn't afford new clothes, but you know how cruel kids can be when someone's different.

Myself, I always just called him Billy.

Every day Josh would call out to Billy in the halls: "Hey scarecrow! Come over here so I can beat the stuffing out of you!" He thought this joke was so clever that he repeated it every single day, and if Billy didn't laugh, then he'd end up with his head stuck in a toilet.

Things went on like that for a while.

Nobody seemed to bother sticking up for Billy, and his overlarge clothes hid the scars that had begun to grow like tree roots down his arms. I never understood why the people this world spits on always end up punishing themselves more, but I guess that's just how it goes.

Billy eventually shut down entirely.

He wouldn't talk to anyone, wouldn't look you in the eye; the kid was scared of his own shadow. We all thought things couldn't possibly get any worse, but I guess fate didn't really care too much for our ideas. That week Billy's mom died, and within a few days the whole town knew that she'd been found with a needle in her arm.

If that was cause for a reprieve, then Josh didn't see it.

Rather, he thought the opposite; his prey was wounded, and now was the time to move in for the kill.

"I heard about how your mom died," he'd hiss under his breath when there were no teachers around, "wish I'd have found her. Your mom was a nice piece of ass for a smack-head."

"You're living with your grandma now, aren't you? Maybe I'll pay her a visit tonight. I don't think she'd put up much of a fight."

Nobody seemed to notice as the gashes on Billy's arms spread to his chest and his legs, or how his face would twitch whenever Josh's insults echoed behind his eyes.

Nobody noticed that he'd started writing in his diary about how much he'd like to steal his dead grandpa's gun and put an end to things his way.

Sometimes you'll see a story about a kid like Billy on the news and wonder how nobody stepped in, how nobody saw what was going on in their head. The answer to that is simple: it's just easier to look away.

The uglier the truth is, the more people don't want to face it because then they'll have to ask themselves why they did nothing for so long.

The last day before it happened Josh had cornered Billy after school and beat him within an inch of his life. When Billy got home that day his face looked like a pound of raw ground beef, and as he stared at himself in the mirror, he decided tomorrow was the day he'd end it.

He snuck into his grandpa's gun safe that night and grabbed the old .357 revolver from inside. He didn't know where to find more ammo, but he knew it was kept loaded in case of a break-in.

The next morning he tucked the revolver in his waist-band and slid a long shirt over it. He didn't check to see if it was loaded; he didn't even want to look at it.

And yet his jaw was clenched with determination as he caught the bus. When he got to school, he noticed there was a crowd outside by the football field. Thankful for the delay, he slid his way in between the shoulders and elbows to the front, and that's when he saw Josh.

His former bully was naked, gutted from head to toe and strapped to the field goal post, straw poking out from holes where he'd been sewn back up. His eyes were hollow pits, pecked out by birds before anyone had found him. And on top of his head, someone had placed an old scarecrow's hat.

Billy left right then and came home. He barely glanced at me as he passed, sitting there in my rocking chair and knitting. Rather, he headed straight to his room and collapsed on the bed. It was the first time he slept easy in a long while.

It was only a few days before the news had spread around the town that the boy had been murdered, and that when the police went to notify his dad, well, they found him dead too.

To this day they still don't know who did it.

The police suspected Billy at first, and they must have asked me a dozen times if I'd seen my grandson leave the house that night, but I told them the same thing each time.

I'd been awake all night watching TV in the den and I would've seen him if he had left. I could tell they all thought I was senile, but none of them dared say it to my face.

Well, I'm older now, and I don't think I have much time left, so now I suppose is the time for truth: I don't know what Billy was up to that night because I wasn't there.

I was at Josh's house. And I was making damn sure that no one called my grandson 'scarecrow' ever again. And no one ever did.

THE BLUE-EYED PAINTING

DAVID MALONEY

"So... what are we doing here?"

"We're uh... appreciating art."

"How do you appreciate art?"

"I think you just stand there and look at it."

"That's it?"

"Yeah, pretty much."

"Danny we're staring at a nine foot painting of a triangle. No offense, but even your hipster girlfriend knew this was bullshit. Which is why she crapped out of going and you dragged me along."

I blew air at my bangs from the bottom of my mouth.

"Alright," I said. "Fuck it, let's go get drunk."

Jason grinned, and we started walking towards the exit.

"That's more like it. You know that beard makes you look like a douchebag?"

"I think it looks manly. And Karen likes it."

"Manly? Danny you look like the kind of guy who

owns a special little comb for picking semen out of his beard."

"How long did it take you to come up with that one?"

"About at long as it took you to... whoa, hold on. Look at this one."

Jason had stopped in front of a small painting of a face.

"Shit, yeah."

The painting was of the bust of a woman and looked like something out of the Renaissance. It was strangely out of place in the modernist gallery around us.

"Look at her eyes, Danny. Holy shit, I'm doing it. I'm appreciating art."

The woman's eyes were sky blue, and they bore a sort of dreamy expression which only seemed to enhance the strangeness of her beauty.

"It gives me the creeps." I said.

"It looks like she's naked. Do you think they've got a painting of the rest of her?"

"Seriously, it's creeping me out. Let's go."

But as we turned around to go, we were approached by a woman with wire rimmed glasses and hair pulled back so tight that her forehead was reflecting the gallery lights.

"Do you like this one?" She asked.

"I, uh. Yeah, my friend likes it."

Jason was too busy ogling the painting to respond.

"Who painted it?" I asked.

"An unknown Renaissance artist. It was donated to the gallery and we display it here to demonstrate the contrast between modern and traditional forms of art."

"Is it for sale?" Jason asked.

"You seem really taken with it," the gallery owner smiled. "Go on and take it. Maybe it can inspire a love of art in you."

"Wait, are you serious?" I asked.

Jason shrugged and lifted the painting off the wall.

"Come on, sexy. You're coming with me."

"I CAN'T BELIEVE you brought a painting to a bar."

"It's called peacocking, Danny."

"What-ing?"

"It's when you bring something flashy to a bar to attract the attention of women."

"Sounds like a good idea. You want the girls to think you're some kind of psycho, right?"

"Shit, that could work. Maybe I can hook up with one of those girls that writes letters to serial killers in prison. Besides, I wanted to look at it some more. I've always had a thing for green eyes."

"Are you drunk already? She's got blue eyes, dipshit."

"Dude get your vision checked. This must be why you're such a shitty driver. You think all the traffic lights are blue."

I was about to tell Jason what a dumbass he was when a girl walked up to us and interrupted.

"Cool painting," she said.

"It's mine." Jason puffed out his chest, perhaps taking the word 'peacocking' a little too literally.

"I really like the expression in her eyes," the girl went on. "So vulnerable, it's like she's really baring her soul."

"Yeah," Jason eagerly agreed. "But there's something more, like a fierceness. It's beautiful."

The girl looked at the painting quizzically.

"I don't see it," she said.

Jason and the girl went on talking while I drained my whiskey. I texted Karen that Jason had met a girl and was ignoring me again. He was always like this around pretty girls. He said he fell in love at least twice a day. Eventually they went off to her apartment and I went home to the dorm.

I woke up on the couch the next morning with a splitting headache. Jason must have gotten home last night sometime after I passed out, because his coat was on the rack. As I became more aware of my surroundings, I noticed a powerful burning smell. I jumped up and saw smoke billowing out from the oven.

"Jason, you fucking idiot," I grumbled.

This wasn't the first time he'd stuck a pizza in the oven and then passed out before it was done. I switched off the oven and went to pound on Jason's door.

"Hey, wake up numb-nuts. You nearly burned us alive again last night."

No answer.

"What a lazy fucker."

I turned the knob and saw that he was still in bed, but obviously awake.

"Hey idiot," I said.

"Get up and clean the–" but the words died in my throat.

As I got closer, I saw the black pool of blood that had spilled from his mouth. His eyes were wide open and still.

"Shit!"

I ran over and shook him, but he was already ice cold. When the ambulance got there they took him away in a bag. They asked me if I knew what had happened, but I couldn't answer. I just kept going over the same thing in my mind. Jason had brown eyes, I was sure of it. But when I found him lying there, in a pool of his own blood, his eyes had been green.

The next week was a blur for me. I numbly floated through the days. People's consolations and pitying looks were just mundane platitudes that couldn't reach me. The university held a memorial service for Jason. They printed out a big version of the picture from his student ID and placed it next to the arts building so people could come and pay their respects. I went the long way around the building to avoid seeing it. I didn't want to be reminded of what had happened. But I couldn't hide from it forever–after class on Friday there was an urgent knock on my door, and when I opened it, Karen was standing there looking upset.

"I tried calling you," she said. "Are you okay?"

I shrugged.

"I'm surviving, I guess."

"Have you..." Karen seemed nervous about something. "Been by the arts building?"

"Not recently, why?"

"I, uh... I don't want to upset you. But I figured it had best come from me."

"What are you talking about?"

Karen pulled up a picture on her phone and handed it to me.

"What the fuck?"

It was Jason's picture by the arts building. But someone had gouged out the eyes and spray painted a big red X over his face.

"Who the fuck would do something like this?" I asked.

"I don't know. The university police are looking into it."

I saw red. A thought had been nagging at the back of my mind for days now. I grabbed my keys off the hook and marched out to the parking lot.

"Where are you going?" I heard Karen calling after me.

"I'm going back to that fucking art gallery."

I'm not sure what I expected to find. An answer, I guess. Some sort of closure. But I definitely didn't expect to find what I did. Hanging right there in the very same spot was the painting of the blue-eyed woman. I couldn't believe my eyes. I just stood there staring at it.

"Do you like this one?"

I heard a voice from behind me, and I turned to see the gallery owner.

"Oh," she said. "You're back."

"Where did you get this?" I sputtered out.

The gallery owner stroked the painting's cheek.

"She always seems to find her way back. I think she misses her spot on the wall."

I felt something in me break; my emotional numbness was replaced by a flood of anger. I grabbed the woman's collar and yanked her towards me.

"I know it was you," I said, shaking her. "I know what you did."

"Are you going to hurt me?" she asked. Her eyes moved

over to the painting, and I followed them. The painting's eyes were now a brilliant shade of green. I gasped and let go of her collar, and watched as the eyes slowly changed back to blue. The gallery owner straightened her shirt.

"I don't decide who she goes home with," she said softly. "She does."

I started to back away slowly, and the gallery owner watched me. I could have sworn the painting was watching me too as I turned around and ran.

When I got home, Karen was waiting for me, worry written all over her face.

"Danny what's going on?"

"I don't know," I said breathlessly. "But I know who killed Jason."

"You do?"

"It was the gallery owner," I said. "The place we went last week."

"The gallery owner? Why would the gallery owner kill Jason?"

"Because she's crazy. She's some kind of witch, Karen."

Karen frowned.

"Are you feeling ok?" She asked. "Jason died in bed, Danny. Why do you think he was murdered?"

"I just..." I was breathing heavily. "You didn't see it... The painting..." I trailed off. Even I could hear how crazy the words sounded as they came out of my mouth. I knew what I saw, but I knew no one else would believe me.

"Nothing." I said. "Sorry, I'm just a little upset. Never mind."

"Let's just relax for a while. Do you wanna watch a movie?"

I agreed more for Karen's sake than my own. After all, I was sure I'd just frightened her. We set up the movie and Karen went off to the bathroom like she always did at the start of movies. While she was inside, I saw a text message from her friend Brittany pop up on her phone. Karen didn't mind when I read her messages, so I grabbed the phone and swiped it open. All the message said was: *have u told him about jason yet?*

I heard the toilet flush and the faucet go on, and then Karen walked back and plopped down next to me.

"What is this?" I held the phone up to her face.

"It's nothing, Danny. Why don't we talk about it when you're feeling better?"

"No. Something is going on and I want to know what the fuck it is."

Karen sighed. "Alright. After they put Jason's picture up, there were some rumors that started going around."

"Rumors? What rumors?"

"Some girls said some things about Jason assaulting them. And then more girls started to come forward. The police looked into it, Danny. They're saying..."

"They're saying what?"

"They're saying his DNA ties back to open rape cases a couple years back."

"What!?"

"I'm sorry, Danny. I know he was your friend."

It felt like all the air had rushed out of the room. There was no way it could be true. Jason had always been a bit of a chauvinist, but he was no rapist. Was he?

A few weeks later, the dust had settled and the truth had come out about Jason. It felt like he had died a second time. All of my good memories of him were now replaced by some sick feeling I couldn't even begin to untangle. Seventeen women. And those were just the ones who'd come forward. The school took down the picture and got rid of the flowers people had left. Some people were saying they were glad he was dead. Those were the same people that gave me dirty looks when I passed them in the hallways.

Whatever. It didn't matter. I didn't know what had really happened with the painting, but I decided to just let sleeping dogs lie. Thinking about it hurt, anyway. I eventually went back to the gallery owner to apologize for my outburst. She smiled and told me I had a good heart. As I was leaving I could hear the faint sounds of her talking with someone.

"You seem to really like it," she said. "Why don't you take it home with you?"

WHAT MY WIFE GAVE BIRTH TO

DAVID MALONEY

IN THE EIGHTH MONTH OF HER PREGNANCY, MY WIFE suffered a complication that required emergency surgery. When she woke up and I told her the surgery had been successful, her reaction was nothing short of terrifying.

She didn't say anything at all, she just slowly reached down to her belly; her eyes widened for a moment, and then she started laughing. It was a deep, humourless chuckle that made the hairs on the back of my neck stand up. I had to repress a shudder as I asked her what was wrong, but she ignored me.

Instead of answering she began to scream; her whole body shaking as she thrashed and wailed; tearing out tufts of her hair and throwing them on the ground. I kept asking her what was wrong, but she wouldn't answer.

All of a sudden she went completely silent. She raised one hand up high. She paused for a moment–our eyes locked–and she brought her hand down with all her strength, plunging her long fingernails into her stomach.

She tore at her stomach with such fevered ferocity that I was sure she would rip it open.

I grabbed hold of her wrists, and with great effort, I managed to wrestle them down next to her sides. I used the restraints on the rails of the bed and her whole body suddenly went limp as if she was too weak to move. I sat down beside her bed; I could hear my voice shaking as I tried desperately to calm her down.

"It's alright, honey. It was just a small complication after all. Soon we'll have a beautiful baby boy. Our son. It'll all be worth it then."

She slowly turned her head towards me. Her eyes were dead, devoid of humanity. She began whispering, her head lolling limply around on her shoulders. I leaned in close to hear what she was saying. It was just one sentence, repeated over and over.

Get it out of me.

She refused to speak at all for the next week; sometimes she would just lay there, totally limp and motionless. Other times she would scream and pull at her restraints until her wrists bled. I tried calming her down, telling her that this was a good thing. I brought her baby clothes and her favourite foods, but nothing I did reached her. Finally, after a week, she went into contractions.

As soon as the baby came out, it was clear that something had gone horribly wrong. The stench was unbearable; a sick, nauseatingly sweet smell–?but the baby was worse. Its head was overly large, its eyes bulging and bloodshot, and the skin was black and ragged; sloughing off in my hands when I touched it.

It was a miracle that my wife survived the birth. I tell

myself that we're lucky for that, even if our son was born dead. She seems to be relieved that the pregnancy is over, but I just keep going over everything horrible that's happened in my head. It tore my heart out when she gave birth to our third stillborn son, and it was even worse when I had to force-feed her those pills so I could perform the surgery to put him back inside her.

If we're going to hold our marriage together through this tragedy, we'll both need something to look forward to. I think I'll go tell her I'm ready to try again; maybe it will cheer her up this time.

THE DOOR IN THE WOODS

DAVID MALONEY

"WHAT THE HELL?"

"What is it, honey?" My wife's voice called out from behind me.

"It's a door."

She laughed.

"Did you break into the shrooms early? We're in the middle of the woods, why would there be a–oh. Huh."

Karen stopped as she saw it. We stood shoulder to shoulder looking at it, an old wooden door built into the side of a hill in the middle of nowhere.

"It really is crazy what you can find out on these expeditions sometimes, huh honey?"? She grinned. "Should we knock?"

I shook my head.

"I'm not really sure I want to meet the kind of person that lives inside a hill."

"Oh come on." Karen punched my shoulder. "Where's your sense of adventure?"

Karen strode up to the door and gave it a polite knock.

"Hello, I'm looking for a Mister Beard. A Mister Tree Beard?"

I chuckled as I shook my head. Karen never let me forget the little wonderful things about her that made me fall in love with her. She turned to me in mock disappointment.

"I don't think anybody's home, honey," she said.

"Alright, come on." I said. "We've got enough shrooms for now, let's find a good place to trip."

"Are you kidding? God, I married the most boring man in the universe! We've got to go inside!"

"What if someone lives there?"

"What if somebody lives in a hill in the woods? I think the man who built his house underground in a forest will be understanding if we offer to share some of our pot with him."

"You assume that just because he lives in a hill he smokes pot? I don't know, Karen, that's pretty racist."

"Racist? Against who?"

"Tree people, obviously. Who else?"

Karen laughed and punched me in the shoulder again. I feigned being hurt, even though I loved it when she did that.

"Alright," I finally agreed. "After all, if I didn't completely ignore common sense sometimes, I wouldn't be married to you in the first place."

"You're really funny. After I kick you out of the house maybe you can live with Mr. Tree Beard out here in the woods."

I chuckled and tried the knob. The door was unlocked.

As we pushed it open we were greeted by a damp, mossy smell. The room inside was pitch black, but it seemed to be made entirely of rock, not dirt like I had expected.

"Hold on a second," I said, sliding the pack off onto the ground and fumbling around inside for the flashlight.

I flipped it on and scanned the walls.

"What the..."

The walls were all covered in some sort of nonsensical carvings. It reminded me of when we'd studied Egyptian hieroglyphics in school.

"What is this, wingdings?" Karen joked.

I didn't answer. I had gotten the sudden feeling that I was being watched. I swung the flashlight to the back wall, only to discover that there wasn't one. The passage continued on and sloped downwards until the flashlight beam ended on the ceiling about thirty feet away.

"Karen, I think we should–"

"Hold on, what's that?"

Karen pointed to a dark spot on the floor, and I pointed the flashlight down to illuminate it. It was some kind of black liquid.

"Motor oil?" I joked. But Karen wasn't joking around. She knelt down to look at the puddle.

"It's blood, Danny," she said. "And look, it's leading down inside."

I tilted the flashlight up. She was right, there was a blood trail leading deeper into the cavern.

"It's probably just an animal," I said. "We should go." But Karen was already tying her hair up the way she did at work. She cupped her hands to her mouth.

"Hello!" she called out. I heard the call echo down the

chamber, which must have been much larger than we had originally thought. "Is anybody down there?"

Silence. But then, a barely audible call answered.

"...h-help..."

The call sounded like it was coming from deep within the cavern. When I heard it all the hairs on the back of my neck stood up and there was a sinking feeling in my chest. My every instinct started telling me to get the fuck out of this place.

"Karen, it could be some sort of trap," I said. "Let's call the park rangers and then get the fuck out of here."

"Somebody's hurt down there, Danny." She said sternly. But then her expression softened a bit. "Sorry, honey, this is what you got yourself into when you decided to marry a nurse."

I sighed. I knew there was no stopping Karen once she had set her mind to do something, but I kept a tight grip on the heavy mag flashlight as we proceeded down the passageway.

The blood trail got thinner as we walked deeper into the cavern. Whoever it was must have lost most of their blood in the antechamber. But if they were hurt out there, why had they retreated farther into the cavern? Why not go outside where they had a chance of being found? It didn't make any sense.

The air grew hotter and more humid as we went farther down the increasingly steep slope, and a pungent smell of mold invaded our nostrils. I coughed as I breathed the horrid air. Where did all this dust come from? The deeper sections of the cavern walls had been cracked open by tree roots that had burrowed their way through the stone.

"What the fuck is this place?" I whispered to Karen.

"Maybe some sort of makeshift survival bunker?" She guessed. She cupped her hands to her mouth again. "HELLO-O!"

Her shout echoed down the hallway. "If you can hear us stay calm! We're going to help you get out to safety!"

"...h-help..."

The voice was a little louder this time. We must be getting closer, I thought. But the sense of revulsion I felt on hearing the voice only got worse. Did she not feel it?

As we went deeper inside, we found where the blood trail ended. There was a long smear of it on the ground. It looked like somebody had been dragged across the floor while bleeding heavily. And then it just stopped. Not even a drop after that. The walls of the cavern had now been almost completely overrun by roots, and breathing was getting difficult as the air had grown hotter and more choked with dust.

"...h...help..."

The voice was very close now, and I could now make it out more clearly. It sounded strange, all breathy and raspy, like a crude imitation of what a person should sound like. The floor had now become so steep it was impossible to go any further without risking a fall into God-knows-what.

"We've got to get down to him somehow," Karen wheezed. She must have been having even more trouble breathing in the hot, thick dust than me.

"I've got it," I said. "You step back."

I pulled out the length of rope we'd brought in our emergency gear and tied it to one of the thick roots springing through the walls of the cave. I gave it a few firm tugs to make sure it was secure before tying the other end around my waist. I'd never wanted to turn around and go home so badly, but I knew there was no way Karen would leave without seeing this through. I started to climb down carefully, leaning over and moving the flashlight around to try and see what was going on without slipping and falling. I could see the vague outline of a man in the darkness, and I swung the flashlight beam over him.

My blood went cold.

"Karen... run."

"What?"

"RUN!"

My breath was knocked out as the rope yanked back against my waist. I hoped it was Karen pulling, but I knew it wasn't. She wasn't that strong. I landed on the ground hard, and the rope continued to pull me backwards.

"Danny, what the fuck is—"

"RUN GOD DAMN IT!"

She started to back away as the roots on the walls all started to move, slowly snaking their way towards us. I sawed through the rope with my pocket knife and stumbled forward into a sprint, yanking Karen along with me. She wouldn't have hesitated if she'd seen what I had. At the bottom of the cavern a man had been suspended above the ground in a giant web of roots that were writhing and sliding through him. Little bulges were moving slowly up the roots that led away from his collapsed and shriveled body, one root jutting into his throat and twisting around every time he called for help. The plant was working his voice box like a puppet.

We abandoned our flashlight and gear bag in the cave behind us as we sprinted towards the exit in total darkness, hacking and coughing as the moldy, dusty air of the cavern filled our lungs. I could feel myself tripping on roots that had not been there on the way in. I felt a yank on my hand as Karen fell, and we both tumbled down onto the writhing roots which circled around our limbs and began to drag us backwards. I started hacking desperately at them with my pocket knife. The roots recoiled as I struck them, and I managed to free my legs. I pulled at Karen's hands, but the roots were stronger.

"Just leave me!" she shouted at me.

"Fuck no!" I swung blindly at her legs, and the knife connected with a sick thud. I swung a dozen more times, slashing her legs once by mistake before she was loose enough to yank free.

We kept running towards the door, and I could feel the air getting cooler and fresher, the floor beginning to level out. We'd almost made it. I could see the outline of light around the door now. We ran full force into it, ricocheting off and bouncing back onto the ground. I scrambled up. Please be open. I grabbed the knob and yanked, and a torrent of fresh air and sunlight poured into the cavern. I grabbed Karen's arm and half dragged her through open door before collapsing exhausted on the ground.

"We made it," I gasped out. My chest was heaving up

and down as I lay on my back coughing up all the dust from the cavern air.

"Yeah." Karen was bright red with exhaustion, her arms and legs covered in scratch marks. I don't imagine I looked much better.

"What the fuck was that?" I said breathlessly, getting to my feet.

Karen shook her head. "I don't know... but let's get the fuck out of here." I helped Karen to her feet, and we both stood there panting and coughing with our hands on our knees. Karen coughed something up into her hand.

"Danny?" she said, showing it to me.

It was a small leaf. I watched her face as little green tendrils began to spread out and coil around under her skin, and I realized with horror that it hadn't been dust we were breathing in. It had been spores.

WHEN FREDDY FOLLOWED THE
SCHOOLGIRLS HOME

DAVID MALONEY

WHEN WE WERE KIDS, WE ALL THOUGHT FREDDY MUST BE the biggest person in the world. He was six foot five and broad as a refrigerator, and though his sheer size was certainly impressive, his intellect was not. From the mismatched and sloppy clothes featuring children's cartoon characters to the disheveled hair and his slack look of disinterest that perpetually graced his features, one look at Freddy was enough to let you know that he was slow. Nobody on our street had ever heard him say a word. As far as we knew, he couldn't talk at all.

He was in his early twenties, which meant that he'd been in the neighborhood for as long as any of us kids could remember, so most of us paid him no mind. And he really wouldn't do much of anything exciting; just stand in the front yard and watch the girls as they came home from school.

So, when Freddy followed the schoolgirls of the neighborhood to their homes one day, we found it a little odd, but certainly nothing to be overly worried about. The strange thing was that he did it again the next day, and the day after that. At this point us girls started to get a little unnerved, but we didn't think about telling anyone what was going on. After all, we all knew Freddy. He was harmless, right?

So we just ignored it. A couple of the braver girls tried asking him to stop, but all they got in response was Freddy's slack-jawed stare. I guess he really couldn't talk after all. It seemed like things would just go on like this forever, until what happened to Sarah.

Sarah was the one in our group who lived the farthest away from the school, which meant that every day she walked the last half mile to her house alone. Well, not exactly alone: she had Freddy.

One day Sarah never came home. Her mom waited, called our moms—no one knew where she was. That's when Eleanor finally piped up about Freddy.

Eleanor's mom called Sarah's mom, and Sarah's mom called the cops. When they went to Freddy's house, they found her in the living room, shaking like a leaf as Freddy sat on the floor and stared at her. Her story went that he had grabbed her up out of the street and tucked her under his arm like a football, sprinting the distance to his house, and setting her down on the living room sofa. She was too afraid of what he'd do to her if she screamed for help so she just stayed there and closed her eyes.

But Freddy didn't do anything to her. For the two hours that he had her there, all he did was stare.

After that there was talk of locking Freddy up, but seeing as he hadn't actually done anything to harm the girl, the police let him off with a slap on the wrist and sent an escort to walk the girls home from school every day. That's just the way things are done in small towns I guess.

Well, this didn't sit right with us girls for obvious reasons, but what could we do? We all figured we'd be safe as long as the officer was there.

Unfortunately, the officer didn't much care for his 'babysitting' duty, and one day when an emergency call came through dispatch he decided to ditch us and head off to do some 'real police-work.'

That day we decided we'd all walk Sarah to her house together. Safety in numbers, right? We were about a half mile from the house when we heard a noise like a wounded animal, loud enough to make our ears hurt. We all turned around to find the source, and Sarah screamed as she saw it–Freddy was barreling towards us as fast as his tree-trunk legs could carry him, mouth agape and wailing.

We all booked it, scattering like balls on a pool table. He ignored us, making a beeline for Sarah, when a gunshot cracked the air like lightning. Freddy's shoulder jerked back, but he didn't slow down. I stopped for a moment expecting to see the officer, but I didn't.

A man had grabbed hold of Sarah with one hand and was waving the gun with the other as he dragged her toward a windowless van. Sarah was screaming and biting the man's arms, but he didn't even seem to notice as he dragged her back. I can still remember how wide his eyes were, the pupils expanded like black bottomless pits, swallowing up the iris.

Freddy's shoulder wound had soaked through his shirt

as he raced towards the two of them. The man raised the pistol again and the air was broken by a loud crack—the crack of Freddy's fist slamming into the man's jaw.

I've never seen anyone hit someone else that hard since. The man's face instantly gave way and he flew through the air like a rag doll.

Sarah wrenched herself out of his limp fingers and just stood there staring wide-eyed at Freddy, but Freddy didn't say anything. He just patted her on the head like you would a puppy and sat down on the ground, staring into space as the blood from his shoulder slowly soaked his shirt.

The police investigation revealed that the man had spotted Sarah one day as she walked home from school and begun following her. Inside the van, they found rope, duct tape, knives, and about a dozen journals filled with psychotic ramblings about Sarah, along with a large supply of PCP. If that wasn't enough to shake us up, the police matched his DNA to three open rape/murder cases of teenage girls in the state.

Freddy ended up being fine—even though the doctors said he should have bled out. The wound hardly seemed to faze him. He lost a little function in his arm, but other than that he was fine. And after that, none of us protested when Freddy wanted to walk us home.

SHE SAYS THE SMELL OF DEATH

SHE SAYS THE SMELL OF DEATH

DAVID MALONEY

THE BEST THINGS IN LIFE ARE FOUR LETTER WORDS. LOVE, fuck, and free.

This is a story about the second one on my list, but the first one makes a guest appearance.

Her name was Marla and she was a real piece of artwork. Not like a Greek statue; more like a high-end sex doll. That may sound like an insult, but it's not. Marla wasn't perfect, but she was the perfect version of what she was. In life, that's all anyone can aspire to be.

I first saw her smoking a cigarette outside our college's art building, looking bored with life.

"I'm out," she announced to no one in particular when she had finished. She looked me up and down like she was appraising a car.

"Suck your dick for a cigarette," she said.

I coughed so hard I nearly swallowed my own cigarette whole. I handed her one, naturally. Later that night, after she was done sucking my dick, she lit up from a full pack in her purse. That was just how she was. I never did truly understand Marla; I was just happy to be along for the ride. So when I found out she wasn't actually a student at the college, I shouldn't have been surprised. But I was.

"I just don't get it," I said. "Why do you hang around here?"

She shrugged.

"But–" I was interrupted as her long fingers slid down my pants, and she slid down to her knees. When Marla didn't want to talk about something she always made sure her mouth was otherwise occupied. And Marla wasn't much for talking.

By the end of a day with her my dick would have more lipstick on it than an insecure teenage girl.

But the quickest way to a man's heart is also the quickest way to make him lose half his brain cells. Consequently, I missed a lot of red flags about Marla that I should have noticed.

Like how I never saw her eat or drink. She had always just had a full meal, or was feeling bloated.

Or how she never slept. Whenever she'd stay the night after we'd fucked away the afternoon she'd just lay in bed and stare at the ceiling. I'd wake up in the middle of the night to her staring at me full on in the face, an inscrutable look in her eyes that most resembled hunger.

My conviction that there was something off about Marla only deepened when I found her driver's license. It had spilled out of her purse that she'd tossed carelessly on the table.

It was a picture of Marla, just as she was today, but the

date of issue was 1979. How could someone not age a day in thirty years?

She caught me looking at it and snatched it out of my hands.

"Like my fake ID?" she asked, tossing her hair and running her hands down my chest.

"Marla, how—oof"

She shoved me hard, and soon I was on the table and she was on me.

"You're a sick son of a bitch, you know that?" she whispered in my ear, her hips twisting in rhythmic circles.

I had already all but forgotten about the driver's license.

We'd been together six months when things began to unravel.

"Marla," I began, as her head bobbed up and down on my crotch, "are we exclusive?"

There was a distinct popping noise as she pulled her mouth off me.

"Why?" She asked. "Do you wanna fuck other girls?"

"What? No, I just wanted to know if I was the only one you're uh..."

"Fucking?"

"Yeah, fucking."

"Yes." She said, sliding her mouth back down my shaft until her lips reached the base.

"But where do you go all the time?" I asked.

She pulled herself off me again.

"I have things to do," she said cryptically.

"What things?"

"Things." She said it flatly. "Do you want me to finish this or not?"

"Oh, uh, yeah."

Marla grinned devilishly and her head began bobbing up and down with renewed vigor.

I know I shouldn't have followed Marla. I should've just been happy I was getting my dick sucked. But sometimes curiosity outweighs our better senses. Well, my curiosity almost killed me.

The first place I followed Marla was to the bathroom. She went into the one-person handicap bathroom in the art building, and I heard the lock click behind her. Then through the door I heard the unmistakable sounds of vomiting, followed by a flush. Was Marla bulimic? It didn't seem to fit with the Marla I knew.

I hid around the corner, then went inside to investigate after she'd left. She'd gotten most of it in the toilet, but around the rim there were tiny droplets of blood.

What the fuck was going on? I thought.

Then Marla went to the hospital. I followed her as she visited dozens of patients, most of whom seemed to be at death's door. After each time she would find a deserted bathroom and vomit. Each time there would be little flecks of blood on the seat. I began to worry for her health. It didn't seem possible that anyone could vomit up that much blood and still be alive.

Finally I followed Marla to a deserted alleyway.

What the hell was she doing here? I thought.

But she just stood there, motionless. And then–

"I know you've been following me," she said. "You can come out from behind that wall."

I stepped out and she turned around to face me.

"How did you know?"

"I can smell you, dipstick."

"Smell me?"

"Oh yeah. I can smell you from miles away. That's how I found you. You think I can't smell you when you're right behind me?"

I gave my armpits a quick sniff. I smelled fine.

"What the hell are you talking about?" I asked.

"You smell like death," she said, staring at me hungrily. "You're a sick son of a bitch."

"You're not making any sense. How am I the sicko?"

Marla shrugged.

"Ask your doctor. What do I care?"

"What?"

"You still don't get it? I'm feeding off your sickness. It's what I do."

It was clear that Marla had lost it.

We parted ways after that, but something in my head kept nagging at me. What if I really was sick? I went to the doctor just to rule it out. When my blood tests came back I got an urgent call to make another appointment as soon as possible. I found out at that appointment that, by all estimations, I should've been dead three months ago. An MRI revealed that the cancer, a rare and aggressive form, had spread all throughout my body. Within a couple days I could no longer walk and barely sit up. I was done for.

I gave Marla a call, just to say goodbye. I started to tell her what hospital I was at when she cut me off.

"I know where you are," she said. "I can smell you."

She was there in five minutes flat. She pulled the

privacy curtains around the bed and started to undo my pants. I appreciated her enthusiasm, but I knew there was no way I could muster up an erection. But I was wrong; soon her head was bobbing up and down on my crotch. I fell asleep after, like I always did. I woke up to the sound of vomiting and flushing, and to my surprise, I felt like a million bucks.

Marla came out of the bathroom and sat at the foot of my bed, reapplying her lipstick.

"Most vampires steal life," she explained. "I steal sickness. But I've gotta get rid of the bad parts. That's where the vomit comes from."

"I don't get it," I said. "You can only keep me alive by sucking my dick?"

"What?" she said surprised. "No, of course not. I suck the sickness out with your blood when you're asleep. I just suck your dick because the smell of death turns me on."

"Oh."

"Yeah... " Marla stared up at the ceiling. "Want a cigarette?"

"Okay."

I've been with Marla ever since, and we've baffled every doctor we've ever come across. She still hasn't aged a day, and I still haven't died. I graduated college, we got married and moved to a little apartment next to a hospital where she visits patients to feed.

I used to think the best things in life were all four letter words, but "Marla" has five.

Marla says "suck" has four, though.

LIFE AS AN IMMORTAL PARASITE

DAVID MALONEY

SOMETIMES WHEN I'M LYING IN BED AT NIGHT AND STARING up at the ceiling, an overwhelming feeling of sadness begins to break over my body in crushing waves.

I think about my past relationships, the girls I never asked out, the friends I let drift away; all the roads I could've gone down but didn't, and my heart throbs with a keen awareness of every loss.

It's a sad thing to put to paper, but the only friend I have left now is regret, the familiar misery of his embrace is strangely comforting as it crushes me more and more each day.

Yet however trying they are, it's in these moments of deep sadness that I feel most like myself. I've hurt for so long that I've forgotten what it feels like to be happy. My pain has swallowed me; it has become me.

I hurt, therefore I am.

These feelings are my humanity, the essence of my being, but I am not a human anymore. I may talk like a human, look like a human, even feel like a human. But my insides are ugly and rotted, and the things that sustain you are poison to me.

Light, food, water.

The base comforts of a warm day, a full belly and quenched thirst are denied me as the price of immortality. My sunshine is darkness, my food hunger, and my water thirst.

Like a vampire, I feed on people.

But I have no fangs to sink into your neck; just a touch of the hand or a brush on the cheek is enough for me to steal away what I need. Another few years of life, and another bad memory to add to the carousel that revolves in my head as I lie awake each night.

My last victim was just sixteen years old. I met her down a dark alley, living under a cardboard box. She had run away from home, and now she had nowhere left to go.

We talked for a long time that night. I asked her why she ran away, and she said she didn't have a reason. Her parents were good to her, she had friends at school; her life should've been perfect.

But there was pain on the inside that pulled her down like a weight inside her chest, a pain that just wouldn't go away. She had thought that if she could just run far enough away, maybe she could escape the pain too.

But it had followed her here, never losing sight of her for a moment.

I smiled at her sadly and asked her to take my hand.

"Where are we going?" she asked, a small note of hope in her voice.

"Somewhere happy," I replied.

As she grasped my hand, I felt the familiar cold flowing through my fingertips and up my arm as I stole her humanity from her.

I sank to my knees as all her pain, her insecurities, and her bad memories became my own, flowing throughout my body like a cold river of misery. When it was over, I lay on the ground, weak and broken. She regarded me with some confusion and then smiled down at me.

"Did you trip or something?" she asked, her voice full of optimism.

"Yes... I... I tripped." I did my best to smile back at her.

"Thank you so much for listening to me," she said. "I guess I needed to talk, and it really feels like a weight has been lifted off me."

I smiled silently back at her as my heart ached with all her pain.

"I uh... think I need to go home," she said.

"Yes," I replied, "I think you do too."

HANDLES

DAVID MALONEY

THE FIRST TIME I SAW ONE OF THE HANDLES I THOUGHT I was dreaming. My mother had just woken me up for school, and when she turned to leave the room I saw a big brass handle sticking out of the back of her head. The hair around it was matted with blood from where it plunged into the skin, and it was slowly and steadily revolving like one of those old-fashioned wind-up toys.

Before I could process what I'd seen, my little sister ran into my room screaming:

"Wake up lazy!"

She started spinning around in circles as she jumped on my bed. She too had a handle, a small silver one that poked through her dark hair, spinning so fast that it was nearly just a silvery blur flicking little drops of blood around as it spun.

When I went to school that day I saw that everybody had a handle, some silver, some brass, some copper, and some even gold. Most of the students had small silver ones like my sister, spinning so fast you could hardly see them, and most of the adults had handles that spun slowly and steadily like my mother's. The old history teacher Mr. Binns had a big copper handle that was creaking so slowly it looked like it could stop at any moment.

Being young and stupid, and wanting to know what would happen if I touched one, I figured Mr. Binns would be the safest choice. After class I walked up behind him and grabbed hold of his handle. As soon as I touched it, Mr. Binns let out a loud gasp and collapsed like wet paper. His handle had stopped and fallen out of the back of his head, and there was black smoke escaping from the hole it left. Someone called an ambulance and the paramedics pronounced him dead on arrival. They later said that it was a brain aneurysm, and that he died instantly. But I felt responsible, whether it had been my fault or not, and I resolved never to touch another handle again.

That resolve lasted until my first girlfriend. I was still young and stupid, and it's amazing what teenage infatuation can do to your decision-making skills. After all, I couldn't be totally sure that it was really me who'd caused Mr. Binns' death, right? I told myself that we could be together as long as I was extra careful never to touch her handle. But of course, as anyone but me could have foreseen, I messed up. One night while we were running our hands all over each other, I strayed just a little too far. I'd no sooner felt my hand brush the cold metal on the back of her head than she collapsed on top of me.

Her breathing went from hot and fast, to wheezing gasps, to nothing at all in the span of a few seconds. I panicked and did the first thing that came to mind—I seized her handle in my hands and began cranking it back with all my might. When I couldn'?t force it back anymore, I let go and it started spinning again, but only barely. Her breath came back to her, but she never woke up again. She died two days later in the hospital, and when I tried to crank her handle up again, it just came off in my hands, that awful black smoke pouring out the back of her head.

I took her death a lot harder than Mr. Binns'. I became a shut-in; swore that I'd never touch another handle again. And that's how I've been living ever since. It's not easy, but I get by. I work from home, and I get supplemental disability checks from the government. My existence has been tolerable monotony, until yesterday morning when I noticed something strange. Overnight my own handle had gone from one that was small, fast, and silver, to a large copper one that spun so slowly it was barely moving.

I never knew that facing death would hit me this hard. After-all, my life has been spent in loneliness and misery. Yet there's something about the imminent finality of total nothingness that makes you want to drink in every detail around you, every sight; every sound; every touch like a tiny droplet of water to a man dying of thirst. And so I've decided break my rule, and to set out and enjoy my last few days on Earth. But I've since seen something strange; something that I cannot explain.

Every person I've seen since leaving the house has the same big, copper handle as mine. And they're all spinning in sync, so slowly they could stop at any moment.

MY NEIGHBOR THE CORPSE

DAVID MALONEY

THE DOCTORS HAVE ALWAYS TOLD MY MOM THAT I HAVE something called 'dissociative hallucinations.' They think that just because I'm a little girl I don't know what that means, but I do. It means they think I'm crazy. Adults all think that just because *they* can't see something that means it isn't real, but the truth is that the things I see are just as real as what they see, maybe even more real.

That's because when I look at people, I see what they look like on the inside. I don't mean that I see their organs and bones and stuff: I mean that I see who they really are. A kind-hearted old woman looks like a radiant angel to me, and a vacuous supermodel like someone suffering from an unfortunate birth defect.

When I look at pictures in my school textbooks of notorious dictators or criminals throughout history, all I can see are bloated corpses with worms poking out of holes in their rotted flesh.

So when our new neighbor moved in, his head caved

in and maggots nesting in his brain, I knew that he was not to be trusted. He came by the afternoon he moved in to introduce himself.

"My name's Jim," he said, extending a hand to my mother and grinning. I gagged as black pus oozed out of the lines in his cheeks.

"Oh, it's nice to meet you!" my mom said. "I was wondering who had moved in across the street."

Jim crouched down so that his rotted face was at eye level with me.

"And what's your name, little girl?" he asked, grinning even wider and sticking his hand out at me.

I didn't say anything.

"Oh Annie, you're being so rude!" my mom said. "Sorry Jim, she's a bit shy."

"Oh that's okay," Jim said, eyeing me up and down. "I'm sure she'll grow out of that soon."

He placed his hands on his knees and pushed himself back to his feet.

"I've got a daughter her age, too," he said. "Annie ought to come visit for a sleepover, sometime. I'd love for little Lucy to have some friends in the neighborhood."

"Oh that sounds like a great idea!" my mom said. "How about we set one up this weekend?"

"Sounds good to me." Jim said. "Well, I've got some errands to run, so I'll see you later, neighbor." He gave my mother a cheerful grin and looked at me one last time before he left.

I looked up my mom as soon as she shut the door.

"That man's a bad man," I said.

My mom sighed.

"Don't be silly, Annie." She paused, then added nervously: "You're not... seeing things again are you?"

"No, mom."

I'd long since learned not to answer that question honestly.

That weekend I met Lucy. She was a pleasant girl, and pretty despite a few scars. Most children are pure-hearted and blemish-free, so I was surprised to see the scars, but they didn't bother me.

The sleepover came and went without event, the only weird part being when Mr. Avery made us sit on his lap so he could read us a story.

The weekend sleepovers continued after that, and although I liked Lucy a lot, I always felt a bit uneasy at her house. At first it was just the walking corpse of her father that set me on edge, but then I noticed that every time I visited, Lucy would have at least one more scar. The longer I went, the more she began to resemble her dad, her flesh slowly becoming a ragged patchwork of scars and bruises, her eyes seething with quiet rage

The day that things came to a head was just a normal sleepover like any other, until Lucy's father came home. Clothes askew and smelling like the bottle of rubbing alcohol my mother kept under the kitchen sink, he barged into Lucy's room, interrupting our game of truth-or-dare. He seized Lucy by the arm, bending down to whisper something in her ear.

As Lucy listened, her eyes widened to the size of milk saucers and a terrified look seized over the patchwork of scars that made up her face.

"Y-you can't..." she mumbled out. "Annie's here..."

Mr. Avery's grip tightened around his daughter's arm until his knuckles were white, and the whispering grew into a hiss. Her shoulders slumped, and her whole body seemed to go limp with resignation. And then, something horrible happened.

As Mr. Avery whispered in his daughter's ear, the skin of her face began to stretch, pulling apart down the middle like cloth tearing at the seams, black pus slowly oozing down from the wound. A new scar was being formed.

I knew I couldn't just stand by and watch, and so I screamed the first thing that popped into my head.

"I know what you are!"

The words sounded stupid coming out of my mouth, but Mr. Avery's jaw dropped a bit, and his grip around Lucy's arm slackened.

"You...what?" he asked, seemingly dumbfounded that a stranger's child had just yelled at him.

"I know what you are," I said. "You're a monster. And you're hurting her. I won't let you do it anymore."

Mr. Avery let go of Lucy's arm and stood up straight as a rail. His startledness had turned to anger, and his eyes narrowed into slits.

"I will not have my parenting questioned by a child," he said through clenched teeth. "You get out of my house right now, and don't you ever come back."

I wanted to hit him. I wanted to grab Lucy by the arm and run away with her, but the sight of that disfigured monster rooted my feet to the ground. And then, like a coward, I turned tail and ran.

I got grounded for two weeks for my disrespect to

Lucy's father, and the next time I saw Lucy around the neighborhood, she was covered in so many scars that she was unrecognizable. I only knew it was her by her clothes and her ragged denim backpack with drawings all over it.

As I saw Lucy becoming more and more disfigured, a boiling rage began to see the inside my heart. That man had taken my friend from me. He had taken away her happiness and nobody around me seemed to care. The more I thought about it, the more hateful I grew, and before long ugly red scars began to rip their way through my face.

I knew I couldn't let him win. I couldn't let him get away with whatever he was doing to hurt my friend. I couldn't let him keep hurting her.

So I hatched a plan.

One day when my parents were working late, I snuck into my dad's closet and opened his safe. I knew the combination was my parents' anniversary. Inside I found what I was looking for: my father's antique Colt .45 revolver and the cardboard box of ammo. I loaded the gun and wrapped it up in grocery bags so nobody would see what it was. Then I walked across the street to Lucy's house.

I rang the doorbell, and as I stood on the porch a panicked thought suddenly rushed through my head–? what if someone else opened the door? What would I do? What would I say?

My heartbeat pounded in my ears as I heard footsteps approach from the other side. The knob turned, my mouth went dry, and the gun seemed to grow heavier in my grip.

The door opened and there stood Mr. Avery, mouth slightly agape.

His expression quickly turned to anger. "I thought I told you that you weren't–"

BANG

The gunshot shattered the peaceful air of the quiet suburban neighborhood, and Mr. Avery stumbled back, clutching his bleeding stomach.

I hit the ground as the gun kicked me back, ears ringing from the shot. I struggled back to my feet as the world span and blood rushed into my head.

BANG

The air shattered again. Mr. Avery fell down, and he didn't get back up. The ground beneath me span so fast I felt as if I would fall off the earth. Then I felt myself falling, and all I saw was darkness.

I woke up in the hospital two weeks later. The doctors said I'd hit my head on the pavement when the gun kicked back, and slipped into a coma when I got to the hospital. In the two weeks that I was out, girls in the neighborhood had come out about horrible things that had happened at Mr. Avery's sleepovers.

The adults assumed he'd done the same to me, and they told me that the DA had declined to press charges against me.

To this day, I still know that what I did that day wasn't justice. It wasn't right. But I also know something else.

I know that every time I saw Lucy after that, she had at least one less scar. And that's good enough for me.

WHY I AM GLAD I ALMOST DROWNED

DAVID MALONEY

I DIDN'T ALWAYS WANT TO BE A LIFEGUARD. WHEN I WAS young, I wasn't even a good swimmer: my physique was more suited to junk food and video games than athletics. But one summer something terrible happened that changed the course of my life forever.

My little brother drowned.

We had all been having fun at the beach, and he had only wandered out of my parents' sight for a few minutes. But those few minutes were enough for him to disappear forever.

The first stage of grief I went through was anger. I couldn't understand why nobody had intervened. How had no one seen him? But I soon learned that when people drown it's not like how it looks in the movies. They don't thrash around and scream for help. If you're looking closely you might see a head bobbing up and down for a few minutes before it sinks down for the last time. You might not see anything at all.

That was the catalyst for my decision to become a life-guard. I wanted to prevent other people from going through what tore my family apart. I practiced for hours every day until my lungs burned and my body was limp. Finally, I was good enough to be hired at the local beach my brother had drowned at.

I was never the Baywatch sort of lifeguard; I was skinny, pale and completely incapable of tanning. By the end of my first week my body was covered in so many freckles I looked like I had a skin disease.

There was a rumor among the other lifeguards that the beach was haunted, that the ghosts of drowning victims stayed there to drag others down to the same fate. I didn't think there was anything to the rumor; I figured they were just messing with the new guy who wasn't part of their clique.

But I was about to find out there was something to the rumor after all.

The beach was closed that night, and I was sleeping in the lifeguard stand. I didn't have a girl up there or anything, it's just that being a lifeguard full-time didn't really pay the bills. I was just nodding off when I heard the scream.

"HELP!"

I sat bolt upright, my heart pounding out of my chest. Nobody was supposed to be here this late. But the scream came again, and louder.

"HELP!"

I heard it more clearly this time. It didn't sound right. It didn't sound like someone in danger; it sounded like someone mimicking a distress call.

But I knew I didn't have a choice. If there was a chance somebody really was in danger, I needed to help them.

I slid down the ladder and scanned the beach around me. It was totally deserted. Where the hell was the scream coming from? I scanned the horizon of water, and that's when I saw it; a head bobbing up and down.

I sprinted through the sand and leapt headfirst into the icy water. I powered towards them with all my might, my nose and eyes burning as the saltwater splashed into them. The head was staying underwater for longer each time. I knew I didn't have much time left.

Just before I reached them, their head went down and didn't come back up.

I dove.

The water was too murky and dark. My head spun in all directions, but I couldn't see a damn thing.

I resurfaced and spat out the saltwater. My mind was racing through a million half formed plans of how to find the person before it was too late.

That's when I felt icy fingers close around my ankle. My head whipped around. No one was there, yet the grip was strong, and its intention was clear as it began pulling me out to sea.

For a flash of a second I wondered if this was what had happened to my brother. If he'd felt icy hands on him pulling him under as his lungs filled with seawater.

I felt my other leg bump into something under the water. I reached down and grabbed hold, and my hand closed around a human arm. I yanked as hard as I could, and a woman came to the surface. It was the woman I'd seen drowning, but she'd been under too long. We needed to get back to shore as soon as possible. I kicked as hard as I could and felt the icy fingers slip off my ankle. But I realized with horror that I'd been caught in the undercurrent, and it was now pulling me even farther away from shore.

I knew there was no way I'd get us both back alive as I watched the shore shrink in the distance. And that's when I felt the icy fingers again. They clasped around each one of my arms and pulled hard. But this time they weren't pulling me out to sea. They were pulling me towards shore, and out of the undercurrent. I kicked my feet as hard as I could, pulling the woman's lifeless body towards the beach where I could perform CPR. With the pulling hands and my kicking combined, we hit the shore hard. I stumbled out of the water and laid the woman down on her back.

It must have only been thirty seconds of CPR, but it felt like an eternity before she coughed up the water and started breathing again.

I sighed in relief and collapsed on the wet sand.

"Th-thank you," the girl stammered out.

"It's my job," I said. "I can't believe you managed to call for help like that."

"Wh-what? I didn't call for help," she panted out.

I sat back up. Was there someone still out there?

I scanned the horizon. My heart stopped.

I never tell people what I saw that night, because I know they won't believe me.

But I saw my little brother.

Standing at the water's edge, he looked just as he did the day he died, still in his powder blue swimming trunks.

He smiled at me and waved. I started towards him, but he shimmered like a mist and vanished into thin air.

After that night the legend of the beach changed. Now, they say there's a ghost of a boy who pulls drowning people back to shore.

And they say he's got powder blue swimming trunks.

SCREAM IN A BOX

DAVID MALONEY

"I'M AFRAID I HAVE SOME TERRIBLE NEWS."

"What is it, honey?" Dean looked over at me worriedly from the driver's seat.

I paused dramatically.

"I have to pee."

"Now? You're joking, right?"

"Yeah, I'm joking. Because 'I have to pee' is such a great punch-line."

Dean half chuckled half groaned.

"Remember the last road sign? The next town isn't for 60 miles."

"Then turn around."

"I'm not going to turn around and drive 20 miles in the wrong direction. Look, I'll pull over here and you can go on the side of the road."

"Sorry to break it to you Dean, but I can't pee standing up like you can. If I could, I don't think we'd be married."

Dean laughed.

"You think that I'd stop loving you just because you had a penis? You really think I'm that shallow? Here," he said, handing me an empty Gatorade bottle.

I cocked an eyebrow.

"What is this for?" I said, hoping he wasn't going to say what I thought he was.

"You know, to go in."

I stared at him silently.

"What?" he said, the ghost of a smirk creeping across his handsome features.

"Oh nothing," I replied. "I'm just wondering whether if I could concentrate hard enough I could make your head explode."

Dean laughed again, this time a little louder.

"Maybe you should try concentrating on finding a place to pee, and then one might appear magically on the side of the road."

"Maybe I will."

I closed my eyes and held out my hands in mock meditation.

"Oh spirits of the great full bladder," I began in a mystical sort of voice. "We pray to you in these dark and troubled times, that you may show us the path to true righteousness. That you might provide us a place to relieve our souls of their wearisome burdens, and our bladders of their wearisome fullness."

Dean laughed so hard that he swerved a little. When he was done wiping the tears from his eyes he pointed to a spot on the horizon.

"Looks like your prayer's been heard, honey," he said.

Sure enough, I looked to where he was pointing and

saw a building ahead. Dean took the exit, but as we got closer, I could see it looked like the kind of place where you put three layers of toilet paper on the seat before sitting down to pee. If somebody had magically enlarged a run-down wooden shack to the size of a small warehouse and then sprinkled it with cobwebs and garbage for good measure, then it would look like this place. There was a crooked wooden sign on the front that read 'Oddments and Curiosities' in peeling white paint. Once we pulled into the lot and saw the garbage up close we could make out that it was mostly rusted out appliances, but there by the front door sat a pile of dirty and dismembered doll heads.

"What the fuck?" I mouthed to Dean.

But he was already unbuckling his seatbelt excitedly. He loves places like this; says they 'keep the spirit of the road alive,' which is his poetic way of saying that he has a morbid fascination for weird and creepy things. We got out and went inside.

If the outside of the place was dirty, the inside looked like someone had set off a garbage bomb. Most of the stuff was old, rusted or broken, and the signs above each item were coated in black grime that made them impossible to read. There were long wooden canes that were topped with little replicas of shrunken heads, keychains with bits of animal bone on them, and little glass orbs that looked a little bit too much like real eyeballs: all kinds of horrible looking stuff. Dean looked like a kid in a candy store, so I left him to wander the aisles while I found the bathroom.

I had just finished up when I heard it, a terrible,

visceral wail that sounded more animal than human. I yanked up my pants and ran outside to find Dean standing next to a large display of what looked like black shoeboxes, grinning like a big kid who'd just found a new toy.

"Honey look," he said, pointing to the yellow plastic sign that hung over the display. I could barely make out the words through the grime.

"Scream in a box."

Dean nodded. "I'm gonna wrap it up and give it to my brother when we get there," he said grinning. "He's gonna hate it."

"Okay," I said. "But let's buy it quick and get out of here. This place gives me the creeps."

Dean took one last wistful look at the items around him before agreeing.

"Yeah alright," he said somewhat sadly. We made our way up to the counter, but there was no one there, not even when Dean called out for someone.

"Did you see a price tag?" he asked.

I shook my head, so Dean shrugged, pulled out a 20 dollar bill and set it on the counter.

"Alright, let's go." He said.

When we got into the car Dean handed me the box and I was surprised to find it was no heavier than an ordinary shoebox.

"How does this thing work then?" I asked. "Does it take batteries?"

"No clue."

I held the box up to my ear and shook it lightly. I could hear something rattling inside.

"What's inside?" I asked.

"Nothing," he said, pulling out of the lot and getting us back onto the road.

I shook the box a little harder and a chill went down my spine. It sounded like the box was... crying?

"There's something not right about this box, Dean."

"What do you mean?"

"Listen," I said, holding it up to his ear and shaking it more vigorously this time.

It wasn't crying that greeted our ears, but a woman's voice.

P-please.... Why are you doing this to me?

There was no answer.

"What the fuck?" I heard Dean swear under his breath.

I shook the box again, but there was nothing. I heard a deep voice in my ear.

I know you're listening, it said. *Would you like to join her?*

I couldn't help what happened next. I threw the box on the ground and began stomping on it like it was a cockroach. And every time my foot made contact it would scream, louder and louder until it felt like little needles were stabbing into my eardrums. And then the blood began to pour, bursting out in spurts and soaking the floorboard. The tires screeched as Dean slammed on the brakes and the car came to a halt. He scooped up the box and hurled it out the open window and then slammed on the gas. I could hear the screams growing fainter and fainter behind us as we sped away.

For the next three hours, neither one of us dared to break the silence. I took off my blood soaked shoes and put them in our road trip garbage bag. When we had almost arrived Dean got a call from his mother; he pushed the hands free call button on the steering wheel and her voice came through the car speakers.

"Oh Deanie, thank God you answered," she said worriedly. "Where are you two now?"

"We're right outside the city limits. Why Mom, what's going on?"

"Oh it's terrible Deanie. We just saw it on the news."

"Saw what?" I could see Dean clenching his jaw, and I began to feel sick to my stomach.

"They found that missing girl, Abby Johnston on the side of the road."

"They did?" Dean's knuckles went white on the steering wheel, and blackness started creeping in at the edges of my vision.

"Oh, yes, it's horrible. So young, and to die like that. It's just too terrible to think about."

"How did she die?" Dean's voice was beginning to shake, and I felt as if I was falling.

"They said her body was covered in shoe prints and road rash." Dean's mom went on in a low voice. "They said it looked like someone had stomped all over her and threw her out of a moving car."

I could hear tires screeching as if from far away, and darkness began to glide over my vision in a solid black line, like a lid sliding over a box.

PAID TO CUT PEOPLE UP

DAVID MALONEY

I was drunk on a Monday night when I saw the link, a spam post on an Internet forum I frequented, dedicated to those suffering from an addiction to plastic surgery.

They'll perform any kind of surgery you want, as long as you've got the cash.

The post was just that simple sentence, followed by a URL that was just a long string of letters and numbers.

How lazy, I thought. *They didn't even bother to disguise the link.*

I shook my head and hit the power button on my laptop. Just before I closed it, I caught a glimpse of myself in the now darkened screen. I closed my eyes and sighed in disgust. The worst time to catch a glimpse of myself was when I wasn't expecting it.

My nose was delicate, small, and obviously plastic, and my chin had been filed down to a needle sharp point by too many surgeries. Most days I could angle my face in the mirror just right and tell myself I was pretty, but the illusion was shattered whenever I'd accidentally catch a glimpse of myself in a reflective surface.

What's worse is that I'd been refused an operation by every surgeon I'd consulted with in the last year on 'moral grounds.'

I tried not to frown as I thought about it. My face was already ugly enough; I didn't need to add frown lines to my laundry list of problems.

I hesitated for a moment, then downed my drink before opening my laptop and turning it back on. I made sure to double check that my anti-virus was on and clicked the link. What loaded was a surprisingly professional looking website filled with those before and after photos where the models eyes were blurred out. Some of the transformations were truly stunning.

The surgeon's name was listed as Dr. Robert S. Ludlum. Googling him came up with nothing, but that wasn't totally out of the ordinary for a lesser known plastic surgeon. I grabbed the vodka bottle and poured myself another glass without bothering to add more orange juice. I was drunk enough that it didn't matter.

I couldn't figure out what was up with the URL... maybe it was just a referral link? I figured that the place looked on the up and up and gave the listed number a call. I expected an answering service as it was close to midnight, but instead an enthusiastic male voice answered.

"Hello!" he said, sounding like what you'd imagine if a border collie suddenly became human. "This is Dr. Ludlum, do you need any surgery done?"

Something about his tone put me off, and I found myself regretting making the call at all.

"I uh... no, wrong number," I slurred out, clicking the hang up button.

But just then the green light above my laptop's screen clicked on, and the webcam software's window popped up, giving me a much clearer look at myself than the black screen of the laptop had. I quickly shut it off, wondering if I'd somehow gotten a virus from this sketchy website.

And yet, having seen my face in the camera like that pushed me over the edge. I called the number again.

"Dr. Ludlum, here!" The chipper voice answered. "Did you change your mind?"

"I uh... yeah. I'd like to make an appointment."

I don't really know what it was that made me have such poor judgment. Maybe it was the alcohol, or maybe it was just that I *wanted* this place to be legitimate so badly that I ignored the misgivings in my gut.

I showed up the next morning at 11 o' clock. I was concerned Dr. Ludlum would be working through his lunch, but he just laughed it off with a 'who needs to eat, ha ha ha.'

The office was in one of those nondescript buildings that people rent out for small businesses. I felt a bit better about the whole weird situation once I saw the other offices full of unrelated companies.

I found door 202A at the end of a long, desolate hallway on the second floor. I gave it a knock and almost immediately a thin, wiry man in a lab coat answered.

"Ms. Stevenson?" he said excitedly, his border collie-ness even more apparent in person.

"Dr. Ludlum?" I hazarded.

"Right you are!" He clapped me on the shoulder as if I'd just won a million dollar prize on a trivia game show.

"So, Ms. Stevenson, we operate a little differently here," he said. He stopped, stared at me for a moment in total silence, and stroked his chin. "Yes!" he went on as if there had been no interruption. "Have you ever gotten a haircut?" he asked, thrusting a white binder into my hands

"Uh...yes?" I replied hesitantly.

"Of course you have!" he almost yelled. "It's the same process. You can take a look at these various faces and decide which one you think is most beautiful, and then I will craft your new face accordingly."

I got another twinge in my gut, telling me to leave, but I made the mistake of flipping the book cover open. The girls in this book were what I always wanted to be. They were flawless, alluring, and most of all, completely natural looking.

No plastic.

And try as I might, I couldn't ignore that little voice in my head, that little voice that had driven me to make poor decisions my entire life: *This is your chance to be beautiful.*

Before I knew it, my finger was on a picture, and I was being ushered into the operating room for surgery.

The last thing I saw before I went under was Dr. Ludlum's too-thin face grinning down at me.

When I woke up, I could definitely feel the difference in my face. I thought Dr. Ludlum must not have given me enough anesthesia, because it hurt with every tiny move-ment. Then, out of the corner of my eye, I saw another bed in the operating room. I could hear Dr. Ludlum's excited babbling behind me, but under the influence of the anesthesia, I couldn't make out a word of it.

For some reason, I just kept staring at that bed in the corner of the room. Something seemed off about the person lying on it. As my vision became clearer and clearer, I realized that her chest was no longer rising and falling. As it become even more clear, I realized that her face didn't match her skin tone. And finally, as the anesthesia wore off, I realized that her face was gone, and she was wearing mine.

"So beautiful, aren't you?" Dr. Ludlum grinned down at me, shoving a mirror in front of me.

My heart stopped as I saw the woman whose face I'd chosen from the book sewn on to where mine had used to be.

"Sadly," he went on, seemingly oblivious to my distress, "your friend wasn't so happy with her transformation and we had to increase her anesthesia to uh... calm her down. You're happy though, right?"

It was then that I caught a glimpse of Dr. Ludlum's white-knuckled hand clasped around a needle with his thumb on the plunger.

I winced with pain as I forced a smile.

"Yes," I said. "I'm happy."

"Yes, yes, and beautiful, right?"

The tears ran like little rivulets of fire down my cheeks.

"Yes," I sobbed. "I'm beautiful."

I gasped as Dr. Ludlum shoved the needle in my neck, and when I awoke I was in an abandoned parking lot. I tried looking for him, but Dr. Ludlum had disappeared, along with the website and the phone number.

Now, when I catch a glimpse of my dead skin mask, waves of shame and self-hatred crash over me until I feel like I'll drown in them. But if I angle my face just right in the mirror, I'm more beautiful than ever.

HELL IS HEAVEN TO THE DEMONS

HELL IS HEAVEN TO THE DEMONS

TOBIAS WADE

JUSTICE ISN'T BLIND. IF SHE CANNOT SEE, THEN IT'S SIMPLY because she doesn't care enough to look. She turned away that dark night my sister was attacked, where even the moon and stars must have hidden their faces in shame. From all accounts it was an anonymous act of brutality: an impulsive flight, a brief struggle, the humiliation of rape, and then the lifetime of silent nightmares that must surely follow such depraved violence.

I've heard it's a common story where the lonely roads meet beyond the protective halo of street lamps. For all the virtues we profess, there is a savagery dormant in us waiting only for our fellow man to blink. It is easy to be noble while someone is watching and the fear of judgment may yet steady our course. In solitude the moral compass will lose its bearing, replaced by whichever base instinct can scream louder than our pounding blood.

It is some consolation that I found the one who valued his greed over human dignity. Through the course of these confessions you will see that I am no better than the animal I hunted, so I will waste no time professing my merit now. I buy substances from a man who knew everything that happened in his neighborhood, and like anyone who seeks profit from another's misfortune, he was willing to sell me the name I required.

I found the rapist when he returned to the street my sister suffered upon: pacing and circling like a hungry animal haunting the doorstep of his last meal. He didn't see me coming, and I made no sound nor spoke no word save for the poetry my bullet inscribed in his skull. I should have departed at once, but the satisfaction that his last throes of life promised lured me into complacent voyeurism. I stayed to tell him that my sister sent her love, hoping to purchase her closure with the death rattle rising in his throat. I wasn't expecting repentance, nor did I receive it.

"It wasn't the first time, and it won't be the last," were his final words to reach living ears.

I have no-one to blame but myself and my zealous retribution for failing to notice that he didn't work alone. They were on top of me in moments, wrestling me to the ground and stomping my gun away from my shattered hand. Knives punctured my back and neck, leaving great sucking wounds which inhaled the night air; wounds breathing in place of my lungs which were swiftly filled with blood. There weren't any magnanimous thoughts or profound revelations as the light went out. One moment there was simply light and pain and noise...

And then nothing.

And then nothing.

And then... I opened my eyes to find I was no longer of this world. I knew at once, despite the fact that I was sitting at a quite ordinary wooden desk in a room no larger than janitorial closet. On the desk was a piece of paper, and on the paper was a question, and in that question was written my fate for eternity:

Welcome to Hell. Would you like to:

*1) Remain **Human**. You will be tortured by those who became Demons.*

*2) Become a **Demon**. You will torture those who remained Human.*

P.S. If there aren't enough people to volunteer to remain Human, they will be chosen randomly.

I do not believe it is within my nature to torture anyone. Even my sister's abuser received death as fast as an executioner's ax. But no more could it be said it is within my nature to receive torture: as unnatural a human construct as can be imagined. But if I had to choose – as I'm sure many of you would have done so far removed from the judgment of both man and God – then I choose to accept my new home and dawn the mantle of Hell I was offered.

I steeled myself against the horrendous transformation I pictured, imagining razor talons growing from my bones to rip holes in the flesh or an entropic decay to wrack my body until my skin ran down my face like candle-wax. No physical transformation came over me though, a phenomenon which I can only account to the Devil's ironic sense of humor. I knew it from the first moment the floor dropped underneath to fling me down into the charnel realm however; I was a Demon now.

And it was Heaven to me. I expected the first time to be harder. The woman was presented to me in perfect physical health. I haven't noticed any discrepancies in age since I've arrived – everyone looks to be their mid-20s here. The room sealed and I was given an hour to work on her. I find it distasteful to dwell on exactly what I did, but I remember rationalizing it cleanly with the knowledge that she was only here because she deserved it. Never mind that I was here too – never mind that it could have been me randomly chosen—never mind that she could have volunteered to suffer like this to spare another. She was in Hell, and it was my job to make sure she knew it.

It wasn't until I'd finished that I learned the second rule to this infernal game. Once the hour of punishment had been completed, the human is offered a choice: they can get revenge on me, or they can accept their pain and continue their journey. Those who refuse the chance to retaliate shall be incrementally elevated, until at last their soul is cleansed and they are set to be reborn on Earth. If however they choose to turn the torture on me instead, I will be nourished by the pain and descend further along the dark road I have chosen. For each blow inflicted upon me, my skin hardens, my muscles tighten, and my power will flourish.

It didn't take long for me to realize how to properly play. The only way for me to progress was to inflict a punishment so foul and induce a hatred so deep in my victim that they choose revenge over the quality of their immortal soul. And progress I must, for untold centuries of this game repeated has refined some Demons into legendary masters of their craft. Those Demons have carved out kingdoms for themselves in this infernal domain, and through their countless successes have transformed themselves into towering behemoths of apocalyptic ability, shattering the landscape with their tread and sending their lessers into groveling servitude. Since the moment I chose to become a Demon the gates of absolution have been closed to me forever. It may be my fate to dwell in this realm, but it was my choice to rule it.

And so I went to work honing my skill. It wasn't enough to simply batter the humans into submission; if I was to force their hand against me I had to get inside their mind, caressing and nurturing their spirit into one of mindless wrath. I learned to expose the subconscious dread lying dormant that even the bravest dare not shed light on. I mastered the art of wetting my brush in nightmares to repaint their memories until all they once knew of life was corrupted by my influence. I promised false salvation, or deceived them into thinking they had escaped, or spoiled their loved ones until they could not contain the anger I imbued within them.

But I didn't stop there. I studied the ancient texts of Demonic lore recounting the torment of dying stars from the beginning of time. I served under the foulest creatures I could find, watching their methods and improving upon their design. Experimentation, research, and endless practice refined my mastery over the subtle art until I could induce a pain so exquisite that Angels would shed their wings for the chance to smite me down. And ever I grew stronger, building a devoted following of my own to gather more humans, ever inventing and facilitating the process of extracting unbearable anguish. My human form twisted into a sentient shadow to reflect the pervasive nature of my approach, each victory making it that much easier to dismantle my prey.

And I loved every second of it. I relished in my progression and thought I could live here until the end of time, prospering and expanding my reign to all corners of the nether realm. Perhaps one day I would supplant the Devil himself, designing my own games to watch the universe fold and decay beneath my guiding hand. And perhaps I would have continued this road forever, had it not been for the fateful encounter where I finally met my match.

A human was pushed into the room with me and the door closed behind. I had an hour to play, but I wanted more. It was the man who murdered my sister: infuriatingly smug and dismissive of my ability to break his spirit. I thought I would enjoy this more than anything, but to my mounting dismay he stubbornly resisted my influence. He remained passive through the acid wash of his nerves. His mind did not falter as I summoned the image of his father's lamentations against him. Every trick, every torment, every mental ravaging left him smirking, until with exasperation I resigned myself to simply goad him into action.

"You must feel cheated. Forced to remain human at the mercy of every lowly criminal who cares to punish you."

"I wasn't forced," he replied. "I made the choice."

"Then you're an idiot who deserves what he gets."

"And what I'll get is freedom. I told you this wasn't the first time, and that it won't be the last," he said. "I've been to Hell so many times that it bores me."

So that was his secret. He had gotten out before. He knew how to play the game. But it didn't matter, because no-one played it like I did.

"So you won't retaliate?" I asked. "No matter what I do?"

He shook his head, the smirk unaltered. "I'm going back to Earth. And when I do, I'm going to remember this like I always do. I'm going to wait until I've grown strong again. And just for this, I'm going to find your sister and I'm going to do it again."

I had almost forgotten about my sister. About the world above, filled with its myriad of joys and sorrows. I missed her in that moment; I missed being alive. And as much as I enjoyed the role I had carved for myself here, I wanted to be back again. The thought that this monster would patiently wait out his trials, cheating the system over and over to return to his life of sin; it made me sick. The tables had turned, and all the hatred I sought to pour into him was rushing into me instead. I wanted nothing more than to flay him down to the core of being and set such a fire in what remained to burn for all of time. But even if somehow I could force his hand against me; even if I broke him so badly that he never escaped; I would still be here forever. And I hated him, and I hated myself, and it was the hardest thing I've ever done to hold onto that hatred and turn it aside.

And harder still to let him walk away. To bide my time, sending the weakest demons in my possession so that he might easily resist their influence. Watching, and waiting, and even helping my sister's attacker elevate through the Hell until the time of his salvation was at hand. It was hard, but it was worth it, because that is when I chose to strike.

I had already learned to infiltrate the mind in my pursuit of torture, and through my mastery I infiltrated the spirit as well. I hid within his soul when his judgment was passed, concealing my hatred within his hatred, tempering my fire with his calculating patience. And when that soul was whisked away, I traveled with it, sleeping so softly within his dreams that even he did not know he bore me as his silent passenger. Until the day when he was born again on Earth, and I with him.

The struggle was violent but brief. It is easy to wrestle an infant's mind from them, and when the child's eyes opened it was I who looked out. He may resist me yet, but I bear with me all the subtle crafts I have honed in Hell, carrying them to Earth where they can be put to better use.

You see Hell is Heaven for the Demons, but all the worst of us have found our way back home.

DO NOT GO GENTLE INTO THAT GOOD NIGHT

TOBIAS WADE

GRAVE MEN, NEAR DEATH, WHO SEE WITH BLINDING SIGHT
   Blind eyes could blaze like meteors and be gay,
   Rage, rage against the dying of the light.

DYLAN THOMAS SAID THAT. My grandfather. I'd heard the name thrown around the house a lot when I was growing up. It was a point of family pride to be descended from such an acclaimed poet, but it never left much of an impact on me. He'd died before I was even born, time reducing even the most brilliant souls to little more than trivia.

After-all, how could I have known that an archaic poem buried away in some dusty volume was written as a warning for what was yet to come?

My father knew better though. And I had the feeling something more was coming too, but my vague foreboding was answered with nothing but his thundering scowl. For the last week he hadn't talked much. He stopped reading like he used to and barely eats at the table, although sometimes I'll hear him prowling the house in the early hours of the morning.

And always, always of late I feel him watching me. From over his newspaper, or parked outside my friend's house after dropping me off. I even caught him sitting outside my room in the hallway, holding a mirror to get an angle through my partly closed door.

"Just checking if you're ready," he mumbled, seeming momentarily embarrassed.

I didn't reply, but it was getting weird and I would have spoken up if he didn't say something first. "Camping trip before school starts," he'd said. His voice carried the insistent authority of a policeman ordering someone to drop their gun. He didn't ask our opinion like he usually did when making plans. Mom must have sensed it too because she volunteered to start packing without hesitation.

"Don't bother," he told her. "It's just going to be me and the boy."

6 AM the next morning, he was hammering on my door. Time to go. He didn't need to tell me not to ask questions. Those sunken eyes and hard-pressed mouth left no room for argument. He was still wearing the same clothes from yesterday when he got in the car.

I kept quiet while he drove. Stoic silence, heavy silence, suffocating all opportunity for conversation. Every now and then he'd pull off the road a little to get out and look around. It felt like he didn't have any clear destination in mind, and it didn't take long for me to realize he wasn't going anywhere in particular; he just wanted to get away.

When he stopped to use the bathroom and get gas I checked the back to see what kind of gear he brought with us. Nothing in the trunk except a backpack. He brought me a sandwich, and after a brief break we were on the road again. A dirt trail cutting straight through the country finally satisfied him. The mood was so dark that I was half-expecting to be murdered the second we'd passed the last hallmark of civilization.

It was night by the time we'd stopped. The sky was a cosmic masterpiece, untainted by the erosion of electric lights. The scattered maple trees we'd passed along the way had grown denser, and dad didn't have any trouble finding some kindling to start a small fire. We didn't have a tent, or sleeping bags, or even food. I couldn't take it anymore.

"What's going on, dad? What are we doing here?"

He grunted and stirred the fire. I was pacing with agitation now, the restless energy from a day in the car overflowing into jerky, frustrated movements.

"Why didn't you want mom to come?" I tried.

"It's none of her business. This is between you and me, and my father before him, and his father before that." He looked up at me, the guttering flames reflecting dolefully in his deep eyes.

Before I could press for more, he'd sat down on a rock beside the fire and produced an ancient book from his backpack. He held it more reverently than a mother with her child, caressing the dust from its thick leather binding.

"From New York, back to Wales, and then Ireland before that," he said, handing me the tome. "Come now, take a look."

I stood beside him as we flipped through the thick vellum pages of the manuscript. Every sheet was dedicated to a single entry, each written in a myriad of separate handwritings and styles.

"Five centuries of verse," he told me. "Each generation has inscribed lines for the last five hundred years, going all the way back to someone named Brodie in 1522. You'll notice some of the earlier pieces written in Gaelic, but they've been reliably English since around the 18th century. Tonight you're going to add yours to the end, and maybe if you're lucky, the book will be finished after that."

He flipped past the continuous stream of thought through the ages to the last few entries. My eye immediately caught the name of Dylan Thomas, who in his own hand had printed his famous poem "Do not go gentle into that good night."

I quickly began to scan the next page where my father had written:

Bloodied, sickened, broken down, we tarry while we may.
For though life has wearied us, from death there's no escape.
One prayer, one stand, one wild charge, before it is too late,
For though dark and dreary thus, there's nothing left to hate.

But father slammed the book shut and pulled it away before I could read on.

"Wait—show me what you wrote," I pressed. He shook his head, roughly dropping the book that he once cradled.

"But how will I know what I'm supposed to write then?" I asked.

He was staring at the fire again, not looking at me even when he finally spoke. "Not long now. You'll know when it's time," he said. "You can't see something like that and not have something to say about it."

I didn't have to wait long, but it was unbearable while it lasted. Every rustling leaf turned to the ominous approach of some nameless horror. A snapping twig was re-imagined into the brittle bones of its latest victim, and even the whispered wind became an unpredictable adversary breathing down my neck.

And always, always, my father's eyes – fixated on me, boring into my skull. His rigid attention sent waves of tension down his face at my slightest movement. That should have been a clear enough sign of what was to come, but I didn't see it then. I just kept watching the woods, or the fire, or the great empty sky, peering and straining my ears against a world which was deaf to us.

But then in the absence of all other sound I heard what he was waiting for: the catching of my breath. I lifted vain hands in feeble disbelief, clutching at the invisible noose around my neck. I wanted to scream, but I could barely draw enough air to breathe. Dad's eyes lit up as the wheezing gasp involuntarily escaped my closing throat. Each breath came shallower than the last; only a few seconds until they stopped altogether. I was getting dizzy, and with the passing seconds mounted a desperate crescendo of my flailing heart and smoldering lungs.

Dad was solemn as the dead, still sitting a few feet away, his eyes an inferno of reflected flames. He didn't say anything, but he withdrew the paper bag which contained my lunch and tossed it into the fire. Blue ribbons of light danced across the open air, although I don't know whether these were a product of my oxygen starved brain or some covert substance revealing their purpose from the chemical fire.

My body thrashed and revolted against the grasp of some unseen specter, yet my whirling consciousness stubbornly refused to abandon me. I felt my body lifted by the pressure around my neck, pitching me to and fro: a cresting ship on its last voyage. The world bled together like running paint, and the meager fire roared into cascading heights to spit sparks like a thousand falling stars.

The dizziness mounted until I couldn't tell left from right, up from down, living from dying. My legs were numb where they beat the open air; my fingers frozen where they scraped helpless against the unrelenting force. Even if I didn't pass out, it was surely only a matter of time before my neck broke. Past the point of all thoughts and prayers a persistent recollection stormed against the closing dark.

Do not go gentle into that good night...

And then another thought that was not my own, coming from within me as though my mind played puppet to its presence. A lighthouse beaming words which carved their way through the midnight of my fading mind. I was struggling again, kicking and biting and clawing at the open air. My wild lashing finally connected with something solid, but the running drool of colors flooded my vision and made it impossible to guess what held me.

Every sense, every muscle, every feral instinct begged for me to close my eyes against the nauseating tumult of color. To let go of the insurmountable force I was thrall to; to find acceptance in defeat, and peace in death. But louder than the diminishing throb of my heart were the words: *Rage, rage against the dying of the light.*

And so I did. I swam through the sea of melting colors, fixating on the black blemish which refused to relinquish my throat. I fought back, tooth and nail sinking into yielding flesh, kicking and screaming as stale air tore through my howling lungs. I lunged after that, digging my fingers into the thing that attacked me until warm wet rivers bubbled over my hands up to the wrist. I wouldn't stop, couldn't stop, pouring all my love for the light and rage against its defiler with one unified assault.

Not until it lay still did I allow myself to fall gasping onto my back. One reluctant star at a time unraveled from the tapestry of madness to find its rightful place in the heavens. My body ached to the core, and were it not for the last utterances of my internal voice still coaxing me back to life, I would have been confident that I had died.

I didn't wake until the next morning. My first shock was that I was alive; my second that my father was not. His body had crumbled beside the ashes of his fire, deep craters gouged into his throat to match the width of my hands. I didn't understand until I had a chance to read the whole book: my unequivocal inheritance.

I wasn't the first, and I won't be the last. My family has been blessed to pursue the secret of the divine spark, and through the years our trials have brought us closer to its unveiling. The voice I heard on the edge of death is the same which inspired my ancestors to write their verse: a further puzzle piece in the enigma of creation. And when the final piece is set to place, then born again is the next God to walk this Earth.

I regret to tell you that such wisdom has exhausted all efforts toward its discovery so far. When we have given up, as my father did and his father before him, it is our place to pass the torch for the child to carry on. Until the day when he too sees his child's mind flare more brightly than his own and knows it is time for them to continue the search in his stead.

I am only writing this now because I have grown so weary of doors without handles and windows looking nowhere. I wish my father had explained this to me before I was thrust upon this quest, but I suppose he thought me too cowardly to end his life and begin my search when such an end was already written by a hundred hands.

That's why I am writing this, my son, so you can make that choice for yourself. And so armed with five centuries of verse, you will listen for that whisper at the end of all light and learn from it what you may. Open the book, when you are ready, and your trial will begin.

DOGS CAN RECOGNIZE
SKINWALKERS

TOBIAS WADE

It's hard to imagine what it's like to lose someone you love before it happens. Of course I've seen it a hundred times in the movies: dramatic affairs for the most part, with lots of screaming and crying and carrying on. The shock, the disbelief, the unconstrained rage; all lashing out at the world for the most ordinary and predictable thing in it.

It wasn't like that after dad disappeared though. He was simply there one day and gone the next, leaving behind nothing but a penetrating dull ache. Weeks of police investigation turned up nothing. It wasn't an act of cruelty which made the world steal him away; it was merely universal indifference. His life was short; his death random and meaningless; and there was nothing left but for the rest of us to carry on.

I got the phone call from mom late at night in my studio apartment. Dad was presumed dead, and the police had officially closed their investigation. I stayed quiet and listened to her all the way through, even though there was nothing left to say after the first line. I thanked her politely for letting me know, and then I hung up. After that I stared at the wall for about an hour, not really thinking anything, just observing idle thoughts as they passed in one side and out the other.

I live in a different state and hadn't even seen him in a couple of months. Eventually I decided that waking up tomorrow wasn't going to be any different than every other day when he was still puttering around the kitchen table a thousand miles away.

But I was wrong. I'd lived alone for years, but my apartment had never felt so empty. I had to keep the TV on all the time just so I wouldn't have to hear the soft gurgle of blood in my veins or listen to the dull monotony of my own breath. I don't know how I never noticed those sounds before, but they were starting to drive me crazy now. I guess I couldn't stop thinking about how fragile my own mortality was, and how pointless my life would have been if it were all to end.

That's why I got a dog. Half-husky, half-coyote, about six months old; I picked her up from the animal shelter where some cowboy was dropping her off. The dog was growling and snarling at him, but she calmed down the instant he left. I figured she must have been abused or something, but she seemed so sweet to everyone else that I decided to take her home with me.

A few days later I got the call that dad wasn't dead. About a month after he'd disappeared, he'd just showed up again. Mom said he just walked in one day and sat down at the breakfast table like nothing had happened.

She couldn't get a word out of him about where he'd been, but she was so happy to have him back she didn't even press. He wouldn't tell me anything either, just grunted something about "needing to clear his head". It seemed like a miracle to me too, but I guess I had already spent so much time fixating on death that nothing much changed for me.

I kept the dog anyway and named her Snoots, and from the very first time I called her that her ears pressed flat with excitement and she started wagging up storm. She was really skittish at first, but she hated being alone and would follow me from room to room, even sitting between my legs when I sat on the toilet.

Snoots was absolutely perfect for me. Her constant attention made me feel like I mattered again. Maybe my life didn't matter in an existential sort of way, and maybe my death wouldn't mean anything on a cosmic scale, but it would mean the world to her. I was warned it might be hard to train her because of the coyote blood, but she learned everything almost immediately. She was so shy that she'd try to walk between my legs when a stranger was nearby, but it felt so good knowing she trusted me.

She did have one bad habit though: unpredictably going off. The first time was a couple months after I got her. We were walking down the sidewalk toward the park when her fur started to bristle and her mouth flared to reveal powerful teeth. Before I knew what was happening, she was snarling and barking and howling at the lady on the other side of the street. The lady started running and Snoots actually lunged at the leash, almost dragging me into the street after her.

As soon as the lady was gone, Snoots was back to normal. I couldn't figure out what happened. She had never even growled at another animal before. The lady didn't have a dog with her, and she wasn't carrying food or anything. She hadn't made the least threatening move. It was so random that I just forgot about it, but that wasn't the only time.

The next time it happened she jumped up from the couch and started snarling at the door. A few seconds later someone knocked and she howled in answer. I looked through the peak-hole, but it was only the pizza guy. I had to drag Snoots into the bathroom and lock her there until he left before she would calm down.

That behavior happened so rarely that I couldn't figure out how to predict or prevent it. I couldn't just keep her isolated, and it was pointless to take her to training when she was usually the sweetest thing in the world. I was terrified that she would randomly attack someone and would be taken away from me though. I kept her daytime walks short after that, only going out early in the morning or late at night when there weren't so many people around.

Another few months went by and I thought her feral side had finally been tamed when it happened again. It was after 9 PM and we were doing a last walk through the park before it closed. I was talking to mom and dad on the phone and wasn't really paying attention to Snoots snuffling along behind. My first warning was when the leash snapped violently taunt, ripping the phone from my hand.

I automatically dove to catch my phone. Snoots was dragging so hard she managed to break the leash free from my grasp. I couldn't stop her from charging head-long into the darkness, a guttural snarl rising in her throat. I chased after her, shouting her name, screaming a warning for whoever was out there... but by the time I caught up with her, Snoots was already on top of some-one. She had his hand in her mouth, savagely thrashing back and forth like she was trying to rip it off. The guy was trying to push her back, but Snoots kept lunging in at him whenever she lost her grip. By the time I caught up with them she had had her teeth around his neck, fero-ciously shaking like wild animals do when they're looking for a quick kill.

I got hold of the leash and pulled so hard Snoots prac-tically did a back-flip. The guy was on his feet now, swaying unsteadily. I started to apologize, but the words died in my mouth. His hand was a bloody pulp, severed digits scattered on the ground. The wounds on his neck were even more brutal. A whole sheet of skin was peeled back, hanging in ragged tatters along his shoulder. Part of his spine had ruptured straight through the side where it had been unmistakably broken. Exposed sinew glistened with blood as he slowly worked his neck in a long circle like someone luxuriously stretching after a long nap.

I don't even know how he was still conscious. I wanted to go back for my phone to call for help, but it took all my strength just to keep Snoots from diving back in to finish her prey. The man started fumbling at the ruined tatters of his neck, not taking his eyes off me. I braced myself, half expecting him to attack us right back in retaliation.

He was too focused on his own injuries though. I was trapped in place holding Snoots back, helpless to turn away from what happened next. He grabbed the hanging folds of his skin with his good hand and started to peel it down the remainder of his neck. Then he reached around to his back and started to peel it there too, the whole mess of flesh flopping away like a diver getting out of a wet suit. I watched, transfixed but mortified as he slid out of the rest of his skin and clothing to leave them both in a soggy pile at his feet.

It wasn't exactly muscle underneath. It was more like a second skin, pale-grey and slick with blood, but it was fitted so closely to the structures underneath that it mirrored the muscle's striations and fibers. I didn't have long to stare though. He was running as soon as he was free, leaving behind the whole wet mess he'd shed on the ground.

I ran home with Snoots as fast as I could. I didn't even go back for discarded phone. I kept telling myself it wasn't real until I got back into my apartment, but it was harder to lie to myself while washing the blood off Snoots's face and fur. She was wagging her tail again, looking like her old self until she opened her mouth to let the last severed finger drop onto the floor.

I couldn't be alone after that. Even Snoots wasn't enough company. I talked with mom for a long time to help calm down, although I didn't breathe a word about what happened. She sensed that I was rattled though, and she convinced me to come back home and visit home for a while.

I kept Snoot with me, more afraid of the thing that discarded its skin than how she reacted to it. I have her locked in the car with me where I'm writing this now

97

though. I want to run in and hug mom and tell her how good it is to see her again. I want to ask dad about what happened – why he left, and why he decided to come back.

I can't get out of the car though. I can't let Snoots out. Not with her snarling since the moment I pulled into mom's driveway. There was only one thing that worked Snoots up like that, and I couldn't lie to myself and say it was something else. The only conclusion I could draw was that dad may have really disappeared, but whatever came back was only pretending to be him.

I left Snoots in the car and knocked on the door. I let out a long breath of relief when mom opened the door. Then a hand fell on her shoulder, and the thing that looked like my dad popped up into view. It made me sick to imagine the bloody-slick grey skin underneath that intimate mask. It was one thing to lose my father, but having to look at him again like this was unbearable.

They invited me in and I sat down, but I couldn't take my eyes off him. The disguise was seamless. His affection genuine. Both of them avoided any mention of his disappearance, and I didn't bring it up either. I had to find some way of breaking the illusion though. I couldn't very well just sic Snoots on him and mangle him in the living room. I had to bide my time and wait until I could get him alone.

I got my chance later that evening. Snoots was out back in the yard, still agitated and restless from his proximity to the creature. Mom was out at the store picking up some things for dinner. I invited "Dad" out to the yard to toss a football around like we used to. I figured we could take him by surprise and get rid of him before mom got back. She'd just think he disappeared again, and if she could accept it once, then hopefully she could accept it again. It was better than letting that thing live inside the house, watching her sleep, just waiting to make its move.

I had one of his hunting knives gripped in my hand. I waited just outside the door. I couldn't wait until Snoots started snarling or he might realize he was caught and get away. I had to strike hard, and fast, and then Snoots could join me and help finish the job. I tried not to think of that thing wearing my father's sweater as anything but a monster. I tried to tell myself it was the thing that had killed and replaced my real father. Anything to make it easier to do the deed before the opportunity was lost.

And then the door opened. He stepped outside, not noticing me pressed against the side of the house. I grabbed him from behind, not wanting to see his face. I plunged the knife into his side, not wanting to let him speak. He pitched forward and I let go of the knife. I still couldn't look at him, so I ran to the yard and opened the gate. Now's the chance! I shouted at Snoots, but she wasn't moving. Her fur was calm. She ran up to lick me and her tail started wagging. I had to drag her out of the yard, thrusting her toward the creature crawling on the ground. Snoots looked back at me, unsure of what to do.

I almost thought I really had gone crazy until at last the fur started to bristle down her back. She bared her fangs, hunching down in preparation to pounce. It wasn't until then that I noticed the sound of tires on the gravel driveway on the other side of the house. Snoots wasn't paying my father any attention. It was my mother she sensed.

Snoots was sprinting around the side of the house and I ran to keep up with her. Mom was just starting to get out of the car with an armful of groceries when the dog sprang. She managed to get the door closed in time, but Snoots wasn't giving up. She beat herself against the window, snarling and slamming herself over and over into the car. Mom was in reverse now, tearing back out of the driveway, out into the street to disappear around the block.

I called the ambulance, but dad didn't look like he was going to last. Snoots came to lick his face, but the blood wouldn't stop and I didn't know what to do. He said he didn't blame me, but every word was getting weaker than the last. I asked him why he left, but I could have already guessed the answer. He'd run when he found out mom had been replaced by one of the Skinwalkers.

"Then why'd you come back?" I had to ask. I needed some closure before he was gone for good this time.

"Because I still loved her," he told me. "And that thing is the closest there is to having her back again."

DREAMS ARE A TWO-WAY WINDOW

TOBIAS WADE

Infinity captured in an hourglass, turn it over and it begins again. That's what dreams are to me. I always romanticized dreams as a window into innumerable secret worlds and forbidden fantasies. It wasn't until I began lucid dreaming that I realized every time I looked out through the window, something else was looking back at me.

The concept of lucid dreaming fascinated me since I first learned about it in my psychology class. I couldn't even believe it was a real phenomenon at first; it seems more like a super power to me.

To create any world or situation with such vivid detail that I become God of my own personal universe. That must be too good to be true, but there it was. Printed clearly in my psychology textbook: a guide how to induce lucid dreams. I even made a photocopy in the library to hang above my bed as a constant reminder to follow these steps until I mastered the elusive and subtle art.

Step One: Reality Checks

The textbook recommended I try to push a finger through my opposite hand at least ten times a day. This will habituate the motion and make it more likely for it to occur in my dreams. When I try the check in a dream, the finger is supposed to pass straight through my hand and prove it isn't real. The self-awareness that I'm dreaming is what triggers lucidity.

Step Two: Set an Early Alarm

I set it for 2 hours earlier than I usually wake up. When the alarm sounded, my goal is to turn it off *without* opening my eyes to make the next transition smoother. This technique is called "wake induced lucid dreaming".

Step Three: Mindfulness

After that I have to try and stay mentally awake while I let the rest of my body go back to sleep. This is known as sleep paralysis because my mind will be awake in a frozen body. It occurs because I've interrupted REM sleep where the dreams occur, prompting the body to return there as fast as possible.

It took a few days of practice before things started to click. At first I kept accidentally falling back asleep after my alarm rang. Soon I was able to maintain concentration, but then I started to see some basic colors and shapes, and I got so excited that I fully woke up. The longer I persisted though, the more real the images became.

Shapes morphed into forms and the dappled specks of light grew and twisted into rich tapestries of color. Sometimes it felt like an ordinary dream, but as I continued to practice I learned to prolong my focus until the imagery fully matured.

Less than a week had passed before I was reliably alert enough to perform my reality checks, and after that came absolute freedom. I began with enacting idle sexual fantasies, but the sheer possibility of exploration made it difficult for me to maintain attention on any one creation for long. My favorite dream to spin was where I stood in a dark room with a paint brush that transformed everything it touched. Mountains ripped through the ground and soared at my command, and a single stroke on my eternal canvas brought flocks of birds into flight. Crystalline caverns, riding dragons, alien encounters, and the entire cosmos stitched onto the back of my hand; I raced through my dreams with insatiable wonder and boundless delight.

And I kept getting better too. I invented a dozen more reality checks involving clocks, mirrors, counting fingers – anything to ensure I would always find a way to become aware. My worlds became more intricate, and I was able to cast distinct characters and plots to entertain me. It's not like this was the only thing going on in my life, but it was the best, and every night I couldn't wait to uncover the latest treasure in my mind.

That is, until I discovered I was being watched. As my awareness became more defined I grew cognizant to certain elements in my dream which remained stubbornly beyond my control. It started off as a vague uneasiness which settled upon dreams like a gathering dusk of the spirit. I couldn't make out anything specifically wrong, but I can only describe the feeling as though I was a character in someone else's dream. All I had to do was tear down my canvas and begin again in a new dream though, and the feeling would be gone...

For a little while anyway.

Each successive escape solidified the presence in my mind, and like an intrusive guilty thought it penetrated my next dream. I built castles only to find eyes I never conceived of watching me from cracks in the stone. A flight through the air went sour as the sun turned to watch my aerial maneuvers. On to an undersea adventure, but my paranoia amplified as an eel followed me relentlessly through the water. Reality checks confirmed my dream, but I couldn't banish these watchers. I could only hope to lose them by starting again, although each time they found me swifter than before.

I became so unnerved that I forced myself to wake up. I found myself in a cold sweat, panting in the cool morning air. The first step of my morning ritual was now a full range of reality checks. I allowed myself to relax as I passed each one. Just a bad dream, I told myself. I swatted the fly away which snuck in during the night and prepared myself for just another ordinary day. But once they've found you, the watchers will never let go.

I felt anxious all day; a source-less, gnawing feeling that made me keep checking over my shoulder. I second-guessed the motives of everyone who turned to look at me, and when my psychology professor asked me a question in class I froze like a hunted prey. I had to try and push my finger through my palm, right in front of everyone, just to make sure. The warm pressure of skin against skin snapped me back to reality and I was able to mumble a cohesive enough answer for him to turn away. But if I wasn't dreaming, then why did his eyes swim through his skin so that they continued watching me after he had turned? Even with his back to me, I could still see them peeking out through his shaggy grey hair.

Growing awareness works the same way in this world as it does in dreams. As soon as I became aware of one discrepancy, I began to notice them all. The same fly which had been following me all day continued dancing orbits above my head. Passing gazes lingered on me longer than they used to, and always, always the eyes would return in the most unlikely places.

A dropped notebook on the floor opened to perfect sketch of an eye looking at me. A sip of coffee left the fleeting imprint of something staring at me from the foam. From knots in the trees to chips in the sidewalk, everything was an eye and all of them were directed at me.

I don't know whether it was a relief or a fresh terror that waited for me at home. Stepping into the bathroom, my reflection had completely disappeared. That was the first reality check to fail all day. At least if I was still dreaming then it meant I wasn't going crazy...

I couldn't will myself to wake up anymore though, no more than I could will myself not to see through open eyes. I tried throwing myself into bed, tossing fitfully until I at last slipped into an uneasy slumber. I was hoping that falling asleep in a dream would be enough to make me wake up for real, but it only threw me into a fresh absurdity of dreams that even my awareness could not tame.

Ghastly specters of thought whirled through a mind so

saturated with fear that I lost track of right from left; of reality and fabrication. Lips began to accompany the eyes in more varied and tortured forms than my waking imagination could conjure. Faces pressed in around me as though struggling to break free from the suffocating cloth that my dream enveloped them in. More than being watched, I was terrified that they would start to speak to me. I don't know why, but just as I had bottled the divine spark of creation, I knew they now dreamed of me and that I would be slave to their slightest utterance.

Faster I spun, willing myself to wake but holding back for the horror of what I might find there. Through the dreams I raced, new ones forming before the searing lights of the last had even faded from my vision. Worlds collided together into maddening abstraction as men with fish-heads rode on horses across the clouds with lances of lightning. Through the clouds the faces pressed, withered lips peeling back to laugh and grunting in mockery of human speech. Endless possibilities are a double-edged sword. An eternity in Heaven is not the same length as an eternity in Hell.

At least now I know why they're watching. They're looking for a way out, just like you're looking for a way in. They've been doing this for much longer than you have, and whatever trick you think you know, you can count on them knowing it too. I know because for as long as I practiced and prepared myself while awake, I've spent many times over learning from the watchers in my sleep.

I'm awake now. For real this time (I think), although I run through my list of reality checks so compulsively that my palm is bloody and raw where the finger keeps pressing in. This isn't a warning against lucid dreaming though, however it may sound. I've seen how shrewdly the watchers hide, and know they were watching me long before I became aware of their existence. They might not reveal themselves to you before you become lucid, but that only means you can't protect yourself from them until it's too late.

Dreams are a two-way window, and if you aren't brave enough to stare down the face on the other side, they can be a door as well.

FOR SALE: HUMAN HEAD. CONDITION: USED

TOBIAS WADE

BEST AD I'D SEEN ON CRAIGSLIST ALL DAY. I'D SPENT THE last hour surfing the site for a passive-aggressive gift for my ex-girlfriend's wedding. Was this a possible candidate for gag gift of the year? Well I certainly thought so.

I didn't think it was a real for a second when I texted the user. I just told him what I wanted it for and asked if he had any left. It didn't even have to look that real – just enough for a little jump scare and a good laugh.

Here's the reply I got a few minutes later:

PLENTY LEFT. DO YOU CARE WHOSE?

Screw the fact that he's shipping heads. There's nothing that labels someone crazy like typing in all CAPS. But hey, let's be fair here. Considering I was asking about buying one, maybe I didn't have a right to condemn his eccentricities. I replied and told him I didn't care, just as long as it wasn't someone I know (I mean come on, he's got to have a sense of humor, right?)

WHO DO YOU KNOW? I'LL CHECK.

I asked for a picture and told him I would let him know if I recognized them. I didn't hear back after that and figured the joke had run its course. Just as well really. Maybe it was petty to try to sabotage the happiest day of her life. Then again, she did sabotage my *entire* life when she decided to wait until I'd finished paying off her college loans to tell me she was seeing someone else ...

It wasn't until that evening when I got the next reply.

SHE WILL LOVE THIS ONE. NICE AND FAT. HE DOESN'T NEED IT ANYMORE.

I almost choked on the pizza I was eating. Fat was a generous description of the picture he sent. Bloated would have been more accurate, like it had been sitting out in the sun for a long time. Congealed blood still clung to the base where several inches of spinal chord extended past the tattered flesh of the neck. The nose was gone, replaced with an explosion of sticky cartilage from where a massive force like a shovel had pummeled it in.

I've had a few hours to contemplate my life choices, and now that I was staring at the picture while trying to eat, I knew this was a bad idea. *Sorry not interested*, I replied before blocking the number.

The next morning I woke up to three more pictures sent from a different phone. Each bore a macabre description:

THIS LITTLE LADY WAS A FIGHTER, SO SHE'S A LITTLE MORE KNOCKED AROUND.

. . .

MY ONLY OLD MAN. THOSE BLOTCHES ON THE
SKIN WERE THERE BEFORE.

IF YOU WANT MINT CONDITION, CHECK OUT
THIS GIRL. POISONED. NOT A MARK ON HER.

THERE ARE some things you just have to ask even if you
don't want to know the answer. Stuff like "do you love
him" and "how long will dad be gone for this time?"

"Where are you getting all these heads from" is
another one of those questions. I typed it in, simultane-
ously eager and afraid for the reply.

I ONLY NEEDED THE BODIES.

I seriously considered reporting this creep to the
police, but again I still figured it was just a bad joke that I
didn't want to waste more time on. I told him not to
contact me again and blocked this number too.

A week later I arrived at the wedding empty handed.
Without a date. My ex gave me a tight smile and that half-
assed hug which is usually reserved for people with a
severe skin condition. She said it was nice of me to be
here and thanked me for the present.

Present, what present? She told me someone dropped
one off with my name on it. I found it sitting on the table
in the reception room; a little brown box about the size of
a bowling ball with a flair of red string tied up in a dainty
bow. A note was slipped underneath which read:

YOU SEEM TO HAVE TROUBLE DECIDING.
HERE'S A FREE DEMO TO TRY OUT. IF YOU AREN'T

100% SATISFIED, YOU CAN EXCHANGE IT WHEN YOU'RE DONE.

So many questions came to mind, like how he found me or what exactly one does to "try out" a head? When I lifted the box up to grab the note I couldn't help but notice the dark sticky stain soaking through the bottom and onto the table. I couldn't exactly leave it there. Shit, what was I thinking? It had my name on it and everything. Most of the people were still arriving and talking outside, so I just grabbed it and made for the door. There was a return address after the "demo period" had expired, so at least I could get rid of it.

I scuttled across the dance room, trying my best to wipe up any errant drips which were soaking through the bottom. I almost made it to the door before I spotted my ex. Quick turn-around, racing for the backdoor instead. More people were flooding in now, including her family and many of her friends who knew me. None of them could have guessed what I was carrying though, so as long as I could make it to the door ...

... or at least I could have if backdoor wasn't wired to the fire alarm. The blaring sound shocked me so much I almost dropped the box. It started to open and I caught a glimpse of the bloody pulp inside. It half-flopped out of the box as it tumbled, and I had to scramble to keep it closed. From the shards of splintered bone to the puddle of dried blood around the base, I had no doubt that it was real. By the time I looked up, the whole room was staring at me.

There was only one thing louder than the alarm after-that: my ex's mother screaming " *he's trying to steal the presents!"*

My panic-stricken brain didn't want people to think I was a thief, so I just dropped the box. If I had been able to think *even a little* more clearly I would have realized it was much worse for them to think I was a murderer, but I couldn't deal with that accusing siren or all those disapproving eyes. I dropped it and ran, swearing to myself that it wouldn't matter as long as I never saw any of those people again for the rest of my life.

I did get some messages though. The next day, my ex told me that my present was a big hit. Everyone loved the gag. They thought the head was a symbolic gesture which meant her past romances were dead, and I was so sweet for giving my blessing like that. I guess no-one looked close enough to decide whether or not it was real.

It's the other messages that bother me more though. All CAPS, sent to remind me that:

YOUR FREE TRIAL IS UP. YOU CAN PAY 10,000 TO KEEP THE HEAD, OR SEND ONE BACK IF YOU'RE FINISHED.

Now where the hell am I going to get another head?

I BUY AND SELL MEMORIES

TOBIAS WADE

You know those people who treat everything like they've just been asked to climb mount Everest? Where every little thing is an insurmountable ordeal, whether it's waking up, taking a shower, or even just going outside? Almost as if the whole world was an elaborate conspiracy designed solely to slightly inconvenience them, god-forbid some effort was actually required to survive.

That was my buddy Craig. What irritated me the most is that he hadn't always been like that. Growing up he read philosophy and filled notebooks with plans about what he was going to do when he grew up, meticulously mapping out possible career paths with their required steps. He graduated high-school with nearly perfect grades, and after he was accepted into MIT, I figured his whole life was pretty much set.

The only thing that could have stopped him from getting what he wanted was getting something he thought he wanted, and her name was Natalie. Controlling, obsessive, jealous, always putting him down for this or chewing him out for that. I have no idea why he stuck with her, but two years later when he dropped out I can only imagine that was the cause.

They broke up soon after, but the damage was already done. Craig was an absolute mess. He couldn't get out of bed without a beer, and every time we talked it was just him bitching about how much he missed Natalie and how worthless he felt without her. I thought it was just going to be a phase and that he'd move on, but the obsession just kept growing in an endless feedback loop.

He couldn't do anything because he felt like shit. He felt like shit because he couldn't do anything. And on and on, doubts feeding doubts. Hating her and loving her, and then hating himself for both. Even though I'd known him since we were kids, I was getting to the point of just giving up on and cutting him out for good. Last week I decided to tell him to his face: one last shot at taking some responsibility for his life.

I hardly recognized the guy who opened the door. Clean shaven and grinning from ear to ear, Craig invited me inside. His apartment was immaculate all the way down to the gleaming grout in his tile floor. His laptop was open to spreadsheets and a color coded calendar. I couldn't believe the transformation. I congratulated him on finally getting past Natalie, but he didn't understand what I was talking about.

"Natalie? Who is Natalie?" he asked.

I thought it was a joke at first, but she was just one piece of the puzzle. He kept talking about high-school like it was yesterday, and how excited he was to start MIT. It didn't take long for me to realize the last two years of his life were completely gone. He seemed obviously better for it though, so I held my tongue in case I accidentally reminded him of something that sent him back into his depressive spiral.

It wasn't until I left when I noticed the business card half-concealed beneath his entry mat. Black card, back and front, with nothing but the words "**I buy and sell memories**" and a phone number.

I wouldn't have believed it if I hadn't just seen the results. It was one thing to discard shameful or destructive memories, but the chance of buying new ones too? Maybe I could remember what it was like to travel the world without any of the expense or inconvenience. Or learn new skills without the effort of practice. My fingers were actually trembling as I dialed the number.

An automated voice guided me through the steps of setting up a free consultation. By the next morning I was in the office building, checking the directories for "Dr. Sinclair". Sure enough, there he was, his office listed as *Cognitive Reconstruction*.

"It's not magic," the beak-nosed doctor told me as I sat down. "My team has mapped a large archive of neuronal patterns which can be replicated with their corresponding electrical signals."

I didn't really understand what that meant, but throughout the session he drove his case home. Folders filled with brain scans, a wall cluttered with degrees, and my own mounting excitement proved an irresistible combination. Within the hour I had signed consent for the treatment.

"We're going to put you under for this part," Dr. Sinclair told me. "The fluctuations of the conscious mind make it impossible to get an accurate reading of baseline activity. Just write down a list of memories you'd like to have when you wake-up."

I did so before reclining on his sofa while he set up the anesthesia mask.

"I'm not going to have to forget anything to make room, am I?" I asked.

"Old telephone numbers, the occasional date or address—nothing but clutter. Deep breaths now."

It seemed too good to be true. I was absolutely euphoric as I inhaled the strawberry scented gas. Dr. Sinclair briefly studied the list I wrote before crumpling it up in his hand.

"These are rubbish," he said, his words distorting like a radio with a weak signal.

The anesthesia was muddling my mind, but a brief surge of panic still flooded my veins. I started to sit up, but he put a hand over the mask and pressed my head firmly back into the couch.

"Most people prefer to hold onto their good memories, mind you," he said. "The ones they sell me tend to be a tad more...*exotic*. Why don't you just relax and let me choose?"

It wouldn't quite be accurate to say I fell asleep then. It was more like I fell awoke, slipping in an and out of consciousness so subtly that I didn't even realize time had passed. One second I was struggling against the mask, and the next I tore it off my face and sat up panting. Only now I was sitting on the sidewalk. The mask lay at my feet, dangling from its severed chords. Dr. Sinclair was nowhere to be seen.

And everything in the world was wrong. The roar of traffic bludgeoned me from the nearby street. I flinched and cowered as my every instinct screamed a warning for the impending collision, even though I was well out of harm's way. Dark clouds had begun rolling in from the sky and I shuddered, imagining some phantasmic presence leering at me from behind them. The eyes of passing strangers cut me with their disdain.

Everything in the world was normal. I was the one who was wrong. In the space of those odd hours on Dr. Sinclair's couch I had lived through the nightmares of a hundred lives. A man like my father had beaten me to within an inch of my life, although I knew he wasn't the father I grew up with. My hand burned as it had when it was torn off by a tractor, even though I could see its perfect vitality at the end of my wrist. I had been shot at, maimed, humiliated, and betrayed a hundred times, and so could I feel the blood of my victims as fresh as the day they were choked to death by hands that were not my own.

I don't know how long I sat there screaming on the sidewalk before someone called the police. I'm vaguely aware of an ambulance picking me up, but my internal world was so much more vibrant and clashed so disorienting with the one I saw that I couldn't keep them straight. The hellish memories were mixed with my own so seamlessly that I couldn't figure out which were true and which were not. Maybe I had done these things, hurt these people. Maybe I deserved to suffer.

But the maddening conflict of a hundred contradictory memories made it impossible to maintain any coherent identity. By the time I got to the hospital, I couldn't have told you my own name. I didn't even know whether I was a man or a woman, having lived distinctly through the most traumatic ordeals of each.

The next time I was able to make sense of the world was within a hospital room. Dr. Sinclair was there as I had seen him last, peering down at me from over a clipboard. His presence was branded into my mind, and I couldn't turn away from him to look at who he was talking to on my other side. He was the point of singularity: the one common aspect in all my separate lives. The person I most feared and most needed in the whole world. I had seen him from so many different eyes and known him from so many different minds that all these thoughts conjoined into an amorphous blob of desperate hope.

"Patient exhibiting signs of psychosis, schizophrenia, and multiple personality disorder," Dr. Sinclair was saying. "He is a danger to himself and others, and must not leave this room until I consent. Is that understood?"

"Yes doctor."

"I know he's your friend, so if you'd like to be reassigned–"

"No doctor. I can handle it," Craig said from my other side. "?I just want what's best for him."

"We all do," Dr. Sinclair replied, his voice oozing with compassion. "?I'll check in again at the end of my rounds. Buzz me if he remembers anything about that man."

I turned to Craig as the doctor exited the room. Craig was wearing a white lab coat as well, his own clipboard hanging limp at his side. My mouth twisted with uncertainty, trying to make sense of which language was natural to its shape.

"Get some rest," Craig said. "The Doctor knows best. He's going to make you better again."

"He did this to me," I managed to match my thoughts to English.

"Me too," Craig grinned. "He was my professor at MIT. He told me I was failing, and that I'd be expelled unless I participated in the experiment."

"But the nightmares—"

"Yeah, I guess I missed that part," Craig said. "I just had my last two years erased. I've been relying on him to fill me in on the details."

My words were failing. There was so much pain, and loss, and suffering spinning around my head. No-one should ever be forced to bury their son or endure their loved ones wasting away from cancer. Not once. How was I supposed to survive it dozens of times?

Craig patted my hand as he stood to leave. I was speechless, comprehending but bewildered by the situation I was forced into.

"And besides," Craig said as he passed through the door. "These memories will make you stronger if you can get through them. Stronger than you thought possible. Nothing will be able to hurt you after this."

"And if I can't get through?" I asked.

Craig shrugged. "Then you'll be left behind, same as everyone who can't move on from the past. Same as you were going to do to me."

FLESH-EATING SEA BUGS

TOBIAS WADE

I'M SURE MANY OF YOU HAVE READ THE RECENT NEWS STORY about the flesh-eating sea bugs. The guy didn't feel a thing standing in the water, but when he stepped out his feet were savaged into a bloody mess, completely perforated by the creatures.

That may sound bad, but after what I've seen, I know it's going to get a whole lot worse.

If you're like me, then your reaction went something like this.

1) WTF, gross. I don't want to look at that.

2) But... a *bug* did that? Actually that's kind of cool. I want to see it again.

First of all, I live in Australia, so assuming all the killer jellyfish and snakes weren't deterrents enough, I'm pretty sure swimming is off the menu for me.

It did give me another idea though. So far I've been

stubbornly refusing to acknowledge my summer break science project (we just get 6 weeks, unlike the States), but class will be starting up again soon and I had to pick something. What could be more fun than studying flesh-eating bugs?

A little research revealed that the perpetrator was probably Lysianassidae, a family of marine amphipods. They're a type of detritivore, which means their diet is primarily comprised of decomposing organic matter. As the unusual case recently demonstrated however, they are perfectly adept at shredding living tissue as well.

I actually live pretty close to the beach where it happened, so I figured I'd just collect a water sample for my display, write a report, post some newspaper clippings on a poster board, and voila. All done.

The only tricky part was that I had to go at night. The beach was temporarily closed for an "Environmental Safety Evaluation", but all accounts online suggested it was an incredibly rare and isolated incident. I figured I wouldn't even find any of them, but just to be safe I was up to my knees in rubber galoshes and didn't wade in very far.

I filled a couple glass vials before I got out of the water, but I couldn't tell much just from eyeballing them. The water was murky, and even though I saw some little critters floating around, they could have been anything. I was all set to hike back to my car when I saw the flashlights scouring the beach.

I wasn't allowed to be here, so my first instinct was to run. There was nowhere to hide on the open sand though, and I figured they'd spot me as soon as I started to move.

All I could do was press myself into the sand and hope for the best.

The beam of light passed right over my head. I clenched my eyes shut, praying they'd missed me. "All clear, sir."

"Good." The voice was deep and gravely like it was obscured from years of smoke. "Back the van up here and keep it moving. We're going to be in and out in 10 minutes."

I heard a car pull up nearby in the closed parking lot. I didn't lift my head because I was terrified that any movement would give me away. I had the feeling that these guys weren't supposed to be here either, but that might make it even worse for me if I was found.

It sounded like they were dragging something heavy through the sand. I wanted to look so damn bad. I lifted my head just enough to see a massive dolly piled high with bags like fertilizer. It was being pushed across the sand on mounted skies by four men in dark blue overalls.

"It's going to get a lot more visible when the activating catalyst hits the water," the gravel voice said. He was an old man, long white hair flowing half-way to his ass. "Line up the bags, and don't pour them until they're all open and ready to go. Three minutes tops, make it happen."

The men in overalls pulled long bone-handled knives from their belt and systematically slashed the bags open. I strained from my prone position, but I couldn't see what was inside. Their attention was all diverted though, so this seemed like a good chance to make my escape. I pushed myself up to my hands and knees and started a huddled dash back toward the street.

It must have been close to midnight then. Around 10 seconds later, it felt like noon. A wave of green light overtook me from behind and illuminated the sky into ghastly pale. I stumbled over myself, pitching flat again before looking behind. The men were pouring the bags into the ocean one by one, and where the powder inside met the water an explosive wave of luminescence blasted out like lightning streaking through the waves.

It took my eyes several seconds to adjust before I realized the old man was staring directly at me. Robbed the cover of darkness, I lay stark under his steel gaze. If I had hesitated any longer, I would have been dead.

A loud crack rent the night air and the sand ruptured directly in front of me. Another shot – this time tearing through the air an inch from my shoulder. I was back on my feet, dodging through the palm trees that flourished densely at the end of the beach.

Shouting interspersed the explosions of light behind me. I didn't trust the open road around my car, so I stayed in the thicket until the shouting passed. A few minutes later I heard the roar of the van ripping out of the parking lot. I counted to a hundred before I could breathe evenly again. As far as I could tell, they were gone.

I crept back to the empty beach to try and figure out what the hell happened. The water was still glowing softly green, but it was nothing like the display I'd seen a moment ago. The ocean silently churned and boiled as dark shapes slipped below the surface. Something was feeding on whatever these guys had dumped into the water.

The tracks from the dolly were hastily swept up all the

way to the parking lot. It looks like they were in a hurry. Approaching the water, I found a small pile of the powder that had been carelessly spilled onto the beach. I gathered it up in one of my extra vials before hightailing it out of there.

I'm not sure who I could contact and be taken seriously about this, so I resolved to do a little experiment of my own. When I got home I poured my samples of Ocean water into a big mixing bowl and then dumped the powder into the water. Sure enough, there was a bright flash upon contact, although nothing compared with the neon splendor in the ocean. Within about 10 minutes the light had all but completely faded, but even my small sample had begun to boil and churn.

I left the mixture out overnight and went to bed, checking it first thing this morning when I woke up. The bowl was nearly overflowing with squirming dark shapes, each almost four inches long. Rows of razor sharp teeth like needles flashed in the light, and a hundred little legs flailed against the walls of the confined space.

Out of a morbid curiosity I dropped a fried chicken drumstick into the water. One of them attempted to swallow it instantaneously, becoming hopelessly encumbered on the bone. The others wasted no time taking advantage of the opportunity, devouring the helpless creature alive. Within seconds even the chicken bone had completely vanished, and all those beady little eyes were turned to fix on me for their next meal. They didn't get it.

By midday, there were only four of them left. They were eating each other with unrestrained savagery, snapping off the legs of any that swam too close. By evening there was only 3, but they'd grown to almost a foot long. I had to dump them into the bathtub to keep them from getting out. I don't know what I'm going to do with them, but the limited space and meager scraps I'm sustaining them with must limit their growth eventually.

I can only imagine what is going on right now in the vastness of the ocean where they're free to reach their full potential.

EVERY SUBWAY CAR

TOBIAS WADE

NEW YORK IS A COMPLICATED CITY TO LIVE IN. HERE, THE
only way to fit in is to be different. I've tried being that
girl who minds her own business, but keeping out of
trouble has only ever invited others to start trouble with
me. That's why I'm done being quiet and submissive. If
you allow yourself to be constrained by social norms,
you're never going to win a race against someone who
isn't similarly burdened. And to me, there's nothing quite
so liberating as singing.

At the bakery while I cook, through the streaming
rivers of huddled faces outside, even on the subway; I'll
just start singing whatever comes to mind. Not that self-
conscious mumbling to echo music from my headphones
either—I throw my shoulders back, open my chest, and
really belt it out. People don't care as much as you'd think.
Most of them don't even notice. Compared to the guy
with a boa constrictor around his neck, or the pair of

homeless people having sex against a wall, singing is a pretty harmless quirk. It gives me what I need to feel like I belong.

There was one time when my singing really caught someone's attention though. There were about a dozen other people on the subway, so I started off with a soft song (Hide and Seek by Imogen Heap) to make sure I wasn't bothering anyone. No-one even looked up, except for one guy wearing a black hoodie. I like matching the beat to the steady th-THUMP of the car on its tracks, and I gradually let the song build in volume until I was able to transition to a Celine Dion power house.

They all just sat there. Reading their papers, staring at their phones or their feet—too awkward or self-absorbed to even look my way. Maybe they thought I was a crazy person and didn't want to mess with me. The chemically radiant sunset of my hair probably didn't help with that, but I didn't need their approval.

The guy in the hoodie though—he wouldn't take his eyes off me. I started to give him a little smile, but then a square-potato masquerading as a human being shoved his way between us. By the time he passed, the guy in the hoodie was gone. Whatever, this was my stop anyway.

The next day I saw that black hoodie again though. His back was turned, and he was spray painting something around a concrete drain pipe. It wasn't the vandalism that bothered me – Hell, I like to make my mark as much as the next—it was what he was painting. My face was blazoned across the pipe, all the way down to my shock of flame hair and the nose-ring I always wore. It was absolutely surreal staring into my own giant eyes which might have been beautiful if the situation wasn't so damn unnerving.

Maybe I should just be flattered that I made such an impression on him. I sat down about a dozen feet away and watched him expertly apply a light drizzle of shadow to define my cheekbones. It was a triumphant pose: a Queen surveying her adoring Kingdom on the night of her inauguration. What was this guy's deal, anyway? I hadn't even gotten a clear look at his face. Did he paint all the pretty strangers he sees, or was it just me? I was about to go ask him when I noticed the caption he was now writing below my portrait.

Kill her

Well what do you know, look at the time. As laudable as New York's diversity is, that unfortunately includes a large population of absolute maniacs. I quietly stood and backed away from the artist. He must have heard me though, because he immediately spun my way.

"Wait! I need you!" He was running after me now, but I wasn't about to stick around for pleasant conversation. I hightailed for the next three blocks until I reached the subway. For a moment I thought I was overreacting, but the two other paintings I passed along the way told a different story.

Death—written under the first one. It was another painting of me, this time from another angle. **Steal her**—the words were splashed right across my face on the next painting. I just wanted to be another invisible face in the crowd now. It was a relief to see the people piling up outside the station. I couldn't hide my red hair, but I don't think my stalker would try something here. Now that there were so many people, I was safe again.

I managed to put it out of my mind for the rest of the day, but I began to get worried when it was time to ride the subway home. I have a defense against fear though, and there's never been a night so black that I couldn't lighten with a song. I sat down at the end of the subway car and just began singing. People filed in and out, odd looks occasionally cast my way, but there wasn't anything they could do to make me stop. As long as I was singing— as long as I was me—somehow that made me safe.

But I didn't make it home before the words choked in my throat. There I was—then another, and another—face after face spray painted along the subway walls. I caught a flash of the words **never grow old**, but I couldn't force myself to look out the window after that.

I turned away, and there he was. He'd just gotten on board and was staring right at me. There were a lot of people getting off now too. Two more stops until I got home—I didn't dare ride with him the whole way. I started shoving my way out with the rest of them, but right before I made it past the door, I felt a hand land on my shoulder.

"Why did you come back for me?" he asked.

"I didn't. I ride the subway every day," I answered.

"Did you see my tribute to you?" he asked. "Is that why you came back?"

I didn't answer. I just pulled away and pushed out the door. I looked back, but I didn't see him get off. Good, maybe he took the hint.

"You know why I did it, don't you?"

I spun. He was right behind me again. The train ground to life, and the crowds were beginning to thin on the platform as the people flooded up the stairs.

"Get away from me," I replied. "Hey! Somebody help me." The uncaring crowd kept moving about their business. Couldn't they see this guy was a creep?

"I just don't think you should be forgotten after you die." he said.

The hand gripped at my shoulder again, but I shook him off. I started walking after the people, but insistent, kneading hands kept clutching onto me.

"Help! Security!" I shouted.

There was a guard barely a dozen feet away. He glanced distractedly in my direction before turning back to his phone. What was wrong with this society? Why didn't anyone care?

"Why are you making this so hard on me?" the man in the hoodie asked. I actually shoved him this time. Hard. He staggered back a half-dozen paces, but then barreled right after me again.

"Hey, cool it over there." The security guard looked up again for a moment, but he didn't make the slightest move to help.

"Can't you see that I love you?" the man in the hoodie howled. "Why won't you stay with me?"

He was there with me every step I took. I couldn't shake him. Another subway car was rumbling into place, and I tried to make my way toward it to get away. Hands were on my back, so I spun and shoved him again. This time he didn't catch himself in time. He dropped his pack as he back-peddled–trying to find his balance, tripping over his own feet. His familiar eyes pleaded an agonizing moment while he seemed to hang in the air before tumbling off the platform –? straight onto the tracks.

The train roared into place. I couldn't look–but I couldn't look away. I saw a pair of hands reaching up over the side before a hideous crack rent the air. I covered my ears and ran, but I couldn't block out the anguished scream. It just kept going and going–rising and falling like a car alarm. I'd thought the train would have killed him on impact, but maybe it just caught one of his legs or something.

Finally. Finally people were starting to notice. The crowd surged to the edge of the platform to watch. Shouting – the security guard trying in vain to hold them all back. Then the train started backing up, and the screaming surged up again. It didn't last long this time though. He must have died as it rolled back over him.

The noise was deafening. The only sign that the man in the hoodie had been there was his backpack still lying on the ground. I should have just left it alone and run, but as long as everyone was distracted, why not? Maybe I wanted a clue as to his obsession, or maybe it was my guilt that begged for closure. Whatever the case was, I couldn't stop myself from opening it and looking inside.

Photographs spilled out. Dozens of them. All of me, although some still showed my unaltered brown hair. He must have been following me for years. I sat on the ground in disbelief while the chaos churned around me.

More photos–these the paintings of my face. Many more than the ones I'd seen–the whole city must be filled with them. So far I must have encountered a random selection, but here they were all assembled in order. As I flipped through the photos, I could clearly read the captions in the sequence they were intended.

LIFE COULDN'T KILL **her** spirit.
   Death couldn't **steal her** soul.
   She's still singing, can you hear it?
   From lips that will **never grow old**.

THEN PAPERS—NEWS-PAPER clippings: the obituary of my death standing most prominently on the top. Two years ago in this very subway. I died when a man slipped his knife between my ribs and ran off with my purse, leaving me to bleed out on the ground while people walked past me and did nothing.

But did I know this man? Why couldn't I remember him? Then again, why had he been the only one to notice me? Of all the careless faces that pass me every day, why didn't any of them seem to look my way?

I was so overwhelmed and terrified—I just did the only thing I knew to calm down. I started singing, but no-one noticed me over the riotous commotion. And every time I can't make sense of where I am or where I'm going, I'll just start singing again. Sometimes I'll catch an odd glance or two, but more often I can be as loud as I want and no-one will even know I'm there.

I keep forgetting things, and places, and people. But I'm writing this because I don't want to forget that he loved me, and that maybe I even once loved him. Now that he's dead, I hope he'll be able to look at my face painted all over the city and remember me. Until then, I'll keep riding the subway where he found me last, singing until he finds me again.

FROM RAGS TO STITCHES

TOBIAS WADE

GROWING UP WITHOUT A DAD, IT WAS SO EASY TO BLAME him for everything that went wrong. Mom wouldn't have to be gone all the time if he was here. She wouldn't be so stressed and angry. I would have done better in school if someone helped me with my homework. I wouldn't be so alone.

It was hard for me to appreciate how hard Mom worked for my sister and I. All I could see were the other families and how much happier they looked. Walking home from school I'd pass dads teaching their sons how to ride bikes or shoot hoops. I'd just walk faster, pretending I had something to do or someone waiting for me when I got home.

It was hard to keep pretending to the locked door and the dark house. Hard to realize that I mattered when most of my interactions with mom were post-it notes on the fridge.

Be back at 10. You're the man of the house. Remember to feed your sister

-Love mom

And then just like that, everything changed. Mom got a new job as a live-in maid with Leroy, a wealthy corporate type living in a big house with extra rooms. His face looked rather like a toad that had been stepped on, and it folded into a vicious scowl whenever he happened across me. Passing my sister or me in the hallway, he'd look the other way and press his body to the far wall as though afraid of contracting a disease.

Mom told us not to take it personally; Leroy didn't like *any* children. At first I couldn't figure out why he invited us to live there at all, but I was 15 then and it didn't take long to translate the leering smiles he gave Mom. He was always watching her when she was cleaning, and it made me sick to be in the same room as them. Even worse, Mom seemed to actually enjoy the attention. She made a show every time she bent over, luxuriously stretching her body when she reached high to dust.

I don't suppose it was my place to fight it though. My little sister Casey was just happy to have mom around all the time, and money was a lot easier now. I still didn't trust Leroy, but I figured mom knew what she was doing and could take care of herself. It wasn't long before Leroy's long looks turned into lingering caresses though. As always, Casey was more optimistic about it than I was.

"He's going to take care of us," Casey said one night. "And if he wants to be our new dad, then Mom is going to make him be nice to us."

"We can't have a new dad because we never had an old

dad," I told her. "And Leroy won't want anything to do with us either."

But both of us were wrong: things didn't improve, and they didn't stay the same. They got much worse, much faster than we could have anticipated. Any noise was too much noise for Leroy. I could barely say good morning to Casey at the breakfast table without him slapping us quiet with his newspaper. He wouldn't look away anymore when I caught him fondling mom either. He'd just stare right through me and keep going, taunting me, daring me to say something. Once I'd left a pile of my school books on the dining room table and he just dumped them into the trash without hesitation. It was clear that Casey and I weren't welcome here.

We weren't invisible anymore. We were openly despised. Casey wouldn't speak up though, and mom refused to see it. She kept praising Leroy for taking us in and saying how much better he was than my real father. I wanted to stand up to Leroy, but seeing mom so happy I couldn't bear the guilt of ruining this for her. That's what I told myself at least. It seemed more noble than admitting I was afraid.

"Our life changed pretty fast, didn't it?" Casey would say. "It's easy to forget that Leroy's life changed pretty fast too. It's going to take time for him to learn how to deal with us. We just have to keep being good, and sooner or later he's going to notice."

I told her we were already being good, but she couldn't look me in the eye. "Not good enough," she said.

Casey hugged me and I held on because I knew she was being strong for the both of us now. She flinched at my touch though, and that was when I first noticed the bruises on her chest. She pulled away from me and put her finger to her lips. *Don't tell,* her eyes pleaded. *Don't destroy our new life because of me.* That time I couldn't lie to myself anymore. I was the man of the house before Leroy arrived, and it was still my responsibility to protect the family. If anyone hurt us, it was my job to hurt them back.

I couldn't lie to myself. It wasn't for mom or for Casey that I was holding back. I was a coward, pure and simple. And it was my fault what happened next.

Less than a week later, Casey didn't get up to go to school with me. When I got home I found dead in her room. Clothing torn. Black and purple bruises around her neck. Her hair was frayed as though she was dragged across the floor. Cuts and abrasions all along her little body. The only thing that didn't look spoiled was her pure white hands. She hadn't fought back. She'd stayed good, even with that monsters hands around her neck.

And still, I was afraid. More than ever now. I wanted to storm down to his office and break open the door. I wanted to gut the bastard, to scream at him for every silent suffering we took in stride. I wanted to let him bleed out on the floor, take his money, and run somewhere I could protect mom. But I couldn't stop thinking about what he did to Casey, or what it must have felt like to be bludgeoned and dragged; choked and killed. I wasn't as brave as she was.

I went to mom instead. Even if we didn't get revenge, we could still get out. Mom didn't answer when I knocked, but I heard her crying inside. My hand froze on the door knob, terrified that he was with her now. I forced myself to open the door anyway. Thank god, she was alone—sitting on the bed, looking up at me as I entered.

"You already know." It was a statement, not a question. Mom nodded, stifling back sobs. "I'm so sorry."

"It's not your fault." I sat on the floor in front of her, pressing my face against her legs. "It's his fault. He did this to us."

"You're right," she said, breathing easier now. "His fault."

"But it's not too late for us. We're going to go away now, right? We're going to be good. We'll start a new life."

She hugged me close, her hands running through my hair. "We have gotten away. This IS our new life. Even though it was your father's fault for leaving me with two kids, it's going to be okay. I'm free now."

"Dad? I was talking about Leroy -" I began, but I couldn't get the words out anymore. She was holding me even tighter. I tried to break free but her hands ran down my face to latch around my neck.

"I had to kill her, don't you see?" Mom's words bubbled out with hysterical insistence. "I had to fix your father's mistake. This is the only way Leroy would marry me. I could never force him to raise another man's children."

Maybe I could have struck her in the face, or broken one of her fingers and escaped. Even with her hands around my neck though, I couldn't bring myself to hurt her. My panicked brain couldn't make sense of what was happening. I struggled to get away, but my head was swimming as her fingers dug holes into my neck.

"Leroy has been so good to us," Mom cooed. "I'm so sorry, baby. This is the only thing I can do to make it up to him."

I toppled backward onto the floor and was able to gasp a greedy lungful of air into my lungs. I screamed as loud as my battered throat would allow, the air escaping me like I was vomiting burning gasoline. Then mom fell off the bed onto me, her whole weight landing on my throat. I must have been on the edge of passing out then because I was only aware of brief slivers of broken time like my consciousness was a strobe light.

The door opening.

Leroy standing over me to watch.

Mom's hands still around my neck.

The door opening again.

Casey standing in the doorway. Bruised and beaten as I saw her last.

And then I passed out for real. When I finally did wake up, I was still lying on the floor with mom on top of me. I pushed her off and struggled to my feet, panting and gasping and spluttering up blood. Leroy was on the floor too. Around both of their necks were the black and purple imprints of little fingers which dug so far into the flesh as to make permanent impressions in the corpse.

I didn't call the police until after I ran back to Casey's room. She was pale and stiff just as I had left her on the bed. The only difference was that her immaculate hands were now stained with dark streaks.

The police later confirmed her fingerprints on both Leroy and my mother. It seems as though they had already gotten married, and without any other living descendants I stood to inherit the house.

It's been four years since then, and I've tried to do my best to make up for what happened. I've given most of Leroy's money away, and I've opened up the extra rooms to foster children without a place to stay. I volunteer every chance I get, and am even taking classes to become a licensed family therapist. I know I should have done more when I had the chance, but I'm doing everything I can now.

I'm writing this because I need to know what is left for me to do. When I lay down to sleep at night, why do I still hear her? It was bad enough when it was just me, but now two of the foster boys have told me they hear it too.

Right before sleep in the broken time between waking and dreams, we all hear the same thing. Some nights it is no more than an intrusive thought that can't be banished. Other times I feel the hot whisper and my throat will start to itch like little fingers brushing the tiny hairs of my neck. Every time the same words, begging, pleading, demanding; I can't tell which.

"Not good enough," she'll say.

And I'll know she was right.

TWO DEAD PLAYING THE ELEVATOR GAME

TOBIAS WADE

I JUST WANTED TO GET HOME THAT NIGHT. AN IMPROMPTU board meeting ran late, and I had to stay until almost 9 PM just to take notes. When I finally did get out of there, waiting for the elevator was absolute torture. My heels were killing me, my bra was a dagger in my back, and all I had to show for my hard work was a legal pad full of inane political drivel and off-colored jokes.

Five minutes. *Ten minutes* before the door opened. Inside a pair of giggling teenagers were shoving each other back and forth. One girl, one boy. Baggy hoodies. Ripped jeans. Smelled like they thought marijuana was a perfume. It didn't take a legal secretary to guess they had been playing an elevator game by pushing every button.

I thought about reprimanding them, but the moment I stepped inside they went dead quiet. Maybe they knew they were busted. The building should have been locked by now anyway. I don't even know how they got in here, but at my energy was so depleted that didn't really care.

142

"Where are you going?" I asked, just to be polite.

The boy started to giggle again for a second. Then stopped. So abruptly I almost thought I was imagining it. It looked like the girl was holding her breath. She hid her face beneath her hair and went to push floor #1.

Not my kids. Not my problem. What *was* my problem is that the elevator was going up instead of down. I moved toward the row of buttons, and the girl fell flat to the floor and scrambled out of my way like I was made of lava. I mashed the highlighted #1, but we were going up quicker than ever.

Faster than it had ever gone before. There was nothing to hold on to, and I had to press myself to the wall to stop from falling over. It was shaking now too, buckling back and forth as it screeched up the cable. The lights flickered, and a cold wind started to whistle through the crack in the doors. It wasn't like a storm or anything though. It was more like all the heat in the elevator was flooding out into the shaft.

Another lurch. The hardest one yet. I fell straight on my ass. The kids playing the elevator game were holding onto each other and managed to remain standing, but even after we'd stopped they kept clinging on as though holding for dear life. The #1 button went dark. #10 turned on. Slowly, ponderously, as though it were struggling against a nearly insurmountable pressure, the door slid open.

I started to stand, then slipped again as one of my heels snapped cleanly off. I took the other shoe off, so frustrated that I just threw it at the kids.

"Now look what you've done. You broke the fucking elevator."

The boy glanced in my direction, but immediately turned away again. They were straining to look outside, but terrified to get close to me. Good, they should be scared. Vandalizing a legal office was as stupid as picking a fight in a police station.

"I want your names, and IDs. Both of you," I snapped. "You will be held responsible for any damages incurred. As far as the trespassing is concerned—"

But they still wouldn't look at me. The boy grabbed the girl by the hand and darted out into the hallway. I couldn't just let them run amok.

"Hey, you can't go in there!" I had to run to keep up now. "That's Mr. Bogle's office. You aren't allowed to -"

Annnnd they were inside. Of course. I patted myself down for my cell phone, but it wasn't there. I must have dropped it when I fell in the elevator. I half-turned back, but the door was already closing. I took a step in that direction, but then I heard something *crash* from the office. I spun again, sprinting down the hallway in my bare feet.

The boy was sitting on Mr. Bogle's desk while the girl stared out the window.

"Look at the sky!" she said. "And how tall the buildings are!"

"Dude, this is crazy," he replied.

Either they were stoned out of their minds or it wasn't just marijuana. They were running their hands over everything, so I wouldn't have been surprised if they were rolling too. The boy was even poking the potted plant like it was some alien creature he'd never seen before.

"That's enough!" I roared. Finally they both looked at me. Then at each other. Then back at me. Did they regret playing this stupid elevator game yet?

"Let's get out of here!" the boy rammed straight through me with his shoulder, sending me spinning back to the ground. The girl was trying to jump over me now, but I managed to grab her by the ankle and drag her down. She thrashed melodramatically on the ground for a few seconds, but before I could get to my feet she planted a kick in my face and broke free.

The door was already closing by the time I got to my feet. They were both inside, staring at me with wide trembling eyes as though they were somehow the victim in all of this. I felt absolutely feral as I lunged at them. I managed to get my fingers in the crack before the elevator closed and the sensor reflected the doors open wide. Half a dozen buttons had already been pushed, glowing like one big middle finger. The final stage of the elevator game had been played.

They were cowering in the corner as I loomed over them, an inferno of retribution burning in my eyes. Fine, let the elevator take the long trip down. That was just longer for them to be trapped in here with me. Now that they couldn't run, the struggle was absolutely pitiful. The boy's throat was almost comically fragile, and I was amazed how little pressure I needed to ram my broken heel through it. The girl was almost gone by the time I got to her, withering to a husk in seconds after the venom from my nails coursed through her leg where I had grabbed her.

I got out of the elevator at the bottom, straightening my dress. I'd found my phone again and fixed my hair, and after snapping the other heel off my shoe, I was able to look almost presentable again.

I thought I could finally go home after that, but it didn't take long to realize that I'd never been further from home in my life. What strange green plants they have here, and the dark blue sky was nothing like the purple and orange we have at home. No wonder they were so surprised by everything in my world. If everyone here is as fragile as those two little ones, then I think I'm going to have a lot of fun here.

ONE DEATH IS NOT ENOUGH

TOBIAS WADE

GILLES GARNIER WAS LESS THAN HUMAN. I DON'T MEAN HE didn't have two hands, or two feet, or opposable thumbs – I mean that his spirit was so vile that his mere existence was an insult to the human race.

That's why he was nicknamed the "Werewolf of Dole," so we could think of him as a beast and pretend that each of us did not possess that same capacity for evil. Whatever he was, the creature was famous for strangling and eating four children in 16th century France before he was burned at the stake in 1572.

But that isn't where his story ends. Even the grotesque agony of burning alive was deemed incomparable to the suffering he caused those children and their families. That's why the secret sect known as "The Order of the Forgotten" was founded that same year, honoring Gilles with their very first sentence.

. . .

ONE LIFE IS ENOUGH to be forgotten by Heaven.
  But one death is not enough to be forgiven by Hell.

THAT WAS THEIR MOTTO. They would wait until the body (or ashes, in Gilles' case) were buried before retrieving the remains. The Order of the Forgotten was initially established by the alchemists who used their macabre ingredients to trace the soul of the departed until it found its next iteration of reincarnated life.

The records indicate that Gilles Garnier was born again in 1574 under the name of Alisa Hathoway. Once the child was located, she was burned as well, serving as further punishment for the original sin she still carried in bearing Gilles' corrupted soul. Although subsequent judgment from the Order of the Forgotten was later restricted to a maximum of five deaths, the soul of Gilles Garnier was fated to serve as a warning for all those who would lend an ear to the goading darkness.

That is why Gilles was sentenced to an everlasting death. Every single time he was found. Every reincarnated animal, or child, or plant that possessed a shred of his original essence would sooner or later be located, and without fail, burned to ashes. These would then be preserved in order to find next soul on his eternal journey.

Now in 2017, the Order of the Forgotten has spanned six continents and over 140 countries, and they have entrusted me with killing Gilles for the 28th time.

"These ashes have been preserved for twenty years since his last death," Father Alexander told me. We were standing in the choir room of his church, now deserted to the lengthening shadows which grew restless with the deepening night.

"Ordinarily," Alexander continued, "we would have found him again much sooner, but the flames of his last death had spread to a nearby forest which consumed him utterly. His remains were contaminated with other ashes, and for a long while we were afraid that his remaining link would be too weak to trace. Although it has taken longer than usual, we have finally been able to succeed."

I'd never killed anyone before. The thought of carrying out this deed should have been abhorrent to me, but my oath to the Order was enough to reassure me that I was doing the right thing. After all, I had been a lost soul as well, and I was in debt to the father for sparing me from a similar fate. I will never forget that night when he found me when I was 14, camping in the woods with my friends. Through the trees he came, bearing a flaming brand which burned with the rage of an angry God.

"You are a sinner." he told me. And there with his billowing robes, basked in the glory of fire and pierced by the wild intensity of his eyes, I could feel my very soul laid bare to him.

"You have killed in your past lives, and you have fallen from grace." My friends had run, but I stood alone with my back to a tree. I was terrified by him, but somehow dependent as well. He knew me as I did not know myself, and it was not only my existence but my very nature which begged for his absolution.

The roaring fire inches from my face – my hair smoldering into my scalp–the exhilarating rush of my eternal realization. Did I remember the evils that I had caused? No, but I felt them like a weight on my soul, and I knew in that moment that I would do them again if I was not purified by the flame.

"You are forgotten by Heaven, but if you do as I say, you will be remembered before you die."

Six years later, I bow to Father Alexander, still fearful of the depth his probing eyes reach.

"Yes Father," I replied, "I will kill Gilles Garnier again."

Through the maturing night I walked, feeling the bag of ashes warm against my skin as I approach my target. I know he is close, which is why the Father has chosen me to do his bidding. *Don't think of it as killing someone. Think of it as killing the part of myself which fate has cursed me to carry.* That's what I tried to tell myself at least.

It was exciting to feel the bag continuing to warm as I entered the restaurant. I walked slowly now, each step resounding with the unswayable purpose of one following God's will. The bag of ashes was starting to burn my leg now. Father told me that it will burst into flame when Gilles is beside me, and that I must use it to return him to ashes once more.

"Excuse me, have you been seated?"

I walked straight past the waiter without a second glance. Too old. It had been twenty years since Gilles was burned, so the man I was looking for must be less than that. It can sometimes take years before the soul to return to life, so there were still plenty of options.

"We're very full, so if you don't have a reservation -"

I felt a hand on my shoulder, but one look was enough for

the waiter to stumble backward. He saw something in me that I had seen in Father Alexander on the night he found me. Such a glorious purpose cannot be seen and turned aside.

"I'm here to meet someone." I told him. His eyes were masks of uncertainty, so I pointed at a table at the far end of the room. "I'm with them."

The teenage couple sitting there glanced up. The waiter bobbed his head, disappearing with the kind of relief you'd expect from a man climbing out of a shark tank. The bag of ashes was searing my flesh now, and the smell of it mingled with the aromatic atmosphere wafting from the table. I smiled through it all, knowing my redemption was at hand.

"We weren't expecting–" the boy started.

"They never are," I answered, sitting down to join them. He couldn't be more than sixteen, face still riddled with enough pimples to make a constellation. Was it him? Or was it the girl, staring at me with her wide blue eyes that quivered around the edges. What was she afraid of, unless she felt the pressing weight on her soul?

"Sorry, but who are you?" the boy asked. I ignored him, digging the cloth bag from my pocket and dropping it onto the table. Sparks forced their way out like smoldering gunpowder.

"Leave us," I told the boy, "I want a word with your friend."

He half-started to stand, but the girl grabbed his arm and pulled him back into the chair. Her blue eyes narrowed, no longer shaking.

"I'm not his friend, I'm his *girlfriend*," she snapped, as

though that made any difference to me. "And you're the one who needs to leave."

She was loud. Too loud. Several tables had turned to stare at me. There was no way to do this quietly here. Not yet.

"My apologies, Gilles." I tested her. She didn't even flinch. And why would she? I didn't remember my past life, so why would I expect her to remember a man who lived hundreds of years ago? I grabbed the cloth bag and excused myself from the table before the waiter could return. As I walked briskly toward the door, I could feel the bag cooling against my skin.

I waited outside for them to emerge, clutching the bag between my hands, desperate for the lingering heat to reaffirm my beliefs. Her soul was corrupt, just as mine was. She must be punished for me to become clean. But how could she be punished for something she never did? How could I be absolved by killing an innocent?

They exited sooner than I expected. Maybe I had ruined the mood. I waited until they left the ring of lights before I fell into step behind them. It didn't matter if I had doubts, because I know God was infallible. If he wanted me to kill, then I would enjoy it knowing I was doing the right thing. The Order of the Forgotten had maintained their charge for hundreds of years, and I wouldn't be weak link in that chain.

The bag was burning again. I watched her say goodbye to the boy in front of her house, hugging him after he seemed too awkward to kiss her. The ashes grew hotter as they held each other close, and then he was gone –

walking down the sidewalk. The bag didn't cool down. That was it then. She was the one.

Dark house. Rustling of keys. She glanced behind her, eyes fixing on the sparkling bag in my hands. Then on my face. I smiled.

"Hello Gilles Garnier," I said. "Would you like to invite me in?"

She shook her head. Back to the door, she fumbled with the keys in her hands. I threw the ashes at her face, watching them come to life as they approached. She threw her arms up to block, but the ashes scattered in fiery impact. She screamed, and I can't deny the satisfaction of hearing my prey realize its helplessness. The burning ashes clung to her like tar, bursting into incandescent color as brilliant as the brand Father Alexander carried when he found me.

I wasn't killing her. I was just sending her back where she belonged.

Only she didn't burn. The light burst around her in a luminous aura. She wasn't screaming anymore either – just staring at her dazzling body in awe. I didn't understand. I wanted to see her soul being purged! I wanted her to suffer for what she'd done! Father Alexander told me that –

"That's enough." It was Alexander's voice. My eyes were stunned from the light and I couldn't see him, but I heard his footsteps approaching from the street. "Gilles has revealed himself to you. It's time to punish him."

"I'm trying–" I spluttered, but Alexander's hand materialized from the shadows to preface his entrance into the light. The hard lines in his skin made it look as though it were carved from stone.

"I'm talking to Lily," Alexander said. His grave face was fully illuminated now, and I could see that he was staring at the girl. "It is as I told you. You do not have to search for the soul in need of punishment. He will find you."

My blood was boiling. My chest was tight. I could barely breath, but I forced the words out like hissing steam.

"The ashes. You told me to–"

"I told you the day I met you," Alexander growled. "That you carried a corrupted soul. Each time you return, you are tested again. Not once in five hundred years have you refused to kill, and so not once have you been spared. So are all the souls tested before they are punished again. There is no reason so grand or order so high that can justify the choice you've made to kill an innocent."

The light had all but faded from Lily now. The ashes still sparkled where they rained through the air around her. It had been a trick then. I may not have remembered being Gilles Garnier, but I hadn't refused the chance to kill again either. I turned to run, and neither of them followed me.

But where can I run when it was my nature that I must flee? How can I hide when they have already found me over 200 times? Sooner or later the Order of the Forgotten burn me again, so there is nothing left for me but to wait. To wait and to pray, that next time I will find the strength to make my own choices, not rely on God.

IMAGINE A NIGHT

TOBIAS WADE

IMAGINE A NIGHT WHEN THE SPACE BETWEEN WORDS BECOMES like the space between trees: wide enough to wander in.
– Sarah Thomson.

"THAT POOR GIRL," they'd say. "Imagine that happening right in our neighborhood."

"Do you think she suffered much? It's too dreadful to think about."

"We're all holding a vigil in her honor. You'll be there, of course?"

No, I won't be there. I honestly don't understand why people still feel sorry for my sister Catherine. Once pain has passed, it no longer exists. Once life has passed, pain is no longer possible. Her cold body no longer bleeds, nor do her withered lungs cry out as they must have done from the lonely depths of those tangled woods. Sympathy is wasted on the dead.

All my life I've been the one who was pitied. I was diagnosed at four with spinal muscle atrophy which wasted me away until I was too weak to stand. I underwent constant orthopedic surgeries, physio-therapy, respiratory care, and endless new medications. Never once did I think I would be the one to survive. My older sister had always been there to take care of me though. From helping me shower to pushing my wheelchair, she'd supported me literally and figuratively for as long as I can remember.

Now they treat her like she's the victim, but she isn't anymore. I don't care if you think this is selfish, but mother and I are the only victims now. We're the ones living amidst the ashes of a life which burned so bright and brief: a defiant flare from a dying star. Only our unmeasured pain still lingers in her absence.

"She's in Heaven now," my mother told me. "It's the most wonderful place you can imagine."

"Then why are you still sad?" I'd asked.

"Because she got there first, and we must wait." Mother held me close, although I think it was as much for her own comfort as mine. She didn't want me to see, but I could still feel the suppressed trembling of her body and knew she must be crying. At 14, I was too old to be comforted by her facade. Catherine helped me so much while mom was at work, but now that we're alone, I don't know what we'll do. There's a constant source of restless anticipation as though any second could bring her through the door or break the grim silence with her swelling laughter. It still doesn't seem real that she's gone.

Catherine used to sit and read upon that window seat,

now cluttered with the graveyard of her possessions. Or out in the garden, dancing among her sprouting seeds with a triumphant exaltation unmatched by the inauguration of an emperor. She walked in grace, warming each room she entered with boundless vitality. Even now in the heat of summer I shiver to remember what that felt like.

I still talk to her sometimes, but not in the way you might expect. I don't ask her about the night she died, or dwell upon evil thoughts of the creature which devoured everything except her eyes. Instead, I'll break the hungry silence of the night by asking how she lived with such innocent wonder. I'll ask how she was so happy, because sitting alone in the room we shared, it seems that I've forgotten.

"You're such a strong girl," they say. "Your sister would be proud."

"It will get easier. Time heals all wounds."

No, I don't believe that either. Time makes a wound fester and rot, magnifying the pain into brooding despair. If Catherine had somehow crawled from the clutches of the wilds, legs torn to shreds, face mutilated beyond recognition, do you think time would have spared her from pain? Or would life's cruelty compound her injury until isolation and rejection stole what remaining dignity even the beast could not take? Will time ever spare me from the prison of this failing body?

They see me eating, and talking, and forcing a smile through my dried lips. They don't realize that two girls died the night Catherine was attacked. They know that we were close, but do not understand that we were the same. One secret glance between us, and we would see into each other's heart. Half a smile, and we both laughed at an unshared joke. Even now through the veil of death I can see her waiting for me on the other side.

My body lingered for a week after her death, but there was no point in delaying the inevitable. I was calm when I rolled up to the pool last night. The chill waters ebbed and flowed against my feet like an electrical current, but it couldn't disturb the tranquility which ushered my spirit toward her. Catherine was in Heaven now, so what was the point of waiting here in Hell?

It would be only human nature to struggle once I rolled into the pool. The chair would pin me beneath the suffocating water though, and even without it I wouldn't be strong enough to swim. Catherine would have struggled too, but that's over now. When the fluid filled my lungs and my oxygen deprived brain stopped thinking about the world that might have been, we'd be together again.

One deep breath before the plunge.

If only I had died and she had lived. Mother could have been happy then.

One look back at the dark house.

But not dark enough. I could see mom now, watching me from her bedroom window.

She wasn't calling out. She didn't want to stop me. It didn't matter either way though.

One way or the other, I was already gone.

I plunged my chair into the water and sank toward the bottom. The peace didn't last, but I waited as long as I could before letting the first bubbles escape my mouth.

The pressure built into a silent scream. My fingers dug into my neck, but I forced myself to let go. The last wave of air leaked from my burning lungs and my head spun. I thought I caught a glimpse of mother looking down at me, but my eyes swelled shut and I couldn't be sure. The water poured into my nose and mouth, filling my chest, flowing and growing and swelling until I knew I would burst.

It's okay. I told myself. *This isn't the end. This is just a stopping point on between being alone and together again.*

The water was rushing past me now. I sensed a light penetrating into my closed lids. I felt a surge of upward motion. I tried to open my eyes, but the light was so bright that I couldn't see any more than with them shut. My chair was gone. This was it. The wait was over, and I was being carried to Heaven.

My head burst free from the water and I spluttered in the open air. My eyes were still pressed tight, but I flailed until I felt something solid and gripped on for dear... life? Dear existence, perhaps. The water gently pushed me toward the shore, and I pulled myself hand over trembling hand until solid ground welcomed me.

I vomited a veritable river of water. It felt like I must have drunk half the pool. I couldn't still be there though, because instead of the tiles I felt grass and mud squelching beneath me.

The rustle of leaves. The strangled caw of a bird, and then a hooting reply. I wiped my face with dirty hands until a sliver of light broke through my swollen lids. The tangled trees rose around me like specters of the night, and a full moon illuminated the stagnant pool which I'd crawled from. Perhaps I was in the woods behind my house, but I had never seen them by moonlight. Was I dead?

What had my sister been doing, so far out alone? She never went anywhere without me. How did she even get there?

The crack of a branch. More rustling, prompting a surge of wild panic from my already erratic heart. And what *was* it that had attacked her that night?

Everyone had assumed that she had simply snuck off into the woods with a boy. Wouldn't she have told me though? I had been so obsessed with my own thoughts and feelings that I hadn't even stopped to wonder what really happened that night. It had just been an accident, too horrible to think about. Or was it?

I took a hesitant step back toward the pool of water, but looking down I could see that it couldn't be more than a few inches deep. It was impossible for me to be here, but I was.

I took another step, my feet scrambling below me. For the first time in my life I was walking, but it wasn't just that. I was walking on all fours. They weren't hands which had pulled me out of the water, but predatory paws like some primordial wolf from an age where tooth and claw were the only rules governing the world.

The *rustling* was getting closer.

"Hello? Is anyone there?"

Catherine! It had to be her! We could be together again, but not like this. Not with the fur bristling down my back or claws churning the wet mud. I felt my mouth involuntarily twist into a snarl. *Run Catherine! You aren't safe with me!* If only she could sense my thoughts now like she used to. Tension washed through my body as I crouched to pounce, and savage instincts flooded my awareness with an undeniable compulsion to feed.

But it wasn't Catherine. It was my mother who stepped through the trees to stand before me. I was so surprised that I couldn't even move. She was wearing a bathrobe I had seen her in when she watched me from her bedroom window and smiling from ear to ear.

"There you are. I've been looking everywhere for you," she said. "Come along, your sister is waiting."

She took a step toward me, but the vibration of an alien growl rose in my throat.

"Don't be silly." Mother didn't seem the least afraid, and her confidence in the face of my terrifying presence was enough to give me pause. "You're in Heaven now, child. You needn't be afraid. For our family, that means returning to who we truly are. The body may be tamed, but the spirit can never be deprived of its true form. Your father has decided your sister was old enough to become herself, although you have decided for yourself."

This wasn't my Heaven. This wasn't who I was. This wasn't who Catherine – poor innocent Catherine – was meant to be. The feral rage was building inside me again, but I couldn't let myself attack. What would that accomplish, besides allowing mother to transform as well?

"That's right, you understand now." Mother took a step forward. She loosened her robe, exposing her bare neck. "Go ahead. Do it, and we will be a family again."

The flesh was so soft, and I was so hungry. It was so easy to sink my teeth in and shake the life out of her. The freedom of my body was exhilarating as I flew through the air. I wasn't a cripple anymore. I wasn't in pain, or pitied, or a victim. I wasn't alone anymore. In that moment as the blood ran down my jaws, I knew my mother was right. I was in Heaven.

But how quickly that moment passed, and how silent the woods when her body stopped moving. By the morning I woke alone in the woods, covered in my mother's blood. My hands were my own. My feet were my own. And how my body shook as I pulled myself inch by excruciating inch across the forest floor with my degenerative muscles fighting me the whole way.

It's taken time, but I've pieced together what I think really happened to me. The first time I died, it was when I suffocated in my sleep when my failing lungs could no longer support my dying body. That was the night of my first transformation, when I killed my sister and dragged her into the woods.

The second night I died was in the pool, prompting my second rebirth. But just like the first time, it only lasted through the night. I don't know who my father is or where these powers came from, but it seems as though my mother didn't understand as I do now. My mother and sister did not have the gift, and neither of them are coming back. Every night since then, I flee my dying body and relish in the freedom of the hunt. Every night I die, and every night I taste Heaven again.

MAKE MONEY OR DIE TRYING

MAKE MONEY OR DIE TRYING

HAYONG-BAK

HELLO, MY NAME IS JARED AND I AM HOMELESS. WELL. I was homeless. I'm now fighting for my life. How did I find myself in that predicament? Well, I chose to. Why? Because I want to win half a million dollars.

Last Night, I was walking around the streets of downtown Nashville. I finished the day off with around thirteen dollars in my pocket. I'm not homeless because I had shit luck. I'm homeless because I was a stubborn twenty-year-old trying to make it out on my own. I had family waiting for me back home, but I wasn't ready to crawl back to my family yet. Like I said, I'm a stubborn guy. I would rather die than beg my parents to take me back.

With the thirteen dollars I had in my pocket I could buy two Gatorades, three ham and cheese sandwiches, and a pack of smokes. I was on the way to my usual convenience store when a man got out of the back seat of a Bentley and walked up to me. He was casually dressed in a t-shirt and jeans but I knew that the clothes he wore cost a small fortune. As he stuck out his hand towards me he said, "Hey bud my name is Elijah and I would like to buy you some dinner. You look hungry." I shook his hand and asked him, "Why? I have a little bit of money. I can buy my own dinner."

He chuckled and said, "Well. It looks like you haven't had a decent meal in ages. Tell you what. I have way too much money and I like helping out people less fortunate. I'll get you some dinner and we can talk. If you don't like what I say I will personally go to any hotel of your choice and get you a room for 3 months. That sound fair?"

I thought about it for a second before nodding my head nervously at him. He put his arm around my shoulder and led me into his car. He didn't take me anywhere really fancy. Just the local steakhouse and we took our seat at the back of the restaurant. He ordered a salad and I ordered a T-bone steak. The first half of the meal was silent. He wasn't really eating, just kept staring into the salad and moving around pieces of lettuce with his fork.

The silence was broken when he put down his fork and let out a small cough. I looked back up at him with a large chunk of steak in my mouth and he softly asked, "I have an opportunity for you." I swallowed what was in my mouth and asked, "What kind of opportunity? Like a job?" He gave me a small smile and said, "Yeah. Well. Kind of. Let me be completely honest with you. I see you as a strong willed person. Suicide is the last thing on your mind, and that is what I am looking for. I have been watching you for the last three days. Keep in mind. This is an opportunity for you to make half a million dollars.

That should be enough for you to be happy for a very long time."

Half curious and half disturbed, I put down my fork and asked, "What do you mean you watched me for three days? What do I have to do to make the money? How do I know you even have that much money?"

After taking a deep breath, he got up from his chair and sat next to me. He leaned his face towards my ear and whispered, "Five people go in. One person leaves. This is for a, hm, let's just say it's a show. People from all over the world pay fifty grand to watch you guys like it's a reality TV show. Of course, people will die and it might be you, but if you win...you get to take home five hundred grand. No strings attached."

I scooted away from him and pushed the meal away from me. He started to speak again but I held my hand up and told him to let me think.

I know money isn't everything, but this was an opportunity for me. Probably a once in a lifetime opportunity. I knew the probabilities pointed to an early grave for me, but I just couldn't lose this chance.

A chance to finally prove to my family that I was fully self-capable.

I looked back at him and said, "I'm in. When do we start?"

He clapped his hands together and said, "Well we need to head out now. I will drive you to our private airplane. Erm. I'm going to have to blindfold you when we get in the car, but the contest starts the day after tomorrow."

When he got up from his chair I got up and followed him to his car. He grabbed a blindfold from the front passenger seat and handed it to me. I covered my eyes up and sat back. After a couple of minutes, I felt the car start up and he put something in my hand and said, "Take this pill. It'll knock you right out." I shrugged my shoulders and threw the pill into my mouth and swallowed it. As the car started to speed up I slowly drifted off.

I woke up and felt a small pain inside of my ear. Once I managed to stand up I rubbed my eyes and looked around. Within a couple of seconds, I knew I was on a plane. There were two other guys and two women sleeping on their chairs. I sat back down on my seat and stared out the window. I noticed that it was the morning now. We were descending, but all I could see was the ocean. After a couple of minutes, the plane started to descend quickly. I looked out the window and saw an endless amount of trees. As the plane started to quickly go down I sat back in my seat and braced myself. I was completely convinced that we were about to crash into the trees, but as the plane touched down on the ground I saw that we were in a small clearing.

The plane came to a stop and a door opened from the back of the plane. Elijah came out and walked to the front of the plane. I looked around and saw that everyone else was awake. He looked at all of us for a second before saying, "Alright. Let me see if I can remember. Jared, Blake, Cody, Allison, and Elise. Did I get that right?" We all nodded and he smiled before continuing, "Okay follow me out of the plane and I will lead you guys to your room. The contest starts tomorrow. We have a computer for each of you to use. You can call out for help if you'd like too, but it won't help. You see, the island that we're on now is untraceable. Plus, if you get found you won't win the money! So. The nights are your time. The daytime is entertainment time. Your only objective is to not be the last one to finish the challenge. The last one to complete the challenge will provide our lovely viewers with whatever they request."

He snapped his fingers at us and we all got up and followed him out of the plane and saw a small house in front of us. I started to panic, but I reminded myself that this is what I wanted.

A chance to either prove myself or die.

I was the first one to walk into the house and looked around. It was a small house with worn down hardwood floors, blue wall paint that was chipping with age, and a kitchen with surprisingly new appliances. The only thing in the living room was a small brown couch. I walked past the kitchen and into the only bedroom in the house. It was a larger room than I expected. There were five small beds with a laptop on each bed. The others walked up to the room and quietly picked out their bed. I chose the one closest to the door.

Elijah walked into the room and said, "I lied. The contest starts today. Open your laptop and turn it on. There will be a window that pops up. If you turn off your laptop or turn off the screen you instantly lose." He closed the door and I grabbed my laptop and booted it on. When the home screen came up a window came up almost immediately.

The window was completely white for a second before it showed a footage of Blake walking into a store and groping a man's ass before running out of the store. We all looked at him and chuckled while he started to grow pale. The next clip showed Allison sitting in an alley shoving a needle into her arm and slowly injecting herself. I looked at her, but she looked away from all of us. Next, it showed Elise breaking into a house. She walked up to the sleeping man on the couch and she grabbed her pocketknife and sunk it into his throat. She proceeded to stab him 4 more times before running around his house and grabbing whatever valuable thing she saw. When her clip ended none of us looked at her. We didn't want to see a person witnessing a murder they committed.

Right as they showed me on the screen I knew what it was. It was from two days ago. I was in the convenience store I always went into. A woman walked into the store and I don't know what came over me, but she was beautiful. She was wearing a very short skirt and a white shirt that prominently revealed her nipples when under the right light. I reached into my pants and pleasured myself. Right as I climaxed I looked up and saw that she was staring at me in disgust. I gave her a small nod before running out the store. I heard a couple of chuckles coming from the others, but the only thought that was running through my head was how they managed to get that filmed.

Right as the next clip came up I heard Cody yell out, "Fuck that. What the fuck. You show pussy ass shit for everyone else. Why the fuck you show me doing this shit?" I looked back at the screen and saw Cody speaking to an old woman. They were laughing together while sitting on a park bench. She handed him a picture and I saw Cody's face instantly turn sour. He started to yell at her and grab her by the shoulder. She tried pushing off of him, but he then put his hands around her throat and started to squeeze. She tried to get out of his grip, but she became still and he let go of her throat and ran away. The screen zoomed in on the picture. It was of Cody, the woman, and a man. "I love you son, but please know that your daddy loved you just as much."

Cody slammed his laptop shut and started to scream at us, "Don't fucking judge me. I loved my mom, but she always backed up that filthy bitch. He fucking did shit to me man. He didn't love me. He was a piece of shit."

Elijah came into the room with two other men dressed in all black. The two men dressed in black picked up Cody and took him outside. Elijah stayed in the room and said, "Keep the laptops on and stay on the screen you were looking at. Watch Cody's punishment so that you may know what happens when you lose."

The screen came back live and I saw the two men standing behind Cody. He was sobbing and pleading for his life. It was the first time I saw a truly broken man. It took all of my willpower to not shut my laptop off right then.

Messages started to pop up on the bottom of the screen.

The first one said, "Take his eyes out. I don't want him to see what we will do to him next."

I saw Cody's eyes glance down at the screen and he started to scream. The man on the right nodded his head and grabbed a rusty spoon from the table behind him. The other man held on to Cody's face to keep it steady while the first man scooped his eyes out.

The next message said, "I want you to cut off three of his fingers and shove them down his throat." The man put down the spoon and grabbed a kitchen knife. While the other man held on to Cody's hand I looked away from the screen. The sound of bones crunching vibrated my eardrums. I looked back at the screen and saw Cody's scream halting and changing to gagging as three of his fingers were shoved down his throat.

The man that held the knife said, "One last request. Make this one fatal."

The last message said, "Stab him in the head 14 times. Keep stabbing even if he dies."

The man nodded his head and put the kitchen knife down and picked up a pocket knife.

Cody started to whisper, "Please. Please. Just let me go back. I won't tell anyone about this. I just want to go back. I just" His pleading ended when the knife entered and exited his head with forceful stabs.

After the man stabbed Cody for the fourteenth time the screen blacked out and closed out.

Elijah looked at all of us for a couple of seconds before saying, "I will let you guys know when it is lunch time. The next challenge starts tomorrow. Prepare yourselves. Today was a cake walk."

I'm not asking for help. I know I will probably die, but I want to finish this out. That is why I am not posting this on my Facebook or alerting anyone I know. People are paying 50 grand to watch this, but I figure I might as well entertain you with the written version.

One down. Three more to go.

Day 2

When I woke up this morning the image of Cody's open eye sockets flashed in my mind. I looked around the room and everyone was already awake. Blake and Elise looked completely normal but Allison was shaking and looked completely pale. I asked her if she was okay. She looked at me with eyes filled with torment before throwing up all over her bed. Blake jumped out of his bed and ran to Allison and started to pat her on the back. She shook him off and said, "I'm fine. Just, please. Don't touch me. I'm sure you would rather touch pretty boy over there anyways.

Blake stood up from his bed. He opened his mouth but immediately closed it again when Elijah walked into our room. After a small cough, Elijah looked down at us and said, "It's time for breakfast. Get dressed. Allison you um. You take a shower. It smells disgusting in here." Allison put her hand out towards Elijah and asked, "Do you have any, ugh, any heroin? I need it. I can't go on without it. Please. Can you help me?" Elijah scoffed and told her to wait in the room. Elise went into the restroom to change her clothes while Blake and I changed in the room. Allison had her face on the pillow the entire time.

Right as I finished dressing, Elijah walked back into the room and threw a small spoon with brown tar on it, a lighter, and a needle on Allison's bed before walking back out. I didn't want to watch her do that again so I followed Elijah out of the room. We walked into the kitchen and saw two pieces of toast on each plate and a jar of grape jelly sitting in the middle of the table. I took a seat and quietly ate. Blake and Elise came out a couple minutes after I did and started eating.

When I finished my breakfast I got up and walked into the living room. Elijah was sitting on the couch staring out the window. I sat next to him and asked, "So when are we starting today?" Elijah let out a quiet sigh and said, "We start in 6 hours. Relax until then. Meditate if you do that shit. You do any drugs?" I thought for a second and asked, "Shit. I want some cigarettes and the harshest drink you've got." Elijah looked at me for a second before laughing and slapped me on my back. He got up from his chair and walked out the front door. A couple minutes later, he came back with a thermos and a carton of Marlboro Smooths. I gratefully took them from his hands and sat back on the couch.

I ripped open the carton and took out a pack of cigs. I don't know about you, but no matter how stressful anything is. A cigarette somehow takes the edge off. It makes you think that no matter what situation you are in. You have a chance of getting through whatever you find yourself in. Right as I put the cigarette in my mouth Elijah lit it for me. I sat back on the couch and opened the thermos. Took a sip and felt the liquid go down my throat and produce a feeling of warmth and comfort instantaneously.

I closed my eyes for what felt like a second, but Elijah was shaking me and telling me to wake up. I groggily opened my eyes and grunted in response. The thermos bottle was still in my hand. Holding back throw up, I put the thermos bottle down and saw that half of it was gone. After a couple of deep breaths, I got up from the couch and walked into the room. The other three were sitting on their bed staring at a simple white table that was just placed in the middle of the room. Elijah walked up into the room and up to the table and said, "Well guys. It's time. I'm going to use my phone to record you guys tonight." He tapped on his phone a couple of times before pointing the camera towards us.

He let out a whistle and one of the men dressed in all black walked into the room and set four knives on top of the table. Elijah pointed the camera towards the knives and said, "Alright guys walk up to the table and grab a knife. Once you pick a knife walk back to your bed with it and sit down. I got up from the bed and grabbed a knife along with the others and walked back to my bed. Elijah turned his phone around and I could see his face fill the screen along with **42683 viewers** written on the top right of the screen. He let out a dramatic breath before saying, "Okay guys. The game has begun. Do what your gut tells you to do! Show the world who you truly are."

He stood in the corner and pointed the camera back at us.

We all stared at each other dumbly for what felt like an eternity. Elise was gripping her knife extra hard as she stared each of us down. Allison was sitting in the middle of her bed. Clutching the knife with both of her hands. Blake had his head hung down low. He was barely holding on to his knife. I started to look back at Allison, but Blake let out a huge sob. I looked back at him and saw him staring at Elijah. Tears were dripping down his face. He grabbed his knife and with a shout lunged towards Elise. Her eyes were wide and her body was still as Blake plunged a knife deep into her left shoulder. A scream erupted from her mouth as she tried to push Blake off of her. He took the knife out of her shoulder and started to bring it back down on her when Elijah grabbed him and threw him on the ground. Elijah's helper ran up to Blake and kicked the knife out of his hand. Blake tried to get back up, but the man pushed him back on the ground and tied up his wrists tightly with rope.

Elijah nodded at the man and walked up to Blake and held him down. The man then walked up to each of us and took the knives from us.

Once he gathered all of the knives he grabbed Blake by his hair and sat him on his bed. Elijah grinned at Blake while he pointed the camera towards him and said, "Well that was awfully quick. Blake. Blake. Blake. Were you mad? What made you stab poor little Elise? What did she do to you? Huh? Made fun of you for liking men's butts?" Blake looked up at him and stared him down. Elijah let out a small laugh before saying, "Well honestly. I don't really give a fuck. You proved that lust wasn't your only fault, and because of your little hissy fit, you lost." He turned the camera back towards him and said, "Okay. I have chosen two people to give my lovely assistants instructions on how we should end Blake's life."

He whistled towards the door and his other helper walked in and helped the other man carry Blake and placed him on the table.

Elijah then looked at us and said, "Open up your laptops so you can see that commands that come on the screen. I opened up my laptop and instantly saw Blake's face fill the screen.

The first command came on the screen.

"I want you to chop off his hands."

One of the men grabbed a knife out of the bag while

the other held Blake's hands down on the table. The man quickly brought down the knife down and the sound of bones crunching against sharpened metal followed by a loud thud as the knife landed on the table filled the room. Blake didn't scream. He just looked at the bloody stub that was once his right hand. Before Blake even took his eyes off his severed hand the man sliced off his other hand.

I tried turning my head away to avoid watching anymore but I couldn't move. I wanted to help him, but I knew it would only end up with me giving up my life. I looked back on the screen as the next command came up.

"Stab him in the stomach and shove one of his severed hands inside."

I managed to look away right after the man stabbed him in the midsection. He was whimpering but it soon became screams of pure agony. It took all of my willpower to look away. I thought it was over when the room became quiet, but I felt someone tapping on my shoulder. I looked up and saw Elijah standing next to me. He pointed at the screen and I looked at the next command.

"Get Jared. I want him to slice a chunk of Blake's thigh off and take a bite off of it. He must chew it and swallow."

I had to reread it several times before I could even comprehend what I was supposed to do. Elijah grabbed my arm and led me up to the table. Blake was lying down on the table almost completely still. He was slowly blinking as I took the knife from the man.

This is where I doubted everything about me. I thought I would never be the person that would be able to mutilate a person, eat a chunk of human meat, or do it without hesitation, but within seconds I was shoving Blake's severed thigh flesh in between my lips. I took a decent sized bite out of it and soon my mouth filled with the taste of salt and copper. I gagged a little, but I kept chewing until I managed to get it into a texture I could swallow.

Elijah gave me a small tap on the middle of my back before saying, "Okay guys. Last request and we are done for the night."

It only took a couple of seconds for the last command to pop up.

"Let Jared see my face. Let him see my face as I watch him stab Blake 5 times in the chest."

Elijah let out a sigh and clicked on the profile that sent out the last command. It showed a picture of when I was 7. I wanted to scream but I held it in. Elijah then turned on the feed to the person's camera and saw myself looking at my mother and father. They were smiling at me and my mother cleared her throat before saying, "Well what are you waiting for. This is your chance. Your only chance to finally bring us happiness. You were always such a pussy, but I'm glad you finally decided to do something ballsy. Pick up that knife and make mommy and daddy proud."

Without hesitation, I stabbed Blake in the chest. I didn't stop at 5. I kept going. I couldn't stop. I was sobbing and I didn't want to kill him, but he wasn't the one that was in my mind while I stabbed him. I thought about how amazing it would be to stab my parents. Over and over again.

I snapped out of my moment of lunacy and looked

down at the table. Blake's chest was nearly gashed completely open. I dropped the knife back on the table and walked back to my bed.

It's been 3 hours since I ended Blake's life and made a new mission for myself.

I needed to win. I needed to stab my parents as many times as I stabbed Blake. They deserved the death I gave him. I don't care about the money anymore. I needed to get revenge on my parents. The pieces of shit that kicked me out of the house when I refused to kill my grandpa so that they could get what he left for them. The ones that refused to give me a single cent when I called them and told them I was starving.

The ones that told me that the only way for me to go back home was if I killed my grandfather.

Day 3

Elijah woke me up this morning. When I opened my eyes he said, "Your chances of survival increased." He pointed over to the right and I looked over and saw Allison lying on the bed. She was sprawled out on her bed, but she was completely pale. A needle and an empty bag were in her clutched right hand. Elise was already sitting up on her bed staring at Allison's lifeless body. She looked up and stared at me before shrugging her shoulders and walking towards the kitchen. Her arm was in a makeshift sling Elijah made for her, but other than her arm she seemed to be her normal self.

Elijah gave me a light tap on my shoulder and said, "Come on. Time for breakfast. Eat up. We are starting the next challenge right as soon as you guys finish." I gave him a nod and walked into the kitchen. There were only two chairs at the table. I took a seat and slowly ate my eggs and bacon.

In the middle of the meal, Elise cleared her throat. I looked up and she said, "Well might as well learn more about each other before the contest ends."

I wasn't really interested in learning about her, but I nodded my head and said, "Sure. Why not. I mean. It won't really change anything, but at least our memory somewhat moves on if we lose."

I don't know how much this conversation really means to everybody, but for me, it changed everything.

Elise: "I'm an artist. Well. I like to think I am but no one really appreciates my art. Not even my father. He threw me out of the house when I refused to go to college. So I lived out on the streets for the past year. I tried selling my paintings out on the streets but no one really appreciates art created by a bum. It's always been like that. Singers that could have topped the billboard charts die every day. The next Edgar Allen Poe dies on the streets with powder on their nose and dreams still captured in their still heart, but what do they get? Just judgment their whole lives and a sense of absolute loneliness."

Me: "Yeah. Shit. I really wish I had something to live for like you. My family is fucked up. My mother and father kicked me out of my house when I refused to kill my grandfather. They wanted his money, but unfortunately for them, I loved my grandfather far more than empty promises. I don't really have a dream. I don't have anything that I am amazing at, but I want to get my revenge. I want to end their pathetic lives."

Elise: "Wanna make a deal?"

Me: "What kind of deal?"

Elise: "If I win, I will make sure I end your parent's lives. If you win, go to my house. The house I received when I killed my father. He was the guy I stabbed in the video. Just so that something I created can stand proudly on display in the house I forever sought acceptance in. Deal?"

Me: "Yeah. Deal. Um. Well. Good luck."

Elise: "You too. Can I ask you an odd question?"

Me: "Sure."

Elise: "Was I prettier than Allison?"

Me: "Um."

Elise: "Never mind. My dad always told me that Allison was the prettier and smarter one. Turns out he was wrong about her. She definitely wasn't smarter. I was just hoping he chose the wrong daughter to favor."

Me: "Wait. What?"

She was silent after that for the rest of the meal.

Right after we finished our meal Elijah walked up to us and said, "Follow me." He walked out the front door and we followed him. While we were walking, I couldn't help myself. I lightly rubbed Elise's arm and she looked back with a small smile before grabbing my hand and held onto it as we walked towards the back of the house.

Once we got to the back Elijah took out his phone and started up the camera. With a huge grin, he started speaking, "Now our last challenge. Allison had an. Hm. An accident. We have our two final contestants left. Let me tell you. This has gotten quite emotional. Thirty minutes ago I overheard them telling each other their little sob stories." He sarcastically wiped a fake tear from his eye and continued. "So. The last challenge." He whistled and snapped his fingers. His two helpers came out carrying a large bag and dropped it in front of Elijah. He winked at his helpers before continuing. "Okay. So Allison's dead body is in this bag. The challenge is to eat as much of her body as you can. The one that loses will be held down by my two wonderful assistants. It is up to the winner how they will die. If the winner cannot take the life of the other person they will also admit defeat."

I heard a gasp from Elise as Elijah opened up the bag and revealed Allison's dead body. Elijah moved the bag out of the way and pointed the camera towards her body and said, "Alright guys. Dig in!"

I didn't hesitate for a single second.

I knelt beside the corpse and started to bite down on her thighs. With each bite, I felt her meat tearing at the force of my teeth. The meat ripped off and landed on my tongue and I started to chew as fast as I could and before I knew it, a decent sized chunk was taken out of her thigh. Elise was screaming at me to quit ruining the corpse of her sister, but I ignored her and continued to stuff my mouth with as much meat as I could tear off of Allison.

I started to feel sick to my stomach so I sat back. Elise was taking little bites off of Allison in between sobs, but I was unaffected. After my stomach settled I started to bite into her other thigh. It only took me two more bites before I saw Elise start running away as fast as she could.

Elijah's helpers caught up to her before she managed to even get around the first corner. They dragged her in front of me and I stood up. Elise looked up at me with pleading eyes, but with a smile, I kicked her in the side of the head. I was this close to the money I wasn't going to quit now. She started to plead for her life but I ignored her as I knelt down next to her head and started to punch her head as hard as I could.

A gun landed next to my leg and I picked the gun up. Elise looked up as the punches stopped. When she saw the gun she said, "Just make it quick. Remember our deal. Please. Just make it qui-"

I shot her left foot. She started to scream and sob but I ignored it. I shot her in the other foot and she tried to break free out of their grip but she couldn't. I gave a little laugh as I shot her three more times on her back.

She looked at me after sobbing and asked, "Why?"

Before I took my last shot I said, "You made one big mistake. Allison was *my* sister. She was the one that my family favored over me. You thought you could make a lie that big and get away with it? Don't worry. I won't forget our deal, but know that you told the wrong lie."

I closed my eyes after I placed the end of the barrel on the back of her head.

Before I pulled the trigger, I heard her beg me to forgive her. To let her live, but I had come too far to give it all up. With a scream, I pulled the trigger and I heard Elijah say, "It's over. Jared. It's done." I dropped the gun and stood up. He gave me a small smile before the world went black.

I woke up on the same spot I woke up before the "competition." I sat up and felt around my pockets. I found a card in my pocket. There was nothing on it except a black strip on the top of one side of the card. On the other side "#6930" was written on the bottom right corner of it.

I checked it at the ATM. 6930 was the password for the account. I checked the balance and saw that I was 500 grand richer.

I went to the local Walmart and bought the cheapest laptop they had. After that, I went to the cheapest hotel and rented out a room for 2 months.

I keep thinking about Elise. How she struggled on the ground as I kicked and punched her as hard as I could, how she begged me before I shot her in the back of the head, but most of all, how she looked when she found out Allison was my sister.

Then I think about how she would have looked at me if she saw me standing by Allison's bed heating up the rest of the tar on the spoon then filling up the needle and releasing the drug inside of the vein prominently sticking out of her arm three times.

Like I said. I needed to win. I have a mission to accomplish.

My sister was always favored by my parents, but it seems like they picked the wrong child to favor.

THE STORY BEHIND MY EIGHT SCARS

HAYONG-BAK

THERE IS A TOTAL OF EIGHT SCARS ON MY BODY. TWO SCARS are on my face, three are on my back, two are on my chest, and the last is across the knuckles of my right hand.

I never felt comfortable about talking about how I got any of my scars. There has only been one person in the world I decided to tell about my scars until now. That person is my wife. She had asked me several times while we were dating, but I always told her I would just tell her later when I felt more comfortable. I know it bothered her, but I didn't want to scare her away. Today is the day I finally feel brave enough. I decided to tell my wife and then tell you all because I feel like it may contain some important lessons.

As you know yesterday was Valentine's Day. I brought home a letter that I wrote for her with the story of my scars and a heart-shaped box of chocolate. She went to grab for her gifts but I told her to meet me in the bedroom. She followed me in and we sat on our bed. I handed her the letter first.

This is what I wrote.

"Today is Valentine's Day and I want to let you know that I love you. I'm sorry I have kept this a secret for so long, but please do not be afraid of me after you read this.

Ironically, I received the first scar on Valentine's Day. I was seven years old and I accidentally broke the TV my father had just bought. He walked up to me and started yelling at me. I tried to tell him it was an accident, but he refused to listen to a word I had to say. He didn't realize it, but he was holding a small pocket knife in his hand while yelling at me. I closed my eyes while I started to cry, but a pain erupted from the middle of my chest. I opened my eyes and started to scream in pain. I blacked out and woke up on my bed. I had three stitches in my chest and my father was sitting next to my bed. He rubbed my shoulder and told me I was fine.

When I was 11 years old I came home from school and my parents were in the middle of an argument. I tried to sneak past them, but as I was walking past the entrance to the kitchen I feel something hard smash on my back. I tried to keep walking, but with each step, I could feel glass pieces digging and ripping into my skin and flesh. I heard a gasp coming from the kitchen before I blacked out once again. I woke up in the middle of the night. I was laying on my right side, and my father was standing in the corner of the room. When he saw me wake up he put a finger up to his mouth and stood there for a couple of hours. I tried to go back to sleep, but I was afraid of what my father would do to me.

When I was between the ages of 11 to 14 I had trouble sleeping. I tried to still keep my eyes closed because whenever I opened my them I would see my father standing off in the corner of my room staring right at me. I was scared for my life. I tried everything to stay asleep, but it was impossible. I hated my dad, and I just wished that he would go away forever.

The next couple of years I tried to avoid my father as much as I could. I did a pretty good job until I was 14 years old. It all started on a Friday. I got off of the bus and walked to my house. When I got close I saw my father standing in the middle of our lawn. I tried to walk past him, but he jumped in front of me. With a gruff voice, he said, "Don't come in here. Just go. We don't have time to deal with you anymore." I tried to run past him and call out for my mom but my father threw me down on the ground. I looked up at my dad, but he threw some money at me and walked back into the house. I honestly didn't know what to do. My face was bleeding and I didn't want to go anywhere else. I ran to the back of the house and into the shed in our backyard. I stayed there for two days. I didn't leave except the few times I would run to the water hose to drink some water. On Sunday I became desperate. I was hungry and I wanted to be back in my home and sleep in my room. I didn't care if my dad hit me again. My father answered the door and pointed at my room. I ran upstairs and dove under my covers. A couple of hours later my father came into my room with a plate of food. I ate every last bite of the food and placed the plate on the side table.

I thought about reading a book, but I didn't have the

strength to get up from my bed. For a little over an hour, I imagined myself being in a much better family. A family where everyone loved each other and the parents didn't spend the whole time arguing. That is all I ever hoped for, but even at that young age, I knew it was not possible.

I don't know when I fell asleep, but I woke up and screamed in pain. My chest felt like it was on fire. I tried to get up but something pushed me onto my stomach and held my head down. It became hard to breathe and I started to struggle even harder before I felt something hit the side of my head and the world went blank. When I woke back up again it was still dark. I looked to my left and right but didn't see anyone. I slowly rolled back onto my back and saw my father standing in the doorway. He had a knife in his hands and kept both of his eyes on me.

I started to shout for my mother, but my dad ran up to me and put his hand over my mouth. I settled down and stared at him. When he took his hand off of my mouth I remained quiet. He still had the knife in his hands and the last thing I wanted to do was make him angry again.

Now you know why I have the 7 scars.

The eighth scar came from the day of my graduation. Neither my mother nor my father showed up. I wasn't sad, though. I didn't care. I was just glad I was off to college in a couple of months. It was a great day for me. After the graduation, I went with a couple of buddies and went to a party. It was the first party I went to and the first time I drank alcohol. I didn't drink too much, but I still felt happier than I have ever felt in my whole life.

The fun stopped when I got home.

The first thing I noticed was the blood all over our

white couch in our living room. Next thing I noticed was my father lying face down beside the couch. I walked over to him and saw blood all around his chest and midsection area. I turned him around and saw that he had been shot 3 times in his midsection. I was about to lay him back down when his eyes opened and his lips started moving.

Despite the shots he took, he still managed to have the longest conversation I have ever had with him.

Father: S-s-ave you...

Me: What do you mean?

Father: Your m-mom didn't want you. I love her and y-you. I wanted it to w-work.

Me: You're the one that didn't want me. You didn't care about me.

Father: N-no please remember

He took his last breath and never moved another muscle.

I sat on the ground next to him and tried to think of what he said. Why he would even say anything like that about my mother? And then, the memories hit me. My father holding the knife and yelling at me when I was 7; He didn't stab me. My mother bumped into him while he was yelling at me.

When I was 11 she was the one that threw the dish at my back. It wasn't an accident. I don't remember what they were arguing about, but he was just watching over me at night so that my mother wouldn't come in. He stayed there every night so that my mother wouldn't come in and try to do anything.

At 14 he had had it. He didn't want to leave my mother. He loved her. He really did. He loved me too, but he just couldn't handle the stress and torture he put himself through. That was the only time he hit me.

I heard my mother coming downstairs. She gave me a smile when she saw me and walked towards me with the gun still in her right hand.

Before she could do anything I jumped on top of her and punched her in her stupid face for every single scar, for taking the life of the only parent that loved me, for making me hate my father, and for still being able to smile through it all. I don't know which bone on her face cut through the skin on my knuckles, but I know one thing: it is the only scar I can appreciate.

When the cops came they asked me question after question. I answered all of them honestly. I was not charged. It was all self-defense.

That is how I got my 8 scars. I want you to promise me one thing. To still love me the same way you have always loved me. Please don't think of me as an evil person. I love you and I will always love you.

FOREVER YOUR VALENTINE,
Hayong

MY WIFE LOOKED at me with eyes full of love, and I knew I didn't mess up by letting her know. I just wanted to share this with you guys, because we tend to forget who cares for us and who is trying to kill us. Please be careful with whom you trust.

OUR BABY DOLL

HAYONG-BAK

FROM THE DAY MY DAUGHTER WAS BORN I COULD TELL THAT she was something special. We named her Zooey and she was the smartest baby I have ever seen. Every single month I loved my special little girl more and more, but for some odd reason, the more I loved my little Zooey, the more my wife distanced herself from the two of us. By the 6th month my wife barely even gave Zooey a glance. I could tell it made her sad, but I didn't really want to bring it up. I just wanted my daughter to know that I loved her very much.

Zooey said her first word when she was 3 months old. "Daddy."

She never really said "Mommy" or even "Mom", but my wife never seemed to mind. If anything she finally looked to be in a much better mood.

By the time she was 6 months Zooey started to walk. She would still fall sometimes, but I was completely blown away by how strong-willed her young mind was. Instead of crying whenever she fell she would just pick herself back up and continue trying.

On Zooey's first birthday my wife was busy with work so I shared a very special day with my daughter. I got her a chocolate cake for her to smash and devour. She didn't touch it, but she looked perfectly happy with staring at the cake with a look of wonder on her face. We spent the rest of the day playing with her presents until it was her bedtime. My wife didn't come home until 10 pm. I asked her where she was, but she just put her hand up to my face and walked past me and into our bedroom.

I sighed and watched TV until I fell asleep on the couch. I woke up to the sounds of my wife and Zooey talking. My wife was trying to get her to say "Mommy", but Zooey kept clapping her hands while saying "Daddy!" with a wide smile on her face. That was the last time my wife tried talking to Zooey.

On the day of Zooey's 2nd birthday my wife told me she was going to stay later at work. I tried begging and reasoning with her to stay, but she just told me it wasn't worth it. I heard sniffles from behind me when my wife left the house. I turned around to see a tear stricken Zooey staring out the door. She asked me if Mommy didn't love her, but I just hugged her and told her that we both loved her very much. After I pulled away from the hug Zooey asked me, "Why doesn't she talk to me?" I told her that mommy was just stressed, and to not let it bug her. I got her another cake, but she told me that she didn't like to eat cake. She thought it was too pretty to destroy.

With a nod I left the cake on the dining room table and took out three brightly colored bags from under the table. We have this tradition where I take out the presents for her and rip the paper as carefully as possible. She liked using the wrapping paper as little decorations for her room. The first two presents were just little bow sets and a couple of new books. The third present was one of those baby dolls you can feed and change. She was really excited about the doll. She played with it in the living room by herself until it was time for bed.

My wife came back home at 11pm completely drunk. She looked like she was crying, but I was far too tired to even acknowledge that she was there. After all, she did the same thing all of the time to Zooey and now me. Our marriage was falling apart and I really didn't know how to fix it. I thought she was just going to go into the bedroom, but she walked into the middle of the living room and picked up Zooey's new doll. After a couple of seconds she started to hug the doll and rock it back and forth. The bottle and the 3 toy diapers were lying next to it and my wife picked those up as well. She put the bottle up to the baby and started whispering to it.

I was completely in awe at the sight of my wife showing the baby doll more attention than she ever gave Zooey. She sat down on the couch with the doll and took the bottle out of its mouth and continued to whisper to it. The whispering overwhelmed me with curiosity so I snuck up behind her and tried to listen to what she was saying. It was hard at first, but after a couple of seconds, I noticed she was saying the same thing over and over again. "Please call me Mommy."

After a couple of minutes my wife fell asleep with the toy baby on top of her stomach. I walked into the bedroom and grabbed a blanket for her. After I got her settled in I went back into the bedroom and fell asleep. This morning I woke up to the sound of my wife laughing for the first time in several years. I rushed downstairs to see what the source of her laughter was. When I walked into the kitchen I saw my wife twirling around in circles with the toy baby. Zooey was sitting down with tears falling down her cheeks. I picked up Zooey and asked my wife what she was doing. Each time she spun around she said one word at a time.

"Just"

"Playing"

"With"

"My"

"Daughter"

I told her that Zooey was crying, but my wife just shrugged and kept spinning around with the baby.

This annoyed me quite a bit, but I just took Zooey back into the living room and played with a couple of her older dolls with her. After about an hour later my sweating wife came out of the kitchen and said that she was going to the mall with her daughter. Zooey got up quickly and rushed into her room to change. By the time Zooey came out changed into her outside clothes my wife and the doll were already gone.

Zooey's bed time rolled around and I put her to bed. While I put her covers over her she asked me, "Does Mommy really love me?" I nodded my head at her and smiled. I just told her that momma wanted to surprise her with some new clothes. Zooey fell asleep a couple of minutes later with a tiny smile on her face.

Tonight my wife came home around 9 pm. I walked up to her and asked what was wrong with her. She tried to ignore me, but I kept blocking her way until she stopped and glared at me. She shoved the baby doll in my face and shouted, "She's at least fucking real! Do you know how hard it is to play fucking pretend with you? Zooey is dead. She's been dead. When are you going to stop playing this stupid game?"

I shouted back at her to stop lying, but my wife just fell into my arms and started sobbing. Zooey came downstairs and stared at us hugging. She gave me a smile and walked back upstairs. I started to sob with my wife as memories started to flood in. Our beautiful daughter died 10 days after we brought her home from the hospital. There was nothing wrong with her. She just fell into a deep sleep she never woke up from. The doctors told us that it was SIDS, but I just never wanted to believe it.

After my wife finally settled down I sat her on the couch and walked upstairs. I walked into Zooey's room and saw all of the little wrapping paper from her presents taped on the walls. The toys I got for her were there and the new bed I bought for her just 2 months ago was there, but Zooey was nowhere to be found.

With a heavy sigh, I closed the door to her bedroom and walked into my room. I looked through all of the photos on my laptop that I thought I took with Zooey, but it was just me taking photos of myself.

I was about to close my laptop down, but I decided to

reach out to you guys. I am now in the grieving process. My wife was acting crazy, but I was the crazy one all along. My baby is gone, and I just wish I could experience just one last day with her.

MY SON'S EXPERIENCE IN HEAVEN

HAYONG-BAK

SEVEN DAYS AGO, I WAS DRIVING MY SON, ZACH, HOME from school when a drunk driver t-boned us. The para-medics managed to drag us out of our flipped over car. As soon as I woke back up I looked around the room for my son. I tried to get out of my bed, but a nurse rushed into the room and settled me back in. He looked at me for a second before saying, "Your son is in critical condition right now, but you need to stay on your bed for at least another day before we can let you leave your room." I tried to argue back, but the words wouldn't come out of my mouth. The nurse left after a couple of seconds.

The rest of the day I sat on the bed and forced myself to stay strong for my son. I knew he couldn't see me right now, but I was all he had now after my wife was found in front of the Wal-Mart parking lot. She was stabbed a total of 12 times and her purse was emptied out. They never found out who killed her. That was 2 years ago, and Zach was just 6 at the time. The day of the funeral was the hardest day of my life. I had to explain that his mother was gone. He didn't cry. He just nodded and stared at the ground for the rest of the day. It took over a year for things to go back to some type of normality.

The thought of Zach dying did go through my mind several times, but I quickly dismissed the thought and remained hopeful. The doctor came into my room around 7 at night to run a couple of tests. I tried to ask him about my son, but he just gave me a sympathetic look before telling me that I was pretty much fine besides a couple of scrapes and bruises. I asked if I could go see my son now, but with a sigh, he said, "Harold. Let me be completely honest with you. There really isn't much you can do right now. You can see him tomorrow after we release you, but just understand that he is a lot worse off than you. There is a chance he may not make it, but our doctors are trying their very hardest. Get some rest and make sure you mentally prepare yourself before you see your son." He gave me a sad nod and walked out of the room.

That night I couldn't sleep. Instead, I sat on my bed and ran through every single memory I had of Zach and me. I thought of every time we sat at the kitchen table eating dinner and laughing, I thought of the times my wife, Zach, and I would sit on the sofa and watch a movie, and I thought of the times we cried together over the loss of his mother. That night was a mixture of half smiles and tears.

At 9 o' clock, the nurse came into my room and gave me a nod before unhooking every little thing that was attached to my body. 30 minutes later, I was following closely behind the nurse to where Zach was. We stopped in front of room 437. I took a deep breath before I walked through the door and saw my son's nearly lifeless body lying on the hospital bed. Each step I took towards my son revealed more and more injuries that his small fragile body had taken. His right arm was rubbed absolutely raw, his left eye was slightly opened from the dent that was now on his face, and his legs and other arm were littered with randomly placed stitches. The room started to spin and I started to go limp, but a doctor grabbed me from behind and placed me on a seat. He handed me a glass of water before saying, "He seems to be a little more stable now, but these next 2 days are the most critical for him. We will have a doctor for him at all hours, and if we get any type of alert we will definitely be there for him. You can stay with him if you'd like." I gave him a nod and told him that I was going to stay with him until he wakes up. He placed a hand on my shoulder before he walked out the room.

The next day and a half went by and absolutely nothing happened. The doctors and nurses would stop in occasionally, but they would leave right after they finished their tasks. That evening at 9:37, my son's heart stopped and my whole world stopped. I saw doctors and nurses rushing into the room, but I was completely stuck on the chair. It took everything out of me to finally get out of my chair and rush up to my son, but one of the doctors held me back. I screamed, pushed, and sobbed during the 18 seconds my son was dead.

For the next 2 days, I stood next to my son. I didn't sleep, eat, or drink anything. I wanted him to somehow know that I was with him. I wanted to somehow help him get out of the coma and into my arms again. At 11:14 pm my son finally opened his eyes and looked up at me. It had taken him 4 and a half days for him to get out of his coma, and the only thing I wanted to do was cry and hold him.

He gave me a small smile before he looked up and frowned. Before I could do anything, Zach went into absolute hysterics. He started off by letting out a series of screams. Screams of absolute agony. He tried ripping off his IV and everything else connected to his body, but I held his arms down as carefully as I could before calling for a doctor. It took over 3 hours for Zach to finally calm down. It was 2 in the morning by then; I was absolutely exhausted, but I walked up to him and sat down next to him while gingerly holding his hand.

I fell asleep at around 5 in the morning.

I woke up to the sound of Zach's voice. When I looked up I saw a nurse carefully feeding him. He was telling her about how we go to the park every Saturday, and proceeded to ask her if he would be able to go with me this Saturday. She gave him a smile and said, "Well, if you eat plenty of food and do everything the doctor says you might be able to go very soon. I have to go now Zach, but why don't you talk to your dad now? It looks like he's awake!" Zach quickly turned to me and gave me a smile before talking about how the doctor told him he was being extra good and that he deserves a new toy. I laughed and told him that once we were out I would give him any toy he wanted.

My son was physically hurt, but it seemed like he was back to normal otherwise. The next couple of days went by in a blur. Throughout the day I would talk with him, read a couple of books to him given by the nice doctor, and watched a couple of his favorite shows on the TV. I felt beyond lucky. I had my son still. My one reason to keep living.

Last night, my son started to talk about his experience and I really don't know what the hell he went through. I was reading to him when he held up his arm up and said, "Everything became really black and then it felt like I was dreaming." Before I could say anything back he took a deep breath and said, "I dreamed about when Mommy was here. We were eating dinner, but everything was quiet. Mommy and you were talking but I couldn't hear anything. I tried to say something, but I couldn't hear myself. I started to scream and then everything went black again." I tried to hold his hand to reassure him that he was fine now, but he pushed away and looked up at me with eyes filled with torment. His lips quivered before he continued with his experience.

"Then a bright light was all around me. I started to feel warm and happy. Really happy like when Mommy was here. I tried to move, but I was floating and so I stayed still while I floated to where I was supposed to go. It got too bright so I closed my eyes till I stopped. When I opened my eyes I had to close them again because I saw the brightest light I have ever seen. It spoke to me. It said that I was dead. It told me that I was going to be here for a little while before he sent me back to you. I tried to ask him to take me back now, but it told me that I needed to stay here."

He took a deep breath and a couple of tears fell from his face before he continued, "I started floating again and

I was taken to another room, but this one was smaller. I waited for a long time, but Mommy came into the room. She was happy and she gave me a hug, but then she started to scream. I tried to keep looking at her, but a knife kept going inside of her body. She started to bleed everywhere and I got scared. I closed my eyes and looked away. She stopped screaming and I looked back at Mommy. She was dying but she told me that she loved me and that she will see me again, but she told me it would be a long time."

I gave him a smile and told him that Mommy was waiting for us in a special place. That is when Zach turned to me and said, "No not us. Just me. I saw who was holding the knife. It was you. She told me you were going to another place. I'm sorry Daddy, but Mommy is not waiting for you. She told me that you were clever enough to get away with killing her, but you can't escape death. Everybody dies and so will you."

I didn't know what to say to him.

I loved my wife and my son, but I couldn't handle how I became the third wheel. I knew I couldn't beat the bond between a mother and her child and I did the only thing that would allow my son to fully appreciate me as much as he could.

This morning, I went home to get my laptop and I am now back with my son and I'm writing this out to you guys. Do any of you guys have any proof of an afterlife? Did my son just have an awfully vivid dream or was what he experienced real? It seems like more of a coincidence that he would be able to place the blame on me when the police couldn't even trace it back to me.

A SHORT LETTER TO MY WIFE

HAYONG-BAK

You may not have noticed, but the day you walked into the coffee shop I worked at, everyone stopped what they were doing and stared at you for a quick second. The pair of blue headphones and the pink scarf around your neck made you seem just that much cuter. You may not have noticed, but it felt like every cell in my body was melting while you told me your order or how, when you smiled, I lost the feeling in my knees. That is why I fell a little while walking towards the machine to make your coffee. You gave me a small smile and laughed, not in a teasing way, but in a way that made me feel like you thought I had a chance with winning you over.

When you left me you left the coffee shop with three other people, I thought I lost my chance with you. You can understand how surprised I was when you asked me out on a date when I saw you walking around our town with the same three people.

From the first date that we went on, I knew I was in

love with you. The soft look in your eyes made me feel like you loved me too. After dating for a little over two years, I knew that I was taking the biggest risk in my life when I knelt down on one knee and asked you to marry me. You may not have noticed, but the moment you said yes, I could have died happily, knowing that my life was finally complete.

You may not have noticed, but when you started hitting me 6 months into our marriage, I was the most depressed I had been. I felt like I truly lost you, and when it continued even after the first year of our marriage, I knew I never really had you. When you were out late into the night, I would watch over our daughter, and see what you once were in her face. It almost drove me nearly insane. Hell, for a period, it did.

The day I woke up and saw a man walking down the stairs with you, the guilty look apparent on your face, I had a lapse of judgment. I told you we could work it out. I told you I could become something so much more. You promised to stay loyal, and I promised to become the best version of myself I could possibly be. The next couple of months, I was finally happy again. You were home when I got off of work, and it really seemed like you were getting closer to our daughter.

I should have known it was all for show. You were just putting on a show, and secretly stashing away money so you could run away. You told me you never loved me, and that you hated our daughter. You may not have noticed, but our daughter was crying in her crib as you ran out the front door and ran into the night.

For the next four days, I took time off of work. I tried

being the best father I could be while keeping the house as clean as I could. If you came back, I wanted to make sure that it was the cleanest it could possibly be. The day you finally came back, I couldn't stay mad at you. It meant you truly loved me. I was ready to forgive you, and the sad look on your face showed me how sorry you truly were. I hugged you, but you never hugged me back.

That night you hung yourself. Right next to our daughter's crib. I woke up to the sight of our daughter playing with your cold feet. That was kinda fucked up, don't you think? At least have the decency of doing that shit where our daughter couldn't see.

You may not have noticed.

Well.

No.

You definitely noticed how different our town is from everywhere else.

You noticed it when a couple of people grabbed you from behind the first time you walked into the cafe. You noticed a voice calling out, "Claimed!" It probably didn't take you long to realize that voice was mine when we went on our first date. The gag over your mouth and the chain around your arms and legs probably made our dates less fun, but I could swear I saw you smile a couple of times. I could see it in your eyes. The day you said you would marry me with tears falling from your eyes and a knife against your throat, that may not have been the ideal proposal you had in mind, but the result was perfect for me. You may not have noticed, but each hit you gave me while pleading me to let you leave, was the reason why I lost my compassion for you. I thought our daughter would help us get closer, but shit, that's life I guess.

You may have noticed that the police officer that promised to help you escape abused your trust, but hell, like I said, our town is different from the rest of the world. Every time you ran away late at night. There would always be someone there to catch you and return you safely back at our house.

Rest in peace, my dear angel.

I'm getting ready to go to the coffee shop again. I need to work as well as find my third wife.

MY TRIP TO HEAVEN

MY TRIP TO HEAVEN

HAYONG-BAK

M Y NAME IS NATHAN, AND I CAME BACK AFTER LIVING IN Heaven for exactly 300 years. I am sure a lot of people would be curious as to how that felt so let me start from how I got there.

I tried to be a good person, but my horrible temper always got in the way. It was to the point to where I no longer had any friends. My family stopped talking to me, including my own mother, father, and two sisters. I was only 21 years old, but I was truly alone. I tried to blame everyone around me, but I knew, deep down, that it was my own fault.

Enough of my sob story.

Let me tell you how I died.

I got off of my shift at the local grocery store and was walking back home. On the way home, a man walked up to me and asked, "Hey man, could you spare some cash? I lost my job a couple of days ago and I need to get some type of food for my kids." He pointed at a hungry boy and girl sitting behind him, but I scoffed and said, "Not that hard to get a job. Why did you even procreate when you're fucking trash?"

I gave him a quick chuckle and walked past him when I felt pain erupt from my lower back. The next couple of seconds were filled with a knife plunging into my chest. I don't know when I blacked out, but the next thing I remember was opening my eyes and seeing a woman sitting close to my head and saying, "Stay calm. We're almost there. Stay with-." I blacked out again and before I knew it I was met by a sense of absolute peace.

Before I opened my eyes, I knew I was floating. When I opened my eyes I saw myself floating through a fog of memories.

Through the fog, I could see myself yelling and cussing out my parents a year ago before storming out of their house. That was the last time I saw them. The next thing I saw was the time I was pulled over by the cops with my best friend since we were 6, Brad. He was there for me whenever I needed someone the most, but I took advantage of that. When a cop pulled us over I took out the 7 grams of coke out of my pocket and threw it on the car seat behind me.

Brad looked at me with pleading eyes while the cops cuffed him, but I acted oblivious to everything.

I closed my eyes again and did not open them until I felt solid ground under my feet. With a deep sigh, I opened my eyes and saw around 20 to 30 people standing in front of me. I looked down and saw that we were standing on a clear glass of some sort. When I looked back up I saw that I was next in line. I rushed up to a man that stood in front of the largest gate I have ever seen in my life. The gate was simple, but it looked to be made of solid gold. After ogling at the gate for a couple of seconds I looked down at the man in front of me. He was maybe a little over 4 feet tall, had poorly maintained facial hair that covered half of his face, and eyes filled with sadness and disappointment.

I opened my mouth to ask him who he was, but before I could get a sound out he spoke in a raspy voice, "Nathan Cliff, enter through the gates." Although I was confused, I rushed through the gates and looked around. I saw a road paved with gold, bodies made of solid light walking around everywhere, and other people walking around with dreamy expressions on their faces.

Besides the people that walked around me, everything around me was a mixture of absolutely pure light. Something far brighter and crisper than anything I have ever seen. The only thing that stuck out like a sore thumb was a man dressed in all red with a piece of paper. Written on the piece of the paper was the date. Somehow, whenever the man flipped the paper over it gave the date of the next day, and an endless swarm of people surrounded the man.

The first 50 years passed by quickly. I met a lot of other people; we talked about our lives, but I quickly became bored. You can only talk to so many people before their lives start sounding the same. We never grew hungry, tired, or thirsty, but it never ended my cravings. I wanted to get a good night's rest. I wanted to eat just one carrot and savor all of the taste. I wanted to quench a thirst with a cool glass of water, but all we had was each other and those damn angels that never said a word to anyone.

For the next 110 years, I reflected back on my life. It may seem like a long time to think about 21 years of life, but you can learn a lot more about your life just by revisiting the same memory thousands of times. You learn to see things in more than just your perspective, in ways much more than the words said.

It took me 160 years to finally snap. I don't know what came over me, but I wanted to leave this place. I wanted to go to hell. Anything would be better than here.

That's when everything around me started to fall apart.

It started with me walking up to the bodies of light we called the angels. I tried talking to them, but they never responded back to a word I said. When I truly became desperate, I tried to attack them in any way possible, but anything I struck them with would just go through them. With every attempt, they just looked at me and said the same thing. "Keep searching. Keep walking. For you will find the answer."

Eighty years have gone by since then, and all I have done was try and fail to attack other angels as well as ask everyone else if they knew what the answer was. Everything has been a failure. I started to give up hope, but I started on the longest journey of my life. I turned around and started running as fast as I could.

I would still see the man flip the sign over and tell us what the next day was. It was annoying at times, but it was really the only thing that kept me from going insane.

55 years went by.

It is now my 295th year in Heaven, and I started to see the gate I walked through three lifetimes ago.

Three years of constant running and I don't feel like I'm any closer, but the scenery around me changes. I am now surrounded by body parts and blood lying all around where I run. I came across a couple of heads, and whenever I see each one I stop running and asking them what happened. Each of them has said the same exact thing, "Don't look for the truth. The truth won't help you. Endure the punishment. It only gets worse from here." I started to get scared. Not just scared for my life. This was far worse. I was scared for my soul. The part that will never die. The part that will suffer for all eternity. No matter how bad we were cut up, sliced open, or just cut into dozens of pieces like the people around me now, I would not be able to leave. This was a punishment that would never end.

After three years of running and hearing the same thing over and over again, I started to second guess myself, but I needed to know. It was beyond curiosity. I was trying to get out of the eternal suffering I had ended up in.

Two years later at the start of my 300th year I approached the gates. I walked up to the man that stood in the front of the gate and fell to my knees, a defeated man. He looked at me with those same eyes full of disappointment and sadness before saying, "Nathan Cliff. Poor Nathan Cliff."

I begged him to let me out. To let me leave, but he simply said back, "Learn the truth and you may leave."

In between heavy breaths of panic, I replied back, "They told me you would tell me the truth. Or that I would find the truth on my way here."

He simply said back, "You know the truth."

I said the first thing in my mind "Is this Hell?"

He chuckled and said, "No. You are in Heaven, but what makes you think Heaven is for the good? You left the paradise created by God. The paradise ruined by us. We can blame the devil all we want, but we are the ones that continue to do wrong. Do you think Lucifer continues to spread his lies to the people when the lies are spread for him?"

I wanted to argue with him, but deep down I knew that was the truth. Humans are truly what ruined the world God made us. Lucifer may have tempted us, but we are the ones that truly ruined it.

I woke back up and saw the woman that was talking to me before I lived through the scariest experience of my life.

She calmly said, "Don't worry. You're back now. Don't go on us. We're almost there."

I knew she was mostly saying it for herself, but I gave her my best attempt of a nod. She put the defibrillator back down and we were silent for the rest of the ride.

I'm in the hospital now.

I learned that I was dead for 45 seconds. 45 seconds that created exactly 300 years for me.

I'm on my phone now. The doctors are done treating

me. Pain is still erupting all over my body, but man does it feel good. I have a tray of food in front of me.

Carrot sticks that I never liked are now bursting with flavor for me. The water is quenching my parched throat, and after I post this experience to you guys I am going to enjoy a good night's rest.

THE IMMORTALITY PROJECT

HAYONG-BAK

THE IMMORTALITY PROJECT IS SOMETHING I STUPIDLY signed up for 3 days ago. It was only a 2-day job, and previous experience was not a necessity. I first heard about the project on Craigslist while I was browsing through job openings. Just like everybody else would have been, I was skeptical when I saw the bland ad, but I couldn't help but be a little interested.

You see, I'm a 27-year-old that still lives with his parents. They both make a decent living so they never felt pressured to get rid of me. I have tried moving out once before, but after going through a brief 3-month marriage that ended in a divorce that lasted even longer, I just never felt comfortable moving out. But, for the past three months I have wanted to live out on my own again. I wanted to feel the absolute freedom I briefly had, but I just don't have the money to move out. My ex-wife took pretty much everything from me. Now, I don't blame her for where I am now, but it helps me sleep better at night. Anyway, the Craigslist post read like this.

The Immortality Project has been in progress for the last 12 years, but recently, we have made a breakthrough. We are currently looking for 8 participants for the next two days. Your job will not be hard. In fact, it is quite simple. The tasks may be a bit tedious at times, but we the compensations will make up for that. Please arrive at 825 Smith Road by 3. Late arrivals will not be considered,

Pay Rate: $25,000 to be paid at the end of the 2nd day.

Please note that if you decide to leave in the middle of the project, you will not be paid. We will receive full consent from all participants prior to beginning and we will give all of the specifics before you sign our forms.

The first thing I noticed when I arrived at the location was how new the building looked. The bricks that covered the house still had an undisturbed deep red color to them, and the immaculate glass door and windows glistened in the sun. There were 7 others waiting outside, and after a quick glance at everyone I stood off to the side and remained silent.

Normally, I'm quite social, but I'm sure we were all a bit thrown off because we all looked somewhat similar. We were all around 5 feet 8 inches, with sandy blonde hair and a little extra bulk. There weren't any females, and though we all had certain distinct characteristics, any person that passed by us would think we were all related.

After a couple of minutes, I walked up to the building and tried looking inside, but the only thing I could see was white floors, white walls, and a small black desk placed in the middle of the room. While I was staring through the doors I heard someone walk up to me and without even giving me a chance to turn around he said, "Shit is weird, isn't it? I thought they would open the doors a little earlier when we came, but fuck, I don't even think anyone is inside."

He walked up beside me and stuck out a hand.

"Hey man, call me Jeff, do you know if we are staying here for the whole two days?"

I took his hand and shook it while saying, "I don't know. That ad didn't really tell me much. William, but everyone calls me Will. Where did you hear about this?"

"Shit, Will, my buddy from Kansas told me about it. Told me that they were coming here. I tried asking him what it was, but all he told me was that they were giving us 25k to do some easy shit. I figured I don't have much to lose. I've been living off of my brother for the past two years, and he told me he was gonna have to kick me out since his fiancé is moving in with him."

As he finished speaking, the door rattled a bit and I jumped back. An older man slowly opened the door and motioned for us to come inside. I quickly walked through the doors and Jeff walked closely behind me. Once we were all inside the older man walked around us and to the back of the desk. One of the other guys tried to walk up to the desk, but the man held out his hand and said, "Stay where you are. He will come out soon, and he will tell you what you need to do.

I looked around the room. There was a glass door behind the desk and another door on the right side of the room. The floors were completely clean except the spot that we walked on, and everything besides the desk was completely white.

While I was looking around the room, a small beeping sound came from behind the desk and a man walked out of the door behind the desk. Every single one of us stared at the man with looks of shock apparent on our faces. The man looked like the perfect version of all of us. He was wearing a gray fitted suit and had zero flaws on his face.

He looked at each of us before smiling confidently and saying, "Hello everyone. My name is Sam, and I'm sure you are all curious why you are here. Well, 12 years ago, I created something called the "Immortality Project". We haven't been exactly successful until several weeks ago. After our first successful test run, I decided to risk my life and test it on myself. As you can see, it worked. Now, don't worry. You don't have to get the procedure. We only need 4 people to go through the procedure and the other four must monitor the guys after the procedure for two days."

Four people, including Jeff, decided to go for the experiment, and I decided to stay because I knew I could deal with handling one person for the next two days. Sam led the four through the door behind the desk and they were gone for the next 2 hours. I tried speaking to the other three guys, but they all ignored me and nervously stared down at the ground. The older man walked up to us and handed each of us a form. I signed it after reading the three rules written on the sheet.

You can talk about what happened in here, but please do not report us to any sort of law enforcement. We will find out and we will deal with you accordingly.

Once you walk into your room, you and the one you are monitoring will not be able to leave. If you need anything, there is a button by the door. Press it and then request what you need through the speaker.

If the person you are monitoring hurts either you or themselves we are not liable. Please understand all of the rules before signing at the bottom of the form.

After I signed the form, the old man took my form and handed me a sheet to fill out my bank account information. Once that was filled out, I sat on the ground and thought about what I was getting myself into.

Jeff was the first to walk back out through the door, and the others followed closely behind. Sam didn't come out with them. Instead, each of the guys walked up to us and stood silently. The older man looked up at us, gave a small grin, and said, "The one that is standing to the right of you will be the person you will monitor for the next two days. They will be mostly quiet for the first couple of hours, but afterward, they should be speaking to you with ease. Follow me to your rooms."

I was slightly glad that Jeff was the one that was standing by me. It felt like he was the closest thing to a friend I had in here.

The old man opened the door on the right side of the room and revealed a small hallway with four doors. We walked up to the first door, and the old man turned around and stuck his hand out towards me.

"We have taken Jeff's phone already. We need anything you can contact the outside world with."

I handed him my phone and walked into the room with Jeff.

218

The door closed, and instantly, it felt like I was locked away in prison.

The room was completely gray. The two beds on opposite ends of the room were tiny but somewhat comfortable. The small TV was barely visible from my side of the room, but it only had two channels, the local news and PBS. I left the TV on PBS and sat down on my bed. Jeff was lying down, staring at the TV with a blank expression on his face. He didn't really look any different. He had a small scar on the right side of his mouth, and his arms were covered with small scratches. I tried talking to him, but he just looked at me with a sad look on his face and kept staring at me until I looked away.

I fell asleep to the sound of cheesy animation theme music and awoke to Jeff shaking me while whispering, "Wake up. They won't stop talking to me. I can't handle it. They just won't stop and I need to get them out. Please."

I pushed him off of me and sat up on my bed. The lights were off in the room, but I could see that Jeff was knelt down beside my bed. He kept whispering the same thing over and over again. I got out of bed and helped Jeff to his feet. Despite the room being warm, his entire body was cold. Once I got him back onto his bed, Jeff became silent, slowly fell back onto the bed, and immediately began snoring.

It took a long time for me to fall back asleep. I know I had someone next to me, but I felt absolutely lonely. A couple of times throughout the night, Jeff started to whisper again, but I couldn't really understand what he was saying. As the light turned back on in our room, I fell back asleep.

The smell of food woke me back up. I opened my eyes to see that Jeff was already taking the last bites of his food. There was a tray with eggs, a piece of toast, and two strips of bacon placed at the end of my bed. I scarfed the food down and as I shoved the last strip of bacon in my mouth, I looked up and saw Jeff staring at me.

Jeff cleared his throat before saying, "Man. Last night. I didn't want to wake you up, but I woke up and I didn't remember anything after I signed the form in the back room. I tried to sleep, but it felt like something was crawling inside of me. All over me. Fuck, I could feel something swimming in my goddamn eyes dude. Shit is weird as fuck. What the hell is wrong with me?"

I shook my head and asked, "Did you see anything back there? Did Sam say anything before you blacked out?"

Jeff let out a sigh and shuddered before mumbling back, "No, I don't remember shit man. I can still feel them. This shit doesn't feel right at all. Do me a favor man. Put your hand over my arm and tell me how many you feel."

He held his arm out towards me and I placed a hand on his arm and immediately recoiled back. It felt like millions of tiny bugs were crawling around.

Jeff chuckled and asked, "I figured you you'd find that shit disgusting. So what did it feel like? They stop moving whenever I try to feel them. Is it a couple?"

I nodded my head and said, "Yeah man. You're good. Probably just something from the procedure."

He let out a sigh of relief and slammed his body back into the bed before watching a couple of unimportant news stories. Lunch time came around and I was given a small sirloin steak with a couple of French fries. Jeff was given a small bowl of what looked like green oatmeal. Before I even managed to cut out a piece of steak, Jeff was already finished with his food. I looked at him with a weird look on my face, and he laughed before saying, "Shit dude. I thought it would taste like shit, but that has got to be the best thing I have ever eaten in my life." I shrugged my shoulders and watched TV with him.

A couple of hours later was when I heard screams coming from the room next to us. I pressed my ear against the wall and tried to listen in, but I heard a loud thud and the door next to us swung open. A couple of seconds later, our door opened and one of the guys fell into our room and looked up at us with desperation in our eyes.

"Please help. I'm going to die. I'm fucking. Fucking. It's crawling. Everywhere. Crawling. Help."

He vomited green shit in our room and fell face flat.

Sam walked up behind the fallen participant and shook his head before grabbing him by the ankles and dragging him out. While being dragged his legs fell off of his body and hung limply from Sam's hands. Thick blood poured out, but as the blood landed on the ground, the liquid split apart into thousands of tiny red creatures and started to crawl back into the man's body.

He was barely speaking. His face was a pale white, and he let out a scream before going completely silent. Sam dragged the rest of his body out of the room silently and closed the door.

Jeff only talked to me once for the rest of the night.

Jeff- "So, that dude is probably dead, huh?"

Me- "Yep. probably. You feeling any better?"

Jeff- "Well I know what the fuck is inside of me now, but I wish I didn't. You know something? I feel smarter now. I know that sounds weird, but I couldn't add worth shit, but I'm actually doing some mental math, and I feel like I'm saying the right answers."

Me- "Anything else seem different?"

Jeff- "Not really. I mean I feel a little more energetic, but that could just be because I saw that fucker's leg pop off. I'm going to sleep. Feel free to wake me up if my body explodes."

He was snoring before I could respond, and I fell asleep shortly afterward.

I woke up yesterday morning and instantly checked on Jeff. He was already awake eating his breakfast of green mush. He gave me a green-toothed smile, and that was the last interaction between us.

Sam walked into our room as soon as I finished my breakfast, and led me out of the room. Jeff was still sitting on his bed when I left.

We walked through the first door and Sam ran behind the counter and handed me my phone. I looked around the room and realized that it looked like it had aged by centuries. The floor was caked with dirt as well as various other unknown stains, and the walls were peeling in over a dozen areas. I walked out of the building with Sam and looked at the outside of the building. The bricks were littered with cracks, gaps, and mold. Sam saw the confusion on my face and laughed before saying, "Don't worry. The building just likes to give off a good first impression."

I was ready to get out of there, but I couldn't bring

myself to do it. I turned around and asked Sam my final question.

"What is going to happen to Jeff?"

He gave me a sad smile and said, "Jeff is fine. In fact, he will make more money than he will be able to spend for the next 3 years. We are going bigger with this. This time, three out of four participants came out fine, and soon they will begin to look completely different. They will start doing what I did for this project. Hopefully, soon, we will have this go world-wide. The body type and facial structure make you guys the ideal candidates. It's fun and easy to mold, but soon, we will be able to do the procedure on everyone. Go home. Forget about us. Enjoy the money in your account."

That was yesterday. I came back home and my parents didn't even ask where I was. They hardly care anymore, but I'm planning to move out soon anyway. I tried looking up The Immortality Project, but there isn't anything about it anywhere.

So I'll take Sam's advice. I'm going to try to forget it and live my life, but if you happen to come across an ad for it, I highly suggest against going for the procedure.

A SITE CALLED "CASH FOR CONFESSIONS"

HAYONG-BAK

I'M NOT USUALLY THE TYPE OF PERSON TO CLICK ON ADS, but I was completely broke and still living with my parents. Before a bunch of you guys come at me and tell me to get a job and to stop being a bum. I want you guys to know. I do have a job. I work 55 hours a week and I give all of my money to my parents. They are the ones that don't have enough to pay their bills. After everything is said and done, I have maybe 40 dollars a month to spend on myself. Fuck, they are my parents, but I make sure they have enough to eat before I feed myself.

That is why when I saw a simple black square take up the bottom right corner of my screen with the words "Cash for Confessions" inside of the box I clicked it. I was using an old beat up tablet and hooked up to really shitty Wi-Fi coming from the modem and router Comcast rents out to us, but the site opened up on my tablet in an instant.

Like I said, I'm not normally the type of person to

click on ads so my guard was up high, but the website seemed completely safe. It was pretty much solid white with a small tan box in the middle of the screen. On the box were two generic words. "Create Account" I quickly made a throwaway e-mail address and clicked on the box. It took me to the next screen. It only asked me for three things.

User Name

E-mail Address...

Currency Desired...

My favorite superhero is Flash so I made my username BarryFlash, I typed in my e-mail address, and then typed in USD on the last slot. As soon as I finished typing the screen turned black. It stayed that way for a couple of seconds before two words appeared on the top of screen. Thank You. The two words faded away and were replaced by a series of rules.

Cash for confessions

1) All of the confessions must be completely true.

2) Do not use the money to help others out. This is your money that you have earned.

3) You may tell others about Cash for Confessions, but you cannot send this into anyone that will cause us any type of trouble."

I impatiently tapped on the screen until it flashed completely white before transitioning to a gray screen. An endless list of confessions filled my screen. I wasn't really interested in anyone else's confessions. I wanted to see if this thing actually paid us. After a couple of seconds of searching around I finally found what I was looking for.

"Once you click this you must confess."

Without a second thought, I tapped on the link the other confessions disappeared from the screen and was replaced by an empty white box. I tapped on the box and my keyboard came up on my screen.

After a small sigh of anticipation, I typed out "I was a virgin till I was 22 years old." Right after I finished typing the keyboard disappeared and the screen went completely black. I waited for a couple of seconds before the tablet vibrated. After a couple more seconds of waiting, I pressed the power button and my tablet came to life. There was a new e-mail. I tapped on the notification and the e-mail app came up and slowly started to load.

I almost let out a scream of joy when I saw that the e-mail was from Cash for Confessions. I tapped on the e-mail and quickly became sketched out and slightly pissed when all it said was, "$15 has been deposited into your bank account. If you would like more money please give us a better confession."

Shit. I would have been happy with just $15, but I knew that there was no way they could have deposited the money into my bank. They didn't have my account number, they didn't even know what bank I used, shit, they didn't even know my name. After letting out a depressed groan, I turned my tablet off and went to sleep.

I woke up in the middle of the night to the sound of my tablet vibrating continuously. Once I got out of bed, I nervously walked up to my tablet and turned on my tablet. E-mails. Thousands of e-mails from Cash for Confessions. I nervously clicked on the first e-mail and almost dropped it on the ground. I closed out of the e-mail and looked through the rest. They all said the same thing.

"Don't doubt us, Samuel Harrison. We know who you are. We gave you the money. Please check your bank account and see that we are a legitimate business. We miss you and we hope you come back."

Curious and scared out of my mind, I clicked on my bank app and logged in. I had 14 cents in my bank account before (I checked earlier to see if I could eat Taco Bell the next day) but I now had $15.14. I was scared. I really was, but I was also excited. I mean, it was the first opportunity I was given to actually make a little pocket change for myself.

I don't really know when I fell asleep, but I do know the sun was rising when I finally did. I kept writing out confession after confession. I mean, they knew who I was, but the people that were reading it had no idea who I was. All they saw were my confessions. I didn't really put anything juicy, but a couple of them managed to make me around 30 dollars. That was 4 days ago.

I woke up the next morning and realized I was already 4 hours late to work. I don't know why I was so dumb, but I called my manager and told him that I quit. In the middle of his rant, I hung up on him and checked my bank account. My jaw dropped when I saw that $1560.14 in my bank account.

For the next three days, I wrote as many of my confessions as I could, but yesterday morning I realized something. I was out of things to confess.

That is when I started to mess up my entire life in the

span of 24 hours. I broke one of the rules. I started to make up confessions.

It started off with small shit like "I stole 100 dollars out of my grandma's wallet when I was 12." and quickly escalated to "I have a gun in my drawer. I am going to kill my parents tonight and they won't be able to do anything about it."

Right after I made that confession I checked my e-mails. A couple of my made up confessions made in between 15 dollars to 750 dollars, but my newest one made me $15,000.

I was ecstatic. Everything finally felt like it was perfect, but about an hour later, my tablet started blowing up again. Nervously, I checked it and saw that I had over 800 e-mails waiting for me. I opened the first one and instantly knew how bad I fucked up. I knew they all said the same thing, but I spent the next hour clicking through all of the e-mails and checking to see if it was maybe just a warning. It wasn't.

They all said the same thing again.

"Samuel, why would you lie to us? You knew we would figure out if you were lying or not, but there is a way to fix it. If you look in your first drawer you will see a gun. Kill your parents if you want to live. Fulfill the confession or we take your worthless life."

I checked my drawer, and sure enough, the gun was in the middle of my drawer. I picked it up and felt goose bumps cover my body.

When my parents sat on the couch for our weekly movie night I took the gun downstairs. I sat next to them for the last time. I enjoyed every single second, every single laugh at dumb moments from the movie, and every single smile we gave each other.

As the movie ended I took the gun out of the back of my pants. Tears filled my eyes as I knew what I needed to do.

I placed the gun behind me and ran out the front door. I didn't look back at them. I didn't want to see their confused and concerned faces as I ran off into the night.

I went to my friend's house that night. I knew I was putting him at risk, but I was honestly hoping they would kill my friend and me off, but unfortunately, I woke up this morning. I woke up and saw my friend cooking breakfast. With a feeling of dread and sadness, I turned on his TV and turned it to the news.

The main story was about my parents. They were found in our house. Both of their heads were mutilated by several bullets. I choked back my tears and sobs. I know they are after me now.

I'm writing this out on my tablet and leaving it at my friend's house while I try to get as far away as possible. It's my fault that my parents are dead, but it is now up to me. It's up to me to get revenge for their deaths.

Until then, I want to leave you guys a warning.

Please be careful if you use Cash for Confessions. It is fine if you need a bit of money, but please don't be like me. Don't make up confessions.

MY SON'S NEW TABLET

HAYONG-BAK

BEING A SINGLE FATHER HAS ALWAYS BEEN HARD FOR ME, but it has been even harder for my son. My wife passed away when my son was 3. She was admitted into the hospital for pains in her midsection. Three days later, she passed away in her sleep. My son never received the attention he needed. Since he was three, I had to send him to my parents' house while I worked all day and then picked him up around 7. We would eat dinner and I'd watch a couple of shows with him, but I would sometimes catch him looking at the empty seat next to him. Whenever he did that I would always feel my eyes start to tear up. It really felt like he knew that was where his mother used to sit.

Until he turned 4, he would go into my room and open up a heart shaped jelly and place it on top of his sippy cup and place it on the desk my wife bought me for our 5th anniversary. The last anniversary we had spent together.

When he stopped doing his nightly ritual he started to grow more and more distant with me.

It broke my heart, but I continued to work and spend less and less time with him. By the time he was five he started to scream and shout whenever I picked him up. My breaking point came when my father walked out of the house to wave goodbye to my son and he yelled, "Take me back to Daddy. I want Daddy. Let me go. Let me go!" With tears welling up in my eyes I got him into the car seat and took him home.

I had money I had saved up to start up my own restaurant, but I didn't want to lose my son. He was the remaining part of my wife I had left, and he meant more to me than my life did. The first weeks of keeping him home with me was rough. They were filled with my son constantly asking me when I would take him to Mommy and Daddy, but I told him that we were going to stay at home for a little while. He would scream and cry for almost for the remainder of the day until I fed him his dinner and put him to bed.

Three days ago we went to Wal-Mart together to pick up some groceries. While we were there I went into the electronics section to get a phone charger. My son was standing close to me the whole time, but when I finally picked out a charger I looked around and saw that he vanished. I started to run around the electronics section until I saw him standing in front of a tablet. When I walked up to him I saw that all of his attention was on the tablet. I looked at the price tag and without a second thought flagged a worker and told him I wanted to buy one. My son looked at me, and for the first time, he was smiling at me.

While I was purchasing the tablet the man that was ringing me up said, "Man, this is the best tablet for the money. I bought it for my son, and he has been learning so much from it. Now, I swear he's teaching me stuff I never knew!" I chuckled and handed him my card.

The entire car ride back my son begged me to take the tablet out of the box, but I told him to wait till the morning. He huffed and sighed, but I could tell he was excited for the morning.

After my son went to bed I spent about and house setting up the tablet. It's one of those "kid safe" tablets that allow the parents to restrict apps, amount of usage time, and websites. Once I was satisfied with the restrictions I plugged the phone and tablet up and went to bed.

I woke up the next morning to my son bouncing on my chest. Teasingly, I asked him, "What do you want?" He started to scream out tablet while I laughed and unplugged the tablet and handed it to him. With a squeal of delight, he ran out of my room. The distant sound of clicking from the tablet made me smile as I fell asleep again. At 9:45 I woke back up again and walked out into the living room to see my son was working on a little puzzle on the tablet.

The day went by smooth. When the 4 hour mark hit my son's tablet locked up and he brought it to me. I told him that he would have to play with something else for 5 hours before he could play with the tablet again. I readied myself for a fit, but he just smiled and said, "Okay!" before running off into his room.

Three hours later, I heard the sound of sirens coming from a distance and stopping close to my house. I peeked out the house and saw two cops running into my neighbor's house. I opened the door and stepped out and saw my neighbor open the door and walk outside with his arms up. My son walked out the door and stood beside me. Before I could get him back inside he said, "He fucked his dead wife. Did it after he bashed her skull with a hammer while she slept."

I turned around and stared at him before asking, "You don't say stuff like that, Eric, who taught you that?" With a smile he looked up at me and asked, "Taught me what, Jared?" While I tried to think of what to say he ran into the house and into his room.

The entire time we ate dinner I tried talking to him, but he would just look up at me and say, "Tablet" before resuming his meal. When he ate all that he wanted he got off of his chair and went to his room. When I finished my dinner I went up to his room and saw that he was already asleep. With a sigh, I walked in and took his socks off before tucking him and giving him a kiss on his cheek.

I plugged up his tablet and my phone and attempted to sleep, but I couldn't keep my eyes closed. The concern for my son overwhelmed me, and after several hours of tossing and turning I got out of bed and went through the entire tablet. Two hours later, I finally plugged the tablet back up to the charger and went back to bed.

Yesterday morning, I woke up to the sound of voices coming from the living room. When I walked out to the living room my son pointed at the TV and said, "Told you." Our local news channel was talking about what my neighbor did. He was convicted of murdering his wife and storing her body in his wine cellar. I felt the blood rush from my face while I turned the TV off. My son got off the couch and ran into my room. He came back out with his tablet and started messing around with a couple of games on it.

I looked over his shoulder the entire time he was on the tablet. The only odd thing he did was click on the browser and stay on the front page while staring at the screen with more fascination the entire time he was on his tablet. He kept staring at it until the screen blacked out and went to the lock screen. Without a word, he handed the tablet back to me, but before he ran off he looked at me and said, "Grandma and Grandpa killed my mom. They poisoned her, but you were too stupid to know."

I picked the tablet up and begged for it to tell me. When I unlocked the tablet it just went to a black screen before white letters appeared on the screen. It said, "Stupid Man."

My son and I went back to Wal-Mart to return the tablet, but when they tried to process the refund they told me that the tablet was never on their system. I took the receipt out of my pocket and gave it to them, but the girl looked at me and said, "You need to leave." When I tried to reason with her she just got madder and said, "I'm tired of people thinking they can say whatever they want to me just because I work here. My son loves me. He will always love me. Fuck off, you piece of shit." She threw my receipt back at me. When I picked it up off of the ground I noticed that the receipt now only said one thing, "Just accept it. You're a sad excuse of a parent. Your son will never love you."

After I put my son to bed I tried sleeping, but every time I started to fall asleep I would hear my wife's voice say, "You could have saved me, but you were just too foolish." Every time I looked up I would see my son standing at the doorway.

I woke up this morning after sleeping for just two hours. This is my last hope, Please guys. Help me. I'm scared, and for the first time in my life I truly don't know what to do.

MY SON'S BABYSITTER

HAYONG-BAK

OUR SON CAME INTO THE WORLD WHEN MY WIFE AND I were just 20 years old. To the surprise of many, we were actually planning on having a child. We were madly in love, had our own house, and my wife had an amazing job that not only paid her extremely well but also gave her up to 3 months of maternity leave. I had a job as well, but I did not make nearly as much as her so we decided I would be the stay-at-home parent.

Of course, it was hard most of the time, but I loved every single second I spent with my son. We named him Jonathan, and he is the best son anyone could ever ask for. When he was 2 years old, he started sleeping through the night. At the age of 7, he skipped the second grade and started his first day of third grade. He loved pretty much every single sport out there, but by the freshman year of high school, he started for the basketball team. I still remember the smile he gave me while he was holding the trophy for winning the state championships with his team.

Shit, he's 14 now, and the worst thing he has ever done was going to the local skate park instead of going to his piano lesson last week. My wife did get a little mad at him for that, but I understood. The kid wanted to enjoy his summer without having to go to his bitchy piano tutor. I also understood why my wife became so angry. She was beyond exhausted. I mean, she worked more than 50 hours a week and still helped me with the household chores while I made the dinner. After dinner, she would try to spend as much time with Jonathan as she could before going into her office and finishing whatever unfinished work she had.

That is why I went behind her back and asked my sister to watch my son for 5 days while we went on vacation. Once my sister told me that she was able to watch him, I went online and reserved a room at the Harrah's in Cherokee, North Carolina. My wife has told me hundreds of times about how she missed going to the Appalachian Mountains with her aunt and uncle. Two days ago, my wife got in the car with me and waved goodbye to Jonathan and my sister.

Though the drive from Nashville, Tennessee to Cherokee, North Carolina was a little over 5 hours, the time flew by for me. For the first time in a long time, it felt like my wife and I was talking like we did while we were in the beginning stage of our relationship. Fourteen years of repressed flirts, jokes, and laughter lasting for the entire car ride. Honestly, I didn't want the car ride to ever end. It was the happiest I had been in a long time, and it truly showed me how much I loved my wife.

Once we checked in, got our luggage in our room, and took a quick shower together we walked down to the casino and took turns playing on the penny slots and got piss-faced drunk. We giggled like teenage horn-dogs while we snuck into our room like we were afraid of waking up the bedbugs and fucked like rabbits on Viagra.

Yesterday morning, I woke up to my phone vibrating in my pocket. Groggily, I slowly sat up and slid my hand into my pocket and took my phone out. As soon as I looked at the screen, I immediately started to panic. There were 6 messages from my sister. I quickly tapped on the notification and unlocked my phone.

Message One: Jerry. Your son was found in the bed with his fucking neck sliced open. I don't know what to do. I haven't even called the cops yet. Please. Call me back.

Message Two: You piece of shit. Fucking reply. I called the cops and they are on the way.

Message Three: Cops are here and they want to know where the fuck you guys are. I told them you guys were probably hiding after killing your son. Good luck fuckers.

Message Four: It was a picture of Jonathan. He was peacefully lying down on his bed. He even had a smile on his face, but his head was pretty much separated from the rest of his body. His blood was all over his pillow and blankets, but his clothes were completely clean. The white t-shirt was unstained.

Message Five: Was pretty much the same exact picture, but this time there was two photos from my wedding day stuck into the neck of my son.

Message Six: Oh hey Jerry, I'm really sorry for bugging you while you are on vacation, but Jonathan asked if he was allowed to skip out on his piano lessons today.

While I stared at the last message from my sister, a call from my her came. Quickly, I answered the phone and nervously said, "Hello?"

She let out a laugh and said, "Oh man, it sounds like you are going through the worst kind of hangover. Did you get my message? Jonathan is literally begging me to let him just go hang out with his friends instead of going to piano lessons. Is that okay?" Without a second thought, I told her that was fine, but I could barely get the words out. As she was telling me to enjoy my vacation I quickly cut her off and asked, "Hey. I know it's weird, but it's the first time not seeing Jonathan for so long. Can you FaceTime me and let me talk to him for a second?"

Once the video connected, I saw my son grinning up at me before saying, "Thank you so much, dad. You know I hate playing the piano. I won't tell mom if you don't tell her!" I gave him a small nod and told him I loved him before hanging up the phone. As soon as I hung up the phone, I looked back at the messages and saw that all of them were gone except the last message.

I know you are going to call me stupid or tell me that what I did after was completely unrealistic, but I'm only human. I don't want to believe that I really saw my son pretty much beheaded on his bed. I also knew my sister would never do anything as fucked up as that. So, I dismissed it. I told myself that I imagined those texts. I believed what I saw in the video. Shit, I saw my son and talked to him. I told myself that everything was fine.

The entire day, my wife and I recuperated in our room. We told each other that we would go sightseeing the next day. It was still a nice day for us. We lied in bed all day and watched random movies. For lunch and dinner, we ordered room service. Hell, it was the lazy day that we both needed for so long. I never told her about the messages from this morning. The last thing I wanted was her getting worried about something my overactive imagination probably made up. Thinking about it now, I know how fucking stupid I was being, but at that moment, it was the easiest thing to believe.

Before I went to sleep last night, I called my son and made sure everything was fine. After talking with Jonathan for a bit, I asked, "Is your aunt treating you well? Actually, can I talk to her for a second?" Right as I finished asking the question my sister asked, "Hey. You enjoying your vacation?" After a couple of seconds, I said, "Yeah. We're being lazy mostly, but it has been going pretty well so far. Thinking about going out to a couple of tours tomorrow, actually." We talked for a couple more seconds before she told me she was going to get back to watching a movie. Before she hung up, I asked her, "So you guys are fine right? Jonathan isn't acting strangely is he?" She laughed before saying, "You know he's never gonna give me any sort of problems. Seriously, enjoy your trip. Make sure your wife gets plenty of rest." I thanked her and hung up the phone.

I woke up this morning at 4 in the morning. My phone was going off on my side table and I picked it up and quickly answered the call. It was Jonathan. With grunts of pain, he said, "Dad. Please. Come back home. I'm in pain. I don't think she can really take care of me. She doesn't even act how she used to. I don't know what's wrong with her." He hung up the phone, and I tried calling him a couple of times, but each time it went to voicemail as soon as I called. I woke my wife up, told her about what the fuck was happening, we packed our shit, and was driving back home within an hour.

I drove at least 40 miles above the speed limit the entire way there.

We got home around 8:45. As soon as I walked into the house, I could smell a coppery sweet scent coming from the living room. When I walked into the living room, I saw my sister sitting on the couch with foam coming out of her mouth. Her neck was littered with blue and purple bumps. Her eyes were bulging out to the point to where I thought they would escape her skull any second and fall into the jumbled mess of bones, flesh, and intestines that were now her midsection.

A mixture of fear and grief rushed out of my body and into my face. With tears falling down my cheeks and blood rushing out of my face, I slowly walked up to my son's room. When I peeked inside of his room, his windows were opened, and he was nowhere to be seen.

My wife was in absolute hysterics now. Shit, I was panicking just as much, but I maintained myself enough to call 911 and report a possible murder and I told them that my 14-year-old son was missing.

The rest of the day was the most stressful time in our life. The officers asked us why we weren't there for the time of the murder, but we showed them the several receipts we had from North Carolina. They asked us if

Jonathan showed any signs of extreme violence when he was young, and we told them that he was always a good kid. He never gave us any trouble, and we were worried that whoever killed my sister had him. They left around 7 in the evening and told us to stay inside of the city until they had everything figured out.

I wish that was all I have for now, but I honestly wouldn't have posted this here for you guys if that were the case.

About an hour ago, I received a call from my son. When I answered the phone Jonathan started to speak without giving me a chance to say a word.

"I don't know why you were always a fucking pussy, dad? Why couldn't you just let my mom know I didn't like doing half of the shit she made me? Is it because you love her more than me? Is that why you guys left me with fucking bitchy Savannah? Well, fuck you. I'm ditching this phone, but I want you to know one thing." In my sister's voice he said, "I'm coming back for you."

TIME IS MONEY

HAYONG-BAK

IN THE PAST THREE DAYS I HAVE LOST MY BEST FRIEND SINCE I was seven and I am 30k richer.

It all started when I was sitting on my bed in my dorm room. My best friend, Alex, ran into our room and excitedly said, "Dude, take your phone out. I thought it was a joke, but man I just made 300 dollars in 10 minutes." Intrigued, I asked him, "Wait. Slow down. What the fuck are you talking about?" He grabbed my phone out of my hand and threw it back at me after a couple of taps. I picked my phone up and saw a treasure chest in the middle of my screen. "Tap Continue to Participate in the Greatest Money Scavenger Hunt of All Time."

Before I could think about it Alex tapped the continue button and the screen bounced to my home screen. An app called "Time is Money" was placed in the middle of an otherwise blank screen. The icon was solid yellow with a small treasure box in the middle.

I looked back up at Alex and he gave me a nod. Once I

opened up the app it went to a solid blue screen with two options.

"Scavenger" and "Quitter" were the two options with "Decisions are Irreversible" written underneath. I tapped on Scavenger and it took me to a white page with 8 nearby locations listed. One of them was the sandwich shop I was going to so I tapped on "Greg's Sandwich's and Homemade Soups." The app closed down and my navigation app came up. Alex and I rushed out and when we got close to the sandwich shop the navigation closed out and Time is Money opened back up and showed a picture of a red brick underneath a water hose.

I walked to the side of the building where the hose was and saw a red brick. When I picked it up I saw five $100 bills underneath with a note that said, "Well done." I don't know why I didn't think something was off, but this was the first time I had extra money. With a smile, I handed Alex a hundred, but he placed the money back into my hand and said, "This is change for us. We will be rich soon man." I laughed and put the money in my pocket and walked into the sandwich shop for my first stress free lunch in a long time.

The next day we spent the whole day on the app and went to every single place the list showed us. Twelve hours of running/walking and a combined total of 9k later we ran into our room with exhausted breaths but a permanent smile on each of our faces. We split the cash evenly, but reached a mutual agreement that searching on our own would allow us to make even more money.

Yesterday was beyond productive for me in the morning. I ran around the town like a madman and made a total of 21k, bringing my total to 25.5k. At 2pm I tapped on the option for the campus library. When I got there a picture of the librarian's desk filled my screen. With a mental nod of confirmation, I ran inside and saw that the librarian wasn't behind the desk. There was a small box in the second drawer of the shelf. When I opened I saw the biggest stack of money I had seen so far. I dug my hand into the box and grabbed the cash, but I felt something thin and hard on the bottom.

Out of instinct, I jerked my hand out of the box to see that my hand was covered in thick red liquid. Swallowing back the vomit that started to come out, I took out the cash and shoved it into my pocket. In the bottom of the box there was a severed finger. Disgusted, I threw the box back in the drawer and rushed out.

I know. I know I should have quit right then, but the thought of more money filled my mind and I kept going back to the app for my next location. It took me three more trips to realize I needed to quit. In the next three locations I have found a toe, another finger, and a heart hooked up to a car battery. It was still beating when I grabbed the money it was on top of.

Last night Alex never came back into the room.

I started to panic when it was 3 am and he hadn't come back yet. I grabbed my phone out of my pocket and saw that I had an unread text message. It was from an hour ago.

It was from Alex and it said, "Man I have been finding some weird shit. Not normal weird. Fucking fingers and other body parts I don't even know. I deleted the app and downloaded it again. This time I chose "Quitter". You might want to do the same thing. This shit. It's not cool man."

I stayed up for another 2 hours waiting on Alex, but as exhaustion from the day hit me I fell asleep.

I woke up at 10 am this morning. Despite the money I earned, I woke up scared and helpless. Alex wasn't in the room. I tried calling him seven times, but each time I called him it went straight to voicemail.

My phone vibrated three times and I picked it up and tapped the power button.

There was a notification from Time is Money.

"Alex Jameson Has Volunteered to be a Donator of the game."

My fingers shaking and my forehead drenched in sweat, I tapped on the notification and a picture of my best friend was on the screen. The friend that beat up my first bully and the one that prepped me up for my first date was lying on the bottom of the picture. There was a hole where his chest once was.

With tears rolling down my cheeks, I screamed out a mixture of pain, hurt, and absolute fear.

I don't know who to turn to. I went to the local police station and tried to show them the app, but it disappeared from my phone.

I made more money than I ever thought I would make during college, but I would give back every single cent and my life for Alex to breathe just one last time.

BONUS STORY

HAYONG-BAK

I work in a company that organizes conferences from the ground up. Basically, we will make sure the right amount of people will register to your conference, make the website to successfully market your conference, and then we will go to the conference to make sure that everything goes according to plan.

Right now I am in the process of maintaining the website and making sure all of the information is up to date while on the phone and calling people to make sure they make their registration payments.

Of course, some people are completely nice and tell me that they are either making their payment soon or that they are not able to participate, and some people are gigantic assholes who tell me to fuck off or to shove the high registration payments up my ass. Whatever response I get, I always thank them with smile and wish them a great day.

Once I make sure the website is completely fine to be

left alone I start giving all of my attention to the phone calls.

I have a full excel list of all of the people who have registered along with the information they have filled out including the phone number so I just put my feet up on my desk and continue to call down the list.

When I get to the participants from Germany I realize that one man only made half of his payment around two months ago.

With a sigh I dial in the number and expect someone to cuss me out about how he paid the full fee, but I get a quiet "Hello" from the person on the other line.

"Yes sir, this is G speaking on behalf of Conference2017. I am calling you because I saw you haven't made your payment yet! When were you planning on making the payment so I can make a note on our registration page?"

Participant: "Yes, I am sorry I will get to that as soon as I can. Can I ask you a question too?"

Me: "Of course sir, what is it?"

Participant: "Well I noticed that every time I go onto your site and try to make the payment I am not able to."

Me: "Well have you tried contacting your bank, sir?"

Participant: "I have tried calling them several times, but I have yet to get anyone on the phone. All I get is a busy signal sound, and it escalates to a high pitched ringing so I just hang up."

Me: "Ok sir, can you please give me the number to your bank and I can call them with you staying on the line as well. Maybe I'll have better luck getting them on the phone!"

Participant: "Thank you so much, sir! Yes, the number is 1-800-867-5309 it's called Herstatt Bank."

So I go ahead and dial the number of his card company, and the card company automatically answers with the bull shit automated message. I know if I dial 0 I can get a service representative so I keep pressing 0 on the dial pad of the phone till I get the notification to stay on the line as they are looking for an available representative.

I keep waiting in silence until the representative picks up the phone.

We talk back and forth about how my participant is having problems making his payment for the conference, and the representative asks if the man is on the phone right now.

The man answers back with a quick "Yes, I'm here."

After about 20 seconds of uncomfortable silence, I ask if the representative needs his bank information.

With a clearly confused voice, the representative tells me that she was waiting on an answer of if he was there or not.

Kind of annoyed I tell the man to confirm he is there. Once he says the same exact thing I wait for 10 seconds before asking if she heard him or not.

Hearing a huff at the other end I get slightly agitated and tell her that maybe the connection isn't good, but I can just relay the message between the two.

With both sides agreeing to it we proceed with all of the basic information.

I relay the following information as I hear it:

Name, address, ID number, account number, and account password.

After waiting for a full minute I ask what the status is, but I do not get a single answer. I ask the participant if he is still on the phone, and all I hear is silence.

Feeling a little uneasy I hang the phone up and redial the participant's number.

When I put the phone to my ear all I get is a busy signal which then progressed to the high pitch noise he was talking about. I try calling the card company in and I get the same exact sounds.

So I looked up the guy's name and the only result showed a well-known doctor who was put to death for the murders of 32 men. He killed them by slicing them up in the midsection then using electricity to see if he could make various organs work through electric wires. Appropriately, he was put to death by the electric chair. Before getting too carried away with my research on this fucked up human being I looked up the Bank's name and realized that it was bankrupted in 1974.

So who the fuck was I talking to?

SHOOTING STARS

KYLE ALEXANDER

JENNA TURNED HER HEAD TOWARDS ME; THE STARS OF THE night's sky glimmered in the reflection of her glossy eyes. She took another drink from her glass.

"You know, Fab, I've always wondered if there were others out there. Another distant planet, far, far away, with people just like us. They'd lay together, same as we do, and watch for shooting stars. I've always hoped we aren't the only ones who feel deep emotions: love, jealousy, anger, excitement. All the things that make us human. What would we be without these emotions?"

I let out a deep sigh.

"I don't know, honey. I could only assume that there are people out there, conscious, aware, living their lives by the day. The only thing is, I hope that they're happy. You and I, Jenna, we have each other. But there are 8 billion people on this planet, and not all of them are as fortunate as we are."

Jenna turned her head back toward the sky. I could see

a single tear stream down the side of her cheek. I wiped it with my finger and refilled her glass with the bottle of wine in my other hand.

"But Jenna, the possibilities are infinite. I bet there's a planet out there with another 8 billion people, only they're all happy, and they all have someone to hold when they're sad. Someone to share their excitement with. Hell, one of these stars," I pointed my finger upwards, "could be a perfect world. There isn't a thing we could do to get there – not in this lifetime."

"Look, Fabio, a shooting star! That's the first one!" Jenna gripped my hand tightly in excitement.

I let out another sigh, took a drink from my glass, and put on a smile. Jenna... she was one of a kind. There wasn't a soul like hers, even out of the infinite worlds that were in front of us.

"You know, Jenna, some cultures believe that a shooting, or fallen, star is a soul being released from purgatory–sent to heaven– finally given their eternal happiness. There are many other beliefs of course, but that one's my favorite."?

Jenna's eyes continued to peer out into the endless, inky blackness. She smiled. "?I like that one too." Another sip of her wine

I closed my eyes. I thought of all the suffering in the world; innocent people being tortured and starved, animals being hurt and used for their bodies, our beautiful planet being destroyed by all of the evil and corruption that mankind had been tainted by. It made me sick. I wished it would all go away, but I can't change the stars. I can't turn back time to when everything was at peace. The only thing I could do is work with what I was given. I hoped that I had done the right thing for Jenna, bringing her to my special place, showing her where I spent many hours alone, thinking about the world and the people that inhabit it.

I felt Jenna's grip fade away. I opened my eyes to see another shooting star. "There's another one!" I shouted in excitement.

I TURNED on my side to see the life had faded from Jenna's eyes; her face still holding that innocent smile.

"I love you, Jenna," I whispered softly, taking the final sip from my glass; a bottle of merlot I had prepared for our special moment lies empty beside me.

She had over-indulged. It was meant for us both to share as we searched the night sky for shooting stars. I wanted ours to be together, I wanted us to ascend into the heavens—side by side. She would've never agreed if I had told her, but it was for her own good. We needed to be freed from this purgatory we called life.

Be patient, sweetheart, it's only a matter of time before another star shoots across the blackness of the sky. I'll see you soon.

BAD HABITS DIE HARD

KYLE ALEXANDER

I LOOKED UP AT THE SKY; A SORROWFUL MESS OF RAIN clouds and misery, and wondered why? Why did I return to this place after spending so many years trying to escape? What lured me back here? It was something I had been asking myself during the entirety of my return, but there were questions left unanswered. My whole life I had been trying to run away from my problems, and they were always in pursuit. I understand that now, and only now, I need to fight my demons.

I lit a cigarette and locked the car behind me. It was a 2-mile walk from here. No Public Access was clearly written on the sign mounted to the iron-gate. I was walking straight into the belly of the beast: the dirt road being its long and rugged esophagus. Many have walked this path only to be swallowed whole, where only a few, such as myself, have been spit back out. It was a place where no one dared to visit, no one dared to speak of, but we are all aware of its existence.

The people of my hometown's ignorance had only allowed these monsters to control their lives. But not anymore. I've watched too many of my friends get taken away—even I had been dragged down that road once before. Never again will I allow this place to swallow another innocent soul.

I was 13 when they first came. They told us they were our saviors. They claimed to be able to provide us with what our struggling community had been deprived of, but at a great cost. They gave us clean water during a long drought and even cured our diseased crops. But the time came for when they wanted a return for their gratitude.

A child. And when we refused—they took her with force. I remember hearing the screams of Janet's mother over the thundering storm clouds of the season's first rain. There were at least two dozen of them: all dressed in black cloaks, masks of the same hue disguised their faces.

They took her. Janet screamed as the men dragged her up towards the mountains. Her mother put up a fight, but they were too powerful and there were too many of them.

But they continued to provide, and every season, they'd demand another payment. Before the rain season, they'd take a child, and during the season of the sun, they would demand a young man. After a few years, the community all accepted their demands, but I never did. Rage and hatred manifested within me, and when they came for me, I fought as hard as I could, but again, I was overpowered. I had prepared for that moment. I took in every detail as they dragged me up, up into the mountains.

I looked for the tree along the path that I had marked

with an "X" during my great escape. For some reason, I must've known I'd be coming back to this place. The forest had grown quite a bit since then, and I had to knock down a few bushes in order to find it–still, the same as it was when I left–the tree that I had marked with a sharp rock and carved an indicator of where to cut off of the main road. And through the sticker-bushes and trees, the memories came flooding back to me.

It was dark–nearly pitch black–and I was running blindly through the woods. I didn't have a destination other than getting far, far away. My feet were covered in cuts and bruises; my hands covered in blood and dirt, and through the weakness and fatigue from dehydration and malnutrition, I continued to run.

The laughter echoed through the woods behind me; closer than it was before—they were gaining. But there was no chance I'd let them take me back there without a fight. They'd be dragging my dead body through those godforsaken woods before I let them take me back to that fucking place.

There was a break in the trees and my feet came in contact with the soft dirt below. I stopped for a moment and picked up a rock and carved an "X" into a large oak just at the edge of the trail. If I were to ever return, I'd know exactly which way I came.

Rainfall. I heard it pattering against the leaves of the trees above before it touched my skin. It was the first rainfall of the season and I knew exactly what was to come. They were going to take another.

I pressed on through the darkness of the woods. Only the sounds of rain and the occasional crashing of thunder were present. I flicked my lighter and drew it to the cigarette between my lips; my only sense of relief. I'd be lying if I said I wasn't scared shitless. I've been dwelling on this for years—mentally preparing myself for the horrors that have been haunting me. But nothing can prepare you for the things that wait at the top of the mountain.

The brightness of the flame had decreased my night sight temporarily. When my pupils began to dilate again and my vision cleared, I saw a figure–?a silhouette–in the darkness ahead. At first I was startled, but when I got a closer look I realized that it wasn't one of them. No, the figure was smaller, one of a child. I slowly approached it, forming it into a more identifiable image as it just stood there, motionless.

I got within arm's reach when the figure spun around. *It...* it was indeed a child, a face I would never forget. The figure that stood before me was the little girl, the one they had taken many years ago. Janet. But that wasn't possible, there was no way it was possible. Her face was emotionless; her eyes looked dead. As if all the life had been sucked from her body and only an empty shell remained. A loud, thundering crash startled me. I turned my head for just a moment, but when I looked back she was gone. Vanished into thin air.

Whether it was my eyes playing tricks on me, or it was the ghost of poor little Janet, I knew there was an evil far more powerful than I could've imagined. This only increased the strength of my determination. I had to end this. I had to put stop to it all. And I was the only one that could.

The river was an obstacle of its own: difficult to cross as I was freezing cold, and the rapids only made it worse. But I had to escape. I was nearly swept away by the sheer force of the water. My determination kept me grounded, and soon I had reached the other side. I didn't bother to look back, but I did, and on the other side was nearly a dozen of those masked figures—all staring at me.

When I approached the edge of the river, I was relieved to see that it had lost its temper. Maybe it was trying to stop me during my escape all those years back, but this time around I made it across with a lot less effort. I was getting close. I could feel it in my bones. My heart picked up the pace and was pounding against the inside of my chest. It took every ounce of self-control not to turn back and run away. That wasn't an option, and if I did, I wouldn't be able to live with myself. I had a duty to fulfill.

The crowded trees slowly started to disperse. They were a great obscurity for the hell that dwelled within them. Mossy brick stuck out from the gap in the trees as I approached the clearing ahead. My hands were shaking by this point; my heart only grew faster. The air was thick, even with the heavy rain and wind, and I caught a whiff of something horribly familiar... death.

Death, disease, sorrow, and shattered dreams. This was the place where the wicked reigned and the innocent suffered. The building resembled a small castle, all made of old stone slabs. It was something that had been around many lifetimes before mine, possibly before even theirs. It was the crypt for those who were unfortunate enough to experience the horrors that dwelled within. And I was going back. I was going back to the place that snatched away my innocence. I still see them in my dreams—?the others—who I promised I'd return for. I'm sorry, I know it has been longer than I had hoped, but I'm here now.

I was thrown into an empty cell. The wooden door behind me slammed shut and a loud thud indicated that a lock was engaged. I was trapped in that room for exactly 35 days. I scratched the sun cycles into the wall with my long, sharp fingernails. I'd wake to a few slices of bread and some water. Nothing in the afternoon, nothing in the evening. I had to purpose a corner of my cell for defecation—although there wasn't much. They were trying to break me, but I had an iron will. A burning hatred so strong it could demolish the very walls that confined me.

Until the time came when it was very dark and the rain pounded on. The clouds overhead blocked any moonlight from illuminating my path as I crept in the shadows toward the exterior of the prison. The mossy, cracked slabs of stone were warm to the touch. Hugging the wall, I circled around the building looking for a back door. I searched my memory, hoping to find a remembrance of where I had vacated during my escape. Only static. I struggled to recall the details of that place's layout. Everything seemed so clear before, why couldn't I remember?

Eventually, I found a point of entry. To my surprise, it was unlocked. It almost seemed as if they were expecting me, but that couldn't be possible. It worried me even more that the place was unusually vacant. Again, I couldn't recall any memories of how I managed to escape. Only static. So I continued; pushing through the door and into a wide corridor. The interior was pitch black, but the temperature seemed unusually warm. My clothes had already started to dry as I navigated through the seemingly endless halls. Doors lead to empty rooms with almost no signs of any presence.

I started to worry. Had I been too late? Was this all for nothing? How would I track them down? I could only hope that the answers would reveal themselves to me as I ventured further, but each room held just as much promise as the next: empty, abandoned, not even a trace of life to be found.

It remained like this until I got to the very last room at the far corner of the wall. All but the trap door had been covered in a thick layer of dust—it was obvious that this door had been used recently. I pulled it open. A beam of bright light burst from behind the door and illuminated the area around me.

I slowly stepped down the grated steps and into a short corridor. The walls were neatly painted a pure white. The fixed lighting above hummed with electrical current. A coat rack on my left held a single pair of scrubs, as well as a pair of boots sitting on the floor below.

I carefully walked the hall; taking each step with great caution. Why didn't I remember this place? Suddenly a sharp pain shot through my skull like a bullet. I cringed and fell to my knees. I tried to think about the faces of those who I had promised to come back for, but I couldn't manage to get a clear image. Their faces were blurred in my mind's eye. Their voices seemed to distort and fade. They must've done something to cause the sudden amnesia. I tried even harder to create a clear image in my head of the horrible memories this place had created, memories I had long struggled to repress. But again, blank, and the voices had become only white noise.

The pain subsided. I took a moment to collect myself. I wondered if I should turn back and let it all dissolve into the collapsing abyss of my memory. But I couldn't do that. I've already gotten so far, and if I was already too late, I at least deserved answers.

The final door stood only a few feet in front of me. As I approached, I could hear the clacking of a computer keyboard coming from the other side. I hesitated for a moment then remembered I had no means of self-defense other than my two fists. It didn't matter at that point; if I died right then and there, it would only be putting me out of my misery.

I kicked the door open. A balding man wearing a lab coat sitting in front of a desk jumped in his seat and spun around to face me.

"Daniel!" he said with a look of surprise.

"Who the fuck are you!? How do you know my name?" I shouted.

The man lightly chuckled and stood up from his chair. I rushed him; running around the desk and grabbing him by his shirt and pinning him to the wall.

"Daniel, relax. I am not your enemy." The man sniffed my shirt and gave me a look of disappointment.

"You've been smoking again, haven't you? Those things are gonna kill you one day."

"WHO THE FUCK ARE YOU?! WHERE ARE THE OTHERS? WHERE DID YOU TAKE THEM?" I screamed.

The man reached up and wiped the spit from his face.

"The others, oh god, not again. Here, follow me." He pushed my arms away, but I resisted.

"Do you mind?" he added. "I just cleaned this jacket."

I was shocked. Who was this man, and what was with his attitude? Had he been the one responsible for all of this? The crippling pain returned and I winced. The man pushed my arms away and stepped towards a door on the opposite side of the room.

"Hurts like hell, doesn't it? It's from the smoking. You need to quit. I have a feeling it's the cause of these episodes."

He swung open the door and held it in place for me, patiently waiting for me to recover.

"Follow me."

I really didn't have a choice other than to comply. There was something about him that just didn't seem threatening. Honestly, it almost gave me a sense of security. By this point, all of the memories of this place had vanished. I couldn't draw a purpose of why I had returned.

We passed through the doorway which led to a room filled with all sorts of medical equipment. A curtain concealed a small portion of the corner, and behind it I could hear a continuous electronic beep.

"Now, Daniel, I know you're angry and possibly confused. Do not worry, it's a side effect of the smoking. It creates a chemical imbalance in the brain, which as a result, triggers those migraines, as well as memory loss. But you're going to be ok."

The man grabbed the edge of the curtain and slowly pulled it back. It was... it was me. It was me, lying there;

machines hooked up to my frail body. I looked sick... like I was on the brink of death. A tube had been shoved down my throat which was connected to some sort of machine. A device on my bedside was monitoring my vitals.

"What is this..."

Pain. Agonizing, crippling pain surged through my head and forced me to my knees. My vision blurred, and soon all the memories I had were erased, others played in my head as if they were replaced with a new roll of film.

There were crying children and parents. Men with white surgical masks held the children's hands and led them onto a bus. I looked down to see that I too was being led towards the bus. Looking up to see a familiar set of eyes. It was his, the scientist's, the one who I had thought I'd just met for the first time.

Static.

Blood. Massive amounts of blood. It covered my hands. I looked down at my medical gown which was also covered in blood. I looked to my left where I met the eyes of a little girl. It was Janet. She was dressed the same as I, tears were streaming down her face, a combination of fear and agony showed in her eyes. She started convulsing. Men with surgical masks rushed to her aid.

Static.

"Daniel, you're going to be ok. Don't be scared. I can save you." I opened my eyes to see that man standing over me.

Static.

I was standing in front of a mirror. I ran my hands down the sides of my face and leaned against the counter.

I looked sick; my face was pale white, I was disgustingly skinny.

Static.

"I've done it!" The man shouted in accomplishment, "Daniel, welcome to your new life. After hundreds of failures, I've finally managed to save someone."

Static.

I was on a jogging on a treadmill. Wires were stuck to my chest with tiny adhesive strips. They were all linked to a monitor which projected a series of lines and alternating numbers. The man stood before me, clipboard in hand, analyzing the monitor.

It all came back to me. This place wasn't some sort of prison or hell, it was a lab. This man, his name was... Craig, Dr. Marshall Craig. We were all terminally ill. Our parents surrendered us with hopes that they could possibly save our lives. But I was the only one. I don't know how I saw these people as monsters. I felt ashamed. I felt terrible. Tears began to stream down my cheeks as I stared into the empty shell of myself.

"Dr. Craig, I'm so sorry..."

"Oh, don't worry about it. I'm just glad you are ok. You've had a few mishaps before, but you were gone for nearly two days this time. I was worried you had—" Dr. Craig's phone started to ring.

"Hello, this is Marshall. Oh. Yes. I'll send someone down to retrieve the delivery. Thank you."

Dr. Craig hung up his phone and looked over at me.

"Daniel, get changed and walk down to the end of the road to meet the delivery driver. Make sure you bring my car back here in one piece. If you lose it again, I'm going to make you walk there and back every time."

I sighed and did what I was told. Dr. Craig was a great man with a lot of weight on his shoulders. He has single-handedly managed to genetically clone a living organism. Not just any, but human DNA. It was beyond that, I've managed to collect a lot of the memories of my past, but it's not all clear. I know that I lived not too far from here. I know that I can't return home since Dr. Craig is trying to figure out how to completely pass on the knowledge of my counterpart. But I am thankful. He has given me a second chance at life, and I would do anything I could to assist him in his endeavors.

I got to the end of the road where I saw Dr. Craig's car sitting just outside the entry gate that prevented any further access towards the lab. The delivery guy, Dave, was leaning against the gate smoking a cigarette and playing a game on his phone.

"Sup, bro?" he said casually.

He walked around to the back of his pickup and handed me 2 boxes. One was labeled with a biohazard sticker and the other was marked flammable. I signed for the packages and tossed them into the trunk of Dr. Craig's car, alongside the others I came for before my disappearance.

Before taking off I turned to Dave, "Hey, can I bother you for a smoke?"

Dave sighed and reached into his shirt pocket, "Ya, but this is the last time. I gave you half a pack the other day and you already burned through 'em?!"

I shrugged my shoulders.

Dave handed me a single cigarette and I put it to my lips. He took off down the dirt road as I was digging around in the car for a lighter. Shutting the car door, I sparked the flame and put drew it towards the end of the unlit cigarette—taking in a lungful of smoke...

I HAVE TO GO BACK. I have to help them, and after all these years, I finally managed to muster up the courage to return. That place. That place is fucking hell on earth, and somehow, I managed to escape. I promised them I'd return. I can only hope that I'm not too late.

TEENAGERS: CHAPTER 1

TEENAGERS: CHAPTER 1

KYLE ALEXANDER

It all started with a bit of innocent curiosity. Over the past few days, I've come to realize there are doors that should've never been opened. That old expression "curiosity killed the cat" had never felt any truer than it does now. I've opened something that I have since learned is far darker than anything I'd have ever expected. Things only seemed to get worse, and like an onion, each layer I peeled back exposed more than my senses could ever handle. But once you start, you're obligated to proceed.

It all began when I noticed strange billboards over the highway. Nothing stood out, but something about them always bothered me. The ads were always so vague: nothing relevant to the website written at the bottom, other than a few smiling children, standing together with their arms over each other's shoulders as though they were best pals.

Another ad was of a teenage boy, hiding in a tree while

2 others below had their backs turned and were looking off into the dark purple background. I'd always notice the new ad whenever I turned onto the freeway. I composed a theory that it was some after-school program where they keep kids out of trouble by occupying their time. I eventually gave in to my curiosity. I decided to enter the URL from the sign into my web browser when I got home one evening.

It took quite some time to load before I was greeted by a message prompt.

"MEMBERS ONLY. Please login or make an account."

I found that odd since they were advertising the website to the public, so why did it only allow access to members? The thought I landed on was: exclusivity creates interest, that alone can be a cunning marketing tactic. I played along and decided to sign up. It asked for a full name, date of birth, and email. After punching in my info, I was denied access since I wasn't within their age range (you had to be 17 or under to become a member).

I tried again, this time changing my last name and lowering my age to 17. Again, access denied. It must've had a IP recognition software. I managed to mask my IP address and made an account under my new identity. That's when things got a little weird...

It didn't ask for email confirmation, but it did ask for proof of age. It required me to upload a photo of a state-issued ID, driver's license, or school ID to prove I was legitimate. Fortunately, I had an old high school ID card in one of my junk drawers. All it took was a few minutes on Photoshop to edit my name and age. After submitting the file, I was told I'd receive an email with my user info after they verified my credentials.

I received a response the next day while I was at work. I was approved and given a username and password which granted me access to the site. I decided to wait until I got home to further investigate. Time felt as if it were moving at half-speed. Finally, the clock turned to 4:30PM and I was on my way home. Traffic was terrible that evening and it didn't help that I was so eager to get home. I pulled into my driveway and tossed my keys on to the kitchen counter, making a beeline to my computer desk.

I logged in to my personal email and opened the message. I copied the username and abnormally long password and was granted access to the site. It looked like something out of a movie: a black background gave the page an ominous appearance. The page was topped with a green text that read "Tyrants" and below were long columns that resembled some sort of blog. I got halfway through the latest entry that described how users can now gain access to anyone's medical history, even private files, through a link on the page. I was suddenly closed out of my browser and that's when it clicked in my head. The email was sent to my personal account! When I signed up under false pretenses, I used a brand-new email address. How did it end up in my own inbox?

I started to panic. I instantly unplugged my internet modem, hoping that it wouldn't allow anyone to track me down. I ran around the house and locked all my doors and windows and pulled the blinds shut. Something about that whole situation scared the living shit out of me. I cowered in my room for the next few hours in complete silence. My anxiety started to dwindle away until I heard a loud knocking at my door. At first, I ignored it, but it persisted.

Quickly, I tiptoed to my front door and peered through the viewer. Two figures stood on my front porch wearing dark clothes with their hoods pulled low over their faces. They pounded several times and even jiggled the knob viciously. Sweat started to pour down my face and my heart shot up into my throat. Eventually, they stepped away and I backpedaled into the hallway. I heard rustling at living room window; the thin pane of glass rattled against its frame as they tried to slide it open. I had to cover my mouth to refrain from screaming.

They continued the attempt to breach every possible entrance to my home. It went on for almost an hour before it finally stopped. When it did, I pushed my couch in front of the door and all other miscellaneous furniture in front of all possible entryways. I didn't sleep a wink that night. I was finally starting to doze off when my alarm began to scream.

5am, time to get up for work. I was already awake, of course, but I did not plan on going to work that day. Then I thought of how I couldn't afford to miss a day at work, and that if I sat at home, maybe they'd come back full force. I made a quick pot of coffee and nearly chugged the whole thing before I started my commute.

I saw the billboard again as I merged into traffic. I couldn't decipher the ad since graffiti writers managed to get to it during the night. Work went by slow in the first part of the day. I couldn't focus, couldn't take my mind off what happened the previous night. But mostly, I was dead-ass tired. I spent the day trying to power nap at my desk between short bursts of productivity when I overheard a conversation between two of my coworkers in the cubicle next door.

"Clay has been wonderful since he joined that after-school program. His grades have improved significantly, he finally gained some manners, and he's just been so involved the community that I don't even have to worry about him getting into trouble!"

"Do you know the name of it? I would love to get Tabitha into one of those. Maybe she'd learn to keep away from that loser boyfriend of hers."

"No, and I don't bother Clay about it much. He's made such a great progress, I don't want to intrude at all. He's graduating this year and the one thing I don't want is to get in the way of that. I'll find out what I can for you though!"

My eavesdropping was interrupted by a phone call to my desk.

"Kyle, you have a visitor here. He says he's you're expecting him...?" I could sense the confusion in her voice.

My blood ran cold, but I knew I couldn't alarm anyone. I wouldn't have been able to live with myself if anything were to happen to my innocent coworkers.

"Oh ya. One second, Phoebe, I'll be right out. Have him wait there for me."

I scrambled to gather my things. I didn't even bother to stop by my boss's office before slipping out the back door and sprinting around the building towards my car.

When I got around the corner, I could see 3 teenagers: 2 boys and 1 girl, standing around my car smoking cigarettes. I knew something was wrong and I didn't want to find out. I turned around and crossed over the property to the adjacent street. After about 3 miles of walking, I decided to take the bus. If I was in public, at least there would be less of a chance of being apprehended.

The bus arrived shortly after getting to the stop and I stepped inside. The smallest bill I had on me was a five, so I slid it into the machine and the bus took off. The front of the bus was crowded; I'd have hoped to find a spot as close to the driver, or the door, as possible. There wasn't even much room to stand, and I had to push through the crowd towards the back of the bus.

The back seats were all occupied by another group of teenagers. They all stared at me as I wiggled my way through the crowd to find an appropriate place to stand. They never took their gaze off me as I tried my best not to look over at them. I made the mistake of turning my head to make sure they were indeed looking at me, and I locked eyes with one of them.

A boy, about 17 with black hair and gray eyes, was glaring at me in a malicious way. The blonde girl sitting next to him leaned over and whispered something in his ear. I got even more nervous. They seemed to be threatening me with their eyes. I couldn't shake the thought that at any moment, one of them would pounce. I decided to pull the string that notified the bus driver to let me off at the next stop.

The bus driver pulled over and I quickly pushed through the crowd that was huddled around the back door. I looked behind me to find that all 4 of the teenagers had stood up and mirrored my movement. They were going to follow me. I pushed through the door before it had even opened all the way and booked it down the sidewalk. I got about a block down the street before I turned around to see that they were following. Their expressions remained blank, but their eyes said it all.

I picked up the pace, running through intersections without even looking. A few cars slammed on their brakes and honked at me, but I didn't care. My only goal was getting as far away from them as possible. I must've ran at least 2 miles in 5 minutes until I became too winded to run any further. I turned into an alleyway between buildings and pulled my phone from my pocket. I had started to dial 911, but a hand smacked it out of grasp. Jumping back, I turned to see all 4 of the teenagers had me surrounded. The boy with the grey eyes was wielding a knife. His expression remained the same.

"Why are you doing this?!" I cried.

No response—only that same, sinister stare. Their faces looked stone cold, like they were under some sort of spell. I stepped away from them but had backed myself into a dumpster. The group got closer, and with each step I became more and more terrified.

Suddenly, the sound of a car horn broke through the silence. I turned around to get a look at my savior: an angry old man shouting obscenities at the group of kids blocking his path. The boy tucked the knife away and gestured to his followers that it was time to leave. They stared at me long and hard before slowly walking back

BRUTAL BEDTIME STORIES

into the street. I dropped to my knees and began to sob. At that moment, I knew my life was in danger.

Worst of all, I didn't even know why. There wasn't any reasonable explanation to what instigated these kids. It was even more stressful knowing that they had made a great attempt to do so. It had to be something regarding that website. Something bad was happening and that website was my only connection.

My phone must've slid about 20 feet away. The screen was shattered but still barely functional. I intended to call the police, but what for? I had no evidence at the time. I didn't even have a suspect other than some vague descriptions of the kids who had attacked me. If I were to get the police involved, there needed to be a crime committed. Until then, I was on my own.

It was well after dusk when I got home. My front door had been kicked in; my home had been destroyed. Furniture was turned over, drawers pulled open with all their contents thrown onto the floor. My bedroom was in complete disarray and my computer had been stolen. At that point, I didn't feel safe in my own home. I was in the process of gathering a week's worth of clothes when I noticed a note pinned to the wall above my desk.

"Go ahead, try and run from us."

I nearly shat my pants at the sight of it. This rabbit hole I had fallen into was far deeper than I could've imagined. And it only seemed to be getting worse...

I called the police. I mentioned that 2 teenagers had been scoping the place out the night before. I gave them the description of the boy who tried to attack me earlier, but didn't tell them why. They claimed that my computer

275

more than likely won't be recovered, but they will open an investigation and keep an eye around the neighborhood for any suspicious activity.

After that, I called my friend Nick. I made up some excuse about how I needed a place to stay for a few days while exterminators come to my house and get rid of a bug infestation. Nick agreed, but said he'd like more of a notice next time since he was going to have another house guest that weekend. I didn't think much of it at the time, but I had been a little too distracted by the whole ordeal to even consider.

"What's up, Kyle?" Nick said as he opened the door. He didn't even bother to put pants on, dressing only in his boxers and a Slayer t-shirt he's had since we were 17.

"Sup, bro," I droned and entered the living room where Nick had a crudely made bed waiting for me on the couch. He didn't bother to clean anything, as his coffee table was covered in beer cans and an ash tray that was overflowing with blunt roaches.

"I was about to roll one up, want to smoke this with me?" Nick asked as he plopped down on the couch. He pulled a large bag of weed from inside a concealed drawer in his coffee table.

I hadn't smoked weed since my senior year in high school, but I thought it might be a good idea since I was under so much stress. Nick and I passed the blunt back and forth. I could tell that I had been high as hell because after only a few hits, I was telling Nick every detail about what happened in the past few days. He stared at me with a blank look and nodded his head slightly every few sentences as I told him the story. When I finished, his blood-shot eyes had grown as wide as they possibly could for the state he was in.

"Whoa. That's some heavy shit, dude. What do you think it is? Do you think they're like brainwashing the kids, or do you think it's like some Fight Club type of shit where you're a threat to their organization and they're trying to kill you since you stumbled across their plans?"

I was surprised by his response, although Nick was pretty fucked up. Something about his level of understanding gave me a bit of relief. Him and I had been best friends since our freshman year in high school. We would always skip 4th period and get stoned behind the gym. Since then, we've always been close. He made a living selling weed, enjoying a simpler life. He was a pretty good businessman, although he was an avid stoner, he was a level-headed guy. He never judged anyone and could always empathize with people. Nick was a great friend.

Nick stepped away for a second to take a phone call. I'd been stoned out of my mind and didn't really think much of it; I was too busy watching a derogatory cartoon on the television about a drunk scientist and an idiot child who got into all types of crazy situations. Nick came back into the living room with a large mason jar in hand and a small scale.

"Yo, my neighbor's gonna swing by and pick up some bud. Is that cool?" Nick asked as he weighed a cup on the scale and dumped a handful of weed inside.

I was too stoned to truly understand his question. I only nodded and continued watching my show. Nick bagged up the weed and soon after, there was a knock at his door. Nick jumped out of his seat and answered it.

"Come in, bro!"

I heard footsteps approaching and the door slam behind them. When I turned to see who it was, I nearly jumped out of my skin. He looked about 16 years old. He had a shaved head and a scar crossing his left eye—like some sort of villain cliché. His expression changed from a casual attitude to a sharp gaze when he saw me. The kid took a seat in the chair across from me and didn't look away the entire time

Nick spoke. He handed Nick the money and stuffed the bag of weed into his pocket without even blinking.

"Thanks," the boy said in a robotic tone. The kid practically turned his neck around like an owl as he made his way to the front door. He didn't look away until Nick shut the door behind him.

"Dude, that was fucking weird. Did you see how he was looking at you?!" Nick squawked.

I was practically shivering in fear at this point. He was just next door to us, and he knew that I was here. He knew exactly where to find me. And worst of all was that Nick had became a potential target too. I worried that they would come after him, using him as leverage to get to me.

"Nick, they know I'm here. They're dangerous. I'm worried that they are going to hurt you now that they know you and I are connected! We have to get out here!"

Nick chuckled. "Dude, I've known Damien since he was 13. The kid just likes to skateboard and smoke weed. There's no way he has plans to hurt either of us. You need to chill. Here, hit the bong and I'll grab ya a beer."

I took a giant pull from the bong and Nick brought me

a 24oz Steel Reserve from the fridge. He always had shit taste in beer. Cheap bastard. I pounded it as quick as I could, hoping it would settle my nerves. Shortly after, my head started to spin and I laid down on the couch. All my worries disappeared and were replaced with a heavy sense of nausea—I passed out shortly after.

Heavy pounding on the front door pulled me out of my intoxicated slumber. Nick stumbled out of his room towards the front door, cigarette hanging from his mouth. When I saw who had been on the other side, I flipped off the couch and fell to the floor.

"Tommy! What's up?! I didn't expect you to be here so early dude!"

A short, frail boy with curly brown hair stepped through the threshold. He had a giant backpack on and a tote bag around his shoulder. I recognized him as Nick's little brother. That didn't make me feel any different as I was already on hyper-alert. Anyone could potentially be a threat—Tommy wasn't an exception.

Tommy dropped his backpack next to the door and let out a deep, relieving sigh.

"Next time you or Mom are driving me. I hate taking the bus here. They're always full of thugs and bums. I could've sworn one of them wanted to steal my computer!" Tommy clutched his tote bag and peered over at me. His face was confusion, which shortly changed to a look of recognition.

"Hi, Kyle," he muttered as he kicked off his shoes and plopped down on the couch.

Nick frantically started to clean up the junk from his

coffee table, trying to hide the 3ft bong which sat in the middle of the mess.

"Nick, you don't have to hide your paraphernalia. Mom and I both know you're a pothead. I honestly don't care," Tommy confessed while pulling his laptop out of its bag.

"What's your WiFi password?"

"Uhh...it's chronic1224 I thin," Nick replied.

Tommy pounded away at his keyboard. I didn't interact with him much when we were kids. He was a lot younger than us and kind of a hermit. His mom got him a computer for his birthday when he was young and he's always glued to that thing. Tommy was some kind of computer wizard.

"Hey, Tommy," I said hesitantly.

"What's up, Kyle. You look like shit, dude. Party hard with Nick last night?"

"No. Actually, I was hoping you could help me with something..."

Tommy stopped typing and glanced over at me. He was always somewhat abrasive, but him and I always got along. Nick came in and set a beer down in front of me and a Mountain Dew in front of Tommy. Nick cracked open his beer.

"Hair of the dog. Isn't that right, Kyle!" Nick playfully smacked me in the back.

I picked up the beer, popped it open, and took a swig. My stomach coiled as the cold malt-liquor slithered down my throat.

"Kyle, what is it you were gonna ask me?" Tommy reminded.

Nick interrupted. "OH SHIT! Dude! So, Kyle was tellin' me about how he found this creepy website, but it blocked him. Now he's apparently being followed by teenagers and they're trying to kill him and shit! Dude it's fuckin' crazy!"

Tommy snorted. "Nick, that's ridiculous. You must've been smoking too much pot because I HIGHLY doubt that is the case. Kyle, please explain."

"No... he's pretty much right. I stumbled upon this website. You have to be 17 or younger to gain access and they make you prove your age and everything." I took in a deep breath. I was speaking way too fast for my lungs to keep up.

"The site was just weird. I didn't get to see much before they kicked me out, but I know there are things that shouldn't be there, I know that much. They're very strict about who can and can't view its contents."

Tommy's eyes grew wide with interest.

"So, after all of that, someone tried breaking into my house later that night. It was 2 teenagers. They were at it for hours. After that, a group of them showed up at my work looking for me. I had to leave my car, but there were even more on the bus and they cornered me. I'm almost positive they were trying to kill me because one of them had a knife and I was trapped in an alleyway before I managed to get away with a stroke of luck."

I'd crushed the beer enough to spill all over the floor. Re-telling the story made me so tense

"Holy shit. You're kidding? I fucking read about something like that this morning. Some guy posted on Reddit about it but the post got removed before I got a chance to read it. Wow. This is insane. What's the URL? I'm gonna see if I can get in."

I told Tommy the website and he typed away at his keyboard for what felt like forever.

"The security of this website is tight. Something you would see on a government page. It's gonna take a while to get in, but I'm confident that I can."

Nick came back with a towel and wiped the beer off the floor. Tommy got up and moved over to the kitchen where he could comfortably sit and plug in his laptop. While Tommy did his thing, Nick and I chatted about the whole ordeal. He rolled up a blunt and we passed it back and forth until Tommy called me into the kitchen.

"Look." Tommy pointed to the screen which was just a jumbled mess of text that I didn't understand.

"Uhh..."

"Oh shit. Sorry. So, Kyle, you're in some deep shit, dude. This isn't just some weird website, or even a cult. This is a deep criminal ring. Maybe like the mafia, only smarter. They have access to any person's medical archives, as well as their criminal backgrounds. They've shared with each other these confidential files that were very well secured. They have a network of personal information at their disposal: Addresses, names, social security numbers, bank account information, everything. Nothing is off limits to them. This is bad, Kyle. This is terrorist level. How is it that a bunch of teenagers are capable of such a thing?"

"Well there's you..." my voice quivered.

"Ya, but I'm an exception. There aren't many people my age who are capable of this kind of stuff. I'm just good with computers, but these people are like a collection of super-geniuses. I tried locating a member list, but I haven't found one yet. I've only managed to bypass their basic security. If I plan on digging any deeper, I'm going to have to get a hold of a few friends. Do they know you're here?"

I paused… the sudden realization forced me to run out of the kitchen. The living room was empty. Nick's still-lit blunt was sitting in the ash tray.

"Nick!" I yelled frantically.

My heart pounded so hard against my chest that the loud, rapid pulse was near deafening. I froze in fear once I realized Nick was gone. His front door was left wide open. At the entrance was a small puddle of blood. I only hoped it wasn't Nick's.

"Tommy, we have to go now!" I howled.

Tommy turned his head and looked at me in confusion.

"Tommy, LET'S GO!"

"What the hell is going on?" he exclaimed.

"Nick! Nick is gone. They took him! We had to go now!"

Tommy didn't question me any further. He swiped up his laptop as I ran through the house gathering necessities. Nick's cell phone and keys were lying on the living room table, and I snatched them up as we headed out the door. I threw our possessions in the back of Nick's pickup and peeled out of there in a cloud of smoke.

"Where are we going?!" Tommy demanded, his arms clenched around his computer.

"We're going to get somewhere safe, then we're going to call the police."

I jumped onto the highway and drove south until dusk. We pulled off exit 126 leading to a small, rundown motel. It was a small junction of rooms, probably about 12 or so. The front had a paved parking lot, but we parked behind the building in the large gravel lot beside a few semi-trucks.

A bell chimed as we entered he rental office. The room was worn down, and an old man sat at the counter was reading the previous day's newspaper. I noticed the head-lining article:

6 casualties and 3 in critical condition in violent bus-jack-ing. A group of teens took control of the bus and lead police on a 2 hour pursuit which ended in a head-on collision with a garbage truck.

There was a picture of the suspects below the title: the kids who cornered me in the alleyway.

Tommy nudged me and I snapped out of my state of shock. The old man at the counter had been looking at me with an annoyed look on his face.

"Can I help you?"

"Ya, we need a room for the night."

"We only got singles available. Is that ok?"

"Ya, sure." I reached for my wallet and saw I only had $80 in cash.

"Credit only."

Fuck. I didn't have a credit card. Before I knew it, Tommy slapped a shiny blue card down on the table. He then signed the roster under "bugs bunny".

We were in room 6 which was smack-dab in the middle of the block of rooms.

"Tommy, whose card was that?"

"My mom's. She gave it to me for emergencies only, but that seemed like an emergency to me," Tommy chuckled.

When we checked in, he paid the extra $10 for WiFi and busted out his computer to start pounding away. I took it upon myself to start fiddling with Nick's phone. When I unlocked the screen, I saw he had 1 new message from an unknown number. It was a picture of Nick with a piece of silver duct-tape over his mouth. His left eye was swollen shut and blood leaked from his nose. The message read:

Do not call the police.

I dropped the phone in shock. In just a few hours, things had escalated to the point where my best friend's life was in danger.

I looked over at Tommy. He had started a video chat with a husky, balding man. A lot of the stuff they were talking about involved computers and hacking and I couldn't really understand. Tommy explained it all to me.

"Ok, so tomorrow we're going to meet up with Tooner. Tooner is going to stay up all night and work his way into their system. He's the best— I learned almost everything I know from him. If anyone can get to the bottom of what's going on, he's our guy."

Tommy carried a surprisingly high level of confidence. It really gave me a sense of relief. At the time, he was my most valuable resource.

I had a hard time trying to figure out what to do with

myself, so I flipped on the TV and ran through the news channels, trying to find anything relevant.

"—was robbed. The suspects managed to get away with 8.2 million dollars, and police have no leads on the case."

"Two teens were shot down by police officers after a shootout in downtow—"

"Police are on the lookout for Kyle Alexander for the kidnapping if Nick Gorie and his little brother, Thomas Gorie."

"Tommy..." I didn't need to get his attention. He was already glued to the TV.

"Kyle is assumed to be armed and dangerous. He was last seen in a white Nissan pickup with the license plate #A734KJ. If seen, please dial 911. Do not attempt to confront him."

Tommy jumped off the bed and snatched the remote out of my hand, shutting off the TV. We both stood there in silence for a few moments. The tension was thick: suffocating and crowding the room like a dense fog. I broke the silence.

"I need a minute."

I stepped outside, slamming the door behind me. I trotted around to the truck and found an old pack of cigarettes underneath the driver's seat. I shook it. Luckily, the last one was rattling inside. I pushed the cigarette lighter in the dash and waited for it to get hot. The sound of a car engine echoed in the distance, followed by silence. I scanned the area for red and blue police lights: nothing but darkness and the glow of the flickering "Vacancy" sign of the motel.

I finished the cigarette and dropped it, smothering the ember with the sole of my shoe. I walked back around the building with my hands stuffed in my pockets. My eyes were pointed at the ground, staring at my feet as I returned to room #6. When I looked up, I saw a brand-spanking-new Dodge Charger parked in front of the rental office. That's when I turned to look at our room. The door... the door was ajar.

My walk turned into a full-on sprint. I charged through the door. The room was trashed. Tommy was missing. The bathroom door was shut.

I bust through the door to see a man. Tommy was on his back, thrashing as the man had him pinned down inside the bathtub. He was choking Tommy to death. I snatched up the soap dispenser from the counter and smacked the man over the back of his hooded skull.

The man let out a sharp grunt and his body went limp, collapsing on top of Tommy and releasing his grip. Tommy sucked in a huge breath of air and started to cough violently. I pulled the dead-weight off him and helped Tommy to his feet. Once he caught his breath, he spun around and started to look at the back of the man's head. Blood was leaking out of the wound, all over the bathroom floor and inside the tub.

"Did you kill him?!" Tommy shouted in panic.

"Fuck, I hope so."

Tommy grabbed a hand-towel and held it firmly against the man's bleeding head. I just stood there. I was baffled at the idea of Tommy trying to perform first-aid on the man who had just tried to kill him.

"Please be okay. Please be okay," Tommy pleaded,

holding the towel over the wound with both hands in attempt to stop the bleeding.

"Tommy, what the fuck are you doing? Let's finish this guy off and call the police!" I growled, readying the ceramic soap dispenser once again.

"It's fucking Nick! It's Nick!" Tommy shrieked. You could hear his voice crack as he tried to hold back the tears.

Pushing Tommy aside, I got closer to the man. He smelled like weed and beer. My stomach flip-flopped as I turned the man's head over to see the bruised and poorly groomed face of my best friend. His eye was still swollen shut, just like the picture, and his nose was bent crooked. I ran my hand over the back of Nick's head. Then I felt something strange...

I gently turned his head back around and parted his brown, oily hair. There were stitches. The blunt object to the back of his head had reopened Nick's wound and I could see something behind the skin. I reached out and grabbed at it with my fingernails. With a little bit of force, it came free. Two long, skinny threads followed as I extracted the device from the back of Nick's skull. I wiped off the blood to reveal a polished silver chip about a square inch in size and maybe a millimeter thick. The two threads appeared to be fine wires that were attached to the side of the device.

I turned around to show it to Tommy who was sitting on the toilet hyperventilating. His eyes widened as I held the strange device in front of his face.

"What the hell is that?" he asked between gasps.

"I don't know. But I found it in the back of Nick's head. Help me get him up."

I waited for Tommy to compose himself, and together we pulled Nick out of the tub and sat him on the toilet. We cleaned him up and got most of the blood off the floor. I found a first-aid kit underneath the bathroom sink and did the best I could to bandage and disinfect his wound. Afterwards, we gently laid Nick down on the bed. I was relieved knowing that my friend was okay, but things were spinning out of control. I didn't realize that I was only making a scratch in the surface.

Nick woke up in complete shock around 4AM the next morning. Tommy and I were each sleeping on the floor next to the bed when we were snapped out of our restless daze. Nick was screaming like a tortured animal. It took us nearly 15 minutes just to settle him down. The bed sheets were soaked in blood, and Nick was obviously in shock. With all that set aside, I was glad he was back to his normal self.

It took almost an hour for us to explain what happened. We explained everything that had occurred after his capture. He told us he didn't remember a thing other than seeing his neighbor who had bought the bag of weed from him earlier that day.

"I'm so sorry, Tommy. I would never do that to you." Nick was becoming hysterical.

Tommy assured him that he understood and didn't hold him accountable for his actions. Tommy got back in contact with his friend, Tooner, and he gave him an update. He was in a video chat with the guy, so he did what he could to show Tooner what we had pulled out of Nick's head. The guy told us to get there ASAP and make sure we aren't being followed or tracked. He gave us an address to a grocery store near his house and told us to meet him there.

This is where I'm going to have to leave you. Tommy allowed me to use his computer to write down the whole thing, and I'll update as soon as I get the chance.

TEENAGERS: CHAPTER TWO

KYLE ALEXANDER

THE DRIVE TOOK ABOUT 6 HOURS. IT WOULD'VE NORMALLY taken 7, but we took the mysterious charger that Nick must've stolen since his truck was under the thumb of the public eye. Before we took off, Tommy ran a diagnostics program to assure there wasn't any tracking program installed in the car. There was, but the little genius redirected the tracking system's compass so that if we were driving south, it would think we were headed north, and vice-versa. He explained it all to me, but I'm no fucking computer expert. I just trusted his judgment and drove.

The brothers nearly slept the entire ride. I was fueled by adrenaline and crippling anxiety, so I didn't have much of a hard time trying to stay awake during the drive. I was also going nearly 120mph the entire way there. A dirty, white suburban was waiting for us in the parking lot. When we all stepped out of the car, the suburban identified us and flashed his lights in our direction. The backseat of Tooner's ride was trashed; littered with wrappers, stale French fries, and other miscellaneous garbage.

We arrived at Tooner's house; his lawn was long and unkempt, toys scattered along the front yard and driveway. He obviously had kids. When we got out, Tooner finally spoke for the first time.

"I need you to know right now that you are in no way going to connect me to any of this. I wouldn't even be helping you if it weren't for Tommy. This is my home, this is where my family lives, do not bring anything back to me. Got it?"

We all nodded in agreement.

Tooner led us around the side of the house and through a door to the basement. Another door was behind it, tightly secured with a deadbolt and another lock attached to a keypad. He covered the keypad with his free hand as he punched in the 12-digit code and we followed him inside. I was beyond overwhelmed by his headquarters, blinded by a plethora of monitors, all running sequences of unintelligible letters and numbers. A large U-shaped desk was placed in the center of the room where countless keyboards and other unidentifiable equipment were placed in a very particular way.

Tooner rubbed his balding head, turned around to face us, and broke the silence. "Welcome to the mothership!" he chuckled and plopped down into his chair.

The man fidgeted with his beard and gave us an intrigued expression. "Let me get a closer look at the thing you showed me, Tommy."

Tommy shoved his hand into his pocket and retrieved the device. Bits of pocket lint were stuck to the wires.

Tooner held the object up to the light and studied it for a moment, then his face lit up. You could almost see the light-bulb of surety appear above his head.

"I've seen something like this before. There's an inscription on the surface. It's subtle, but I can just make it out."

Tooner spun around in his chair and swiveled over to one of the monitors. He pounded away at his keyboard for a minute until he shrieked in discovery.

"Here it is! I remembered this peculiar inscription from a video I'd seen back in 2010. This man, Elliot Kuska, had developed a sort of artificial intelligence. It wasn't like your stereotypical interactive type of AI. It was hardware you'd install that would override its programming and allow you to modify its code by adding your own simplified instructions to it.

I found it interesting. I know it sounds vague, but in the demo, he showed you exactly how it works. Basically, you would install the chip into any piece of technology that was capable of such. Once it was completed, it would adapt to the programming of its host. You'd wire the device up to your computer and open the software, at that point it would give you a simplified version of the host's technological capabilities. From then on, you're able to customize its functions to your own liking just by typing simple commands into the program. The more advanced the host, the more descriptive you'd have to be.

He started with an RC car. He modified the car so it could receive the chip and link up to his computer. Of course, the car only had a few simple functions: forward, reverse, and steer. Elliot commanded the car to drive in a straight line just by typing a few sentences. The car continued to drive until it hit a wall, then it just stayed stationary until it received another command. Next, he commanded it to drive in a figure-eight formation—the car did so. Each demonstration became more complicated than the last until he had the car doing various tasks. It pushed a ball in a circle and was fully capable of following exact instructions by targeting it into a basket which was placed in the corner of the room.

Tooner tried playing the YouTube video for us, but it said it had been removed.

"Fuck!" Tooner shouted.

I was overwhelmed with the whole thing, but I got the idea. Tommy, on the other hand, understood it all.

"Ok. So, what does that have to do with this? I get the connection, but how does that compare to us pulling that device out the back of my brother's head?" Tommy pointed over at Nick, who was sitting against the wall in the corner of the room.

"Well, the demo that Elliot put on was for investors. They didn't seem too interested in the idea, so they denied him. Elliot was forced to seek other sources of funding. I found a tech blog from 2011 saying that a bio-engineering corporation bought the majority of his development solely from the concept of his prototype. Elliot then became the director of their development team, but there haven't been any updates since February of 2012. It seems as if Elliot just disappeared off the face of the earth."

"So, you're saying that this company, and possibly Elliot, are responsible for all of this?" I asked.

Tooner scratched his chin and let out a deep sigh. "It's plausible, but not definite. Bioengineering hasn't even managed to touch close to base when it comes to crossing technology with neuroscience. Unless they managed to obtain an immense amount of funding, as well as made technological breakthroughs without any news being leaked, then yes. But from what you've told me, and from what I've seen, I'm damn near positive that this device," Tooner held the chip out in front of him, "is cram-packed with technology far beyond our generation. If what you're saying is true, we may be on to something far worse than anything we could ever imagine. You have to understand that if they found a way to wire this hardware into the brains of the most powerful people in the world, that could be the end of days as we know it."

"Well so far Nick is the only one who we've seen that is over the age of 18 with one of those inside them," I added.

"I thought that. You said you've only encountered adolescents who have appeared to be under the control of the device?"

I nodded.

"Well, maybe Nick is an exception. There's a chance that they may not be able to control fully developed brains. Would there be any reason why Nick may be more susceptible to this?"

We all looked over at Nick, who had moved from the sitting position and was now lying on the floor. He groaned.

"Hey, toner, do you know where I could get any weed? My head is killing me, dude."

We all looked at each other, the same thought passed through of our minds. We had a solid theory to build from after that.

"Let me do a little more research and see what I can come up with. You can go upstairs and find something to eat if you like. My wife is probably making dinner as we speak," Tooner said.

We did just that. Soon after, dinner was ready and we all sat together: Tooner, his wife, and his two little ones. It was nice to be able to come back into reality. For a minute, I almost forgot what it was like to be normal. It felt as if the entire world around me had shattered like a glass mirror, only to reveal something more sinister than my own reflection on the other side...

I woke to a cup of fresh coffee being handed to me from Tooner's wife.

"They're all downstairs, sweetheart. You were sleeping so soundly that no one wanted to wake you."

I sat up and everything that had just happened replayed inside my mind. Sipping the coffee, I sat on the couch and reflected on everything for a moment while rain peppered the living-room window. I thought about how suddenly my whole world had flipped upside-down. I knew that if this ever came to an end, my life would never be the same. Everything used to be so normal. Average car, decent paying job, everything I had grown so accustomed to was all ripped out of my hands and I was thrown into a boiling pot, fighting off the hand trying to seal my fate.

I went downstairs to find Nick, Tommy, and Tooner, all gathered around one of the monitors. They were so wrapped into what was being projected that they didn't notice me arrive.

The Regional Justice Center is in complete lockdown. 6 armed and unidentified men have taken the entire 3rd-floor hostage. Their motives are unclear and no demands have yet been made. Negotiators are trying to make contact at this very moment.

Tommy turned and noticed me standing behind him.

"This is insane. I bet every penny I have that those 6 are teenagers." He scoffed and spat at the ground.

"Wait. Tooner, what about the website? Can we get a better look at that?" The sudden thought sprang from my lips the moment it came to mind.

Tooner nodded and spun around in his chair. Tommy hovered over his shoulder and admired his role-model's work. I turned to Nick. His face was pale and his eyes sunk low into their dark sockets. He needed rest. There was no way he could do this in the state that he was in.

"Nick, dude, you've been through Hell. Why don't you go upstairs and get some sleep?" I placed my hand on his shoulder.

"Yo, Tanner, do you know where I can find some weed?" Nick pleaded.

Tooner chuckled and slid open a drawer on his right-hand side, and without looking, he tossed a Ziploc bag of weed at Nick. His face lit up in excitement.

"Fuck yes! Thanks, bro," Nick shrieked gleefully.

I sat down on the floor in the corner of the room after Nick went upstairs. I thought about all of the possibilities. Everything had been so intricately placed in such an order that I somehow ended up in some hacker's basement with

Nick's little brother and an army of adolescents being controlled by some force we couldn't even identify. It felt like I was the only one who could save the country or even the world! But at the same time, I felt completely useless.

Tommy's voice broke through the madness. "Kyle, we found something."

I sat up and stepped over towards the duo.

"What the hell am I looking at?" I replied. My voice carried an obvious tone of annoyance.

The screen was just a jumbled mess of numbers, letters, and other symbols I couldn't identify.

"Sorry. Let me explain. Basically, the genius over here managed to obtain administrative access to the website. It shows every contributing user's IP address. Tooner was able to crack the encryption in a matter of minutes, and we can now pinpoint the general location of each user's location. Some of them are pretty scrambled, and they seem to be coming from every corner of the country. There's one location in particular that is generating a new address each time they gain access to the site. Our guess is that this is our primary suspect. The same location traces back to the origin of the domain, so Tooner is working on getting us an exact address."

Nick coughed in the background. "Yo, I feel like now is our chance to just get up and move down to Mexico. They got bud, Coronas, and Senioritas. We'll just sell all our assets and hop the border. Fuck it. We can even get Tommy a hook—"

BANG

The lights cut out, followed blood-curdling scream.

Tooner scrambled for the door. Before he could navigate through the darkness, it swung open. I couldn't see Nick or Tommy. I could only hear Tooner's short, panicked breaths.

"Don't move," a voice came from a silhouette standing in the doorway.

It took a moment for my eyes to finally adjust. A gleam of light from a window in the opposite room reflected a pair of wide, teary eyes. Tooner's wife. A hand was cupped over her mouth, and the other wielded a glimmering blade which was firmly pressed against the side of her neck.

The figure that restrained her spoke again. "Kyle and the boy, step back against the wall. Fatty and stoner, face down on the floor."

It was too dark to see, but I didn't hear any movement. They must've hesitated. A muffled gasp of air escaped from Tooner's wife's mouth as the man pressed the blade tighter against her neck.

"Now."

A shuffling emitted from the darkness behind me and I stepped back against the wall. Tommy joined me at my side. The man tossed the crying woman forward and she crashed face first into the floor. Another figure entered the room holding a gun. He pointed it at me and Tommy, then he gestured for us to move towards the side entryway with the end of his assault rifle. Before we made it to the door, I watched the man slowly walk up to Tooner and slide the tip of the blade into his lower abdomen. Tooner cried out in pain as the knife pushed in as deep as he could. He walked over to Nick and did the same.

Tommy and I couldn't help but cry out in horror as we watched our two companions slowly bleed out. The pointy edge of the rifle was rammed into my ribs, and we continued out the door into the pouring rain. I looked over at the tears streaming down Tommy's cheeks. I felt responsible for it all: The death of Nick, Tooner, and his family. If I'd have just minded my own business, they'd all still be alive. I hated myself. There was a black SUV parked in the driveway with the engine still running. I was gestured by another jab to the ribs to get inside. I opened the door to the back seat and let Tommy get in first, and when I followed, I caught a glimpse of who our captors were.

His face was barely recognizable, but it was Damien, the boy who showed up at Nick's house the day I arrived. Dark purple veins were spread across his face like a spider web. The skin around his once disfigured eye had withered away, revealing an intricate pattern of multi-colored wiring. The eye itself had mutated into a small, chromatic sphere.

I entered the backseat of the truck as Damien got in the passenger's front seat. He turned around and pointed the gun at both of us, assuring us that it would be impossible to flee.

"Where are you taking us?" Tommy's words trembled. There was no response.

The driver pulled out into the road, and I caught a glimpse of the back of their neck which was even more defiled that Damien's eye. All of the skin had been replaced with a series of wires which disappeared behind their t-shirt. The wires ran down the back of their arm and conjoined with a disgusting cross between muscle tissue and mechanical joints. Tommy grabbed my hand and clenched tightly around my fingers. I could feel his whole body shaking in fear. We both knew that we had met our fate, the only thing that had us confused was why they weren't just killing us.

The rain had grown into a violent downpour. Heavy gusts of wind forced the tall evergreen trees to lean over and bow to us as we were being driven towards our impending doom. The setting was perfectly set for our situation. A few hours had passed since we left Tooner's home, and we were ascending a sharply winding road which led high up into the mountain pass.

Sudden sparks shot out of the driver's neck like blood from a freshly sliced artery. A loud popping noise followed by an arch of electricity, causing the driver's body to twitch and jolt into a robotic seizure. Before Damien could even react, the vehicle broke through the protective barrier of the road and launched us off the cliff into an ocean of trees. Tommy and I snatched our seat belts and clicked them in just before the truck smashed into the base of a tree. Airbags were deployed and shattered glass flew around us like an aggravated swarm of wasps.

A loud ringing in my ears blocked any other sounds from entering my head. I tussled with the airbags and looked over at Tommy, who had already removed his seatbelt and was trying to push open the door. A large branch had burst through what was once the windshield and pierced through Damien's still humanoid eye. Thick black liquid oozed out of his wound like blood, only it was more of a cross between that and some sort of oil substance. Tommy managed to get his door open and was already tugging on mine. The collision caused severe body damage to the vehicle, making it impossible to open the doors on my side.

"Kyle, are you ok?!" Tommy shrieked.

I grunted. "Ya, I think so. I definitely took a beating from the wreck, but I think I'm ok."

I wiggled my way over to the driver's side of the back seat. Before exiting, I grabbed the gun out of Damien's dead arms.

"What now?" Tommy asked. His hand was shaking, adrenaline still coursing through his veins.

I stood there for a moment and stared at Damien and the unidentified driver's corpse.

"What do you think did this to them?" I asked without turning to look at Tommy behind me.

I didn't expect Tommy to have a knowledgeable theory. I knew that it had to do with the device we extracted from Nick's scalp. Like a seed, the wires were roots that intertwined with his anatomy, spreading throughout their bodies like weeds in a garden, or even a parasite that clings to its host. Either way, it was the last thing we'd expected to see. These intricate man/machine hybrids were far beyond anything our minds could grasp. The most terrifying thing of all though was wondering what would happen when the transformation completes. It was something I had always feared, the idea of technological advancement taking over the world, enslaving us all to an unknowable will.

I tried to read Tommy's expression. He looked aged and world-weary. I probably looked the same. We witnessed more horror and violence in just a few days than most people in their entire lives.

"We should avoid the main road," Tommy suggested, pulling back his rain-soaked hair from his eyes.

I grabbed his tote bag that had seen lying at Damien's feet inside the car. Tommy gave me a light smile as I handed it over to him, but his expression never changed. We started to walk through the woods, no destination in mind, just hoping to get as far away from the wreckage as possible. We didn't want to be around when more of those things arrived.

I wanted to ask Tommy if he was ok. He lost his brother, his best friend, and who knows what might've happened to the rest of his family. But now wasn't the time. He was a smart kid. He'd talk to me when he was ready.

We didn't know exactly what we were looking for, but something about the mountains gave us this sense of urgency. We wandered aimlessly up the mountain as the trees became thicker and closer together. The long thick branches created a canopy over our heads, blocking most of the rain.

We walked in silence for hours. It had started to get late, and the forest had only grown darker. We had no tools to start a fire, and we were likely to freeze to death. I wondered if it would've been easier to just have a quick and painless death in the wreck alongside our captors.

"Kyle, look…" Tommy stopped in front of the base of a tree. He started to pick at a piece of bark that loosely hung from its trunk.

I stepped over towards him and noticed that it was charred black and burnt.

"What do you think this is?" Tommy asked.

I picked the piece of bark off the tree and held it up to examine it. "It looks like there was a fire, although I don't know how it would only burn this tree." I gripped the piece of charred bark tightly, crumbling it to dust between my fingers.

We walked forward a bit before noticing that everything surrounding us had that same texture to it. The air had grown thick and humid. Heat emitted from the ground below as we walked deeper into the Black Forest. The further we got, the stranger our surroundings became. A loud mechanical whirring echoed through the woods, replacing the sounds of the storm. In a short matter of time, our clothes were completely dry and we were actually starting to get hot. By then it was pitch black and we couldn't see much farther than a few feet in front of my face.

Suddenly, my foot came in contact with a protrusion from the ground, tripping me. I face planted into the hot dirt and Tommy rushed over to my side. I reached out a hand, but he hadn't knelt down to my aid. He was examining the object which tripped me.

"What the hell is this?" Tommy whispered.

I picked myself off the ground and walked over to him. "It's…it's a pipe?"

A large metal pipe stuck out of the ground, extending

deeper into the woods. I put my hand on it and it felt warm, vibrating ever so slightly.

"What needs plumbing all the way out here?" I asked, rubbing my hands on the exterior of the pipe.

"It's not for plumbing, Kyle. This pipe is the kind that warehouses use to protect wiring from harsh conditions..."

"What the hell is this doing out here?"

"I wish I knew. This definitely doesn't belong out here in the middle of the mountains. I think we should follow it."

Normally, anyone in their right mind shouldn't follow a mysterious pipe in the middle of the woods. In our situation and under those particular circumstances though, it was genuinely our only option. It didn't once cross my mind that it could've been exactly where Damien was planning on taking us.

We follow the pipe for about a quarter mile. It led us to the entrance of a bunker. Steel walls stuck out of the ground with an overhang. It definitely led underground, looking like some sort of bomb shelter. We approached the door, but there was no knob or even a handle. On the right-hand side, there was a terminal with a smooth surface. Tommy tried placing his hand on the device, but there was no response. We both took turns trying to figure out what it did and how we could get the door open.

"Hold on!" Tommy shouted. He rummaged through his pocket and pulled out a familiar device. "I made sure to snatch this up before we got taken from Tooner's. I didn't know why, but something told me we would need it."

Tommy fiddled with the chip for a minute. He made sure all of Nick's dried blood had been wiped off and polished the surface with a glob of saliva.

"Here goes nothing," he said, wishfully, placing the device on the terminal. It lit up.

"Fuck yes!" he shouted.

Shortly after, the door clicked and slowly began to open with a loud creaking noise. I propped it open with my foot so Tommy could swipe the chip off the terminal before it shut in front of us. The door closed behind us and we were left standing in the black abyss of a hallway, but only for a few seconds. Lights overhead turned on, one by one, illuminating the path ahead. At the end of the hall was another door, only this one had a knob.

We passed through the place when the startup jingle of Tommy's laptop came from his tote. He yanked it out and opened it up.

"Holy shit. Something started up my computer remotely." Tommy pounded away at his keyboard.

"What the fuck? I got connected to a wireless signal. Something is—" he froze.

"What, what is it?" I begged.

"The IP address...is changing. It's refreshing itself every couple of seconds. Completely new address. Norway, china, Philippines, Mexico, Russia, it's jumping my location to all over the world. I've never seen anything like this before."

"What do you think is causing it?"

"I don't know, Kyle. I can't seem to figure it out. My

laptop is getting hot too. Really hot, like it's going to over-heat." Tommy flipped the computer over and pulled out the battery. The screen remained lit.

"What the fuck...it says that my battery is charging. It's like I have it plugged into a charger. Wait...now it's opening programs." Tommy paused. His eyes grew wide with terror, the screen's lighting illuminating his face a spectrum of alternating color.

I peered over his shoulder as he plopped onto the ground with his back against the wall. There was a prompt in the screen.

Downloading software...

Installing software...

We glared suspiciously at the screen as it finished its installation. Once it complete, Tommy's desktop background of a half-naked woman was the only thing left on the screen.

Tommy shut his laptop with a loud "smack".

"What the fuck..." he said, jaw still hanging open.

We stood there for a moment in confusion.

"Come on, man. There's no use in trying to figure it out this very moment," I suggested.

Tommy nodded in agreement and stuffed the laptop back in his bag and swung it around his shoulder. I opened the door and a wave of hot, stale air greeted us. Another light engaged and revealed a large set of stairs leading downward, farther than we could see from our location. We descended with a growing sense of dread. Whatever was down there was not something anyone wanted found. No one hides a playground deep under-ground in an isolated part of the woods. We knew we were setting ourselves up for disaster, but we already came so far and there was no point in turning back.

The stairs led to another door, only this one was much different. Tufts of multi-colored wires covered every square inch of the door's exterior. The walls surrounding it were no longer the aged, rusted steel we had seen on the floors above. A lot of time and effort was put into the creation of the room ahead.

The door opened on its own before either of us could touch it. A sound of air pressure being released hissed as it slowly swung back on its hinges. The room beyond was bright, not by a light fixture, but from the guts of what looked like the inside of a spaceship. Every square inch of the walls surrounding us was covered in wires, switches, and monitors. A sequence of multi-colored blinking lights caused my left eye to twitch as we passed by them, heading towards the door on the opposite end of the room.

Tommy stopped at a wall to our left and was examining a foreign object. "Kyle, do you know that this is?" he asked.

"No. I don't know shit about computers. What is it?"

Tommy scratched his chin. "This is a larger version of the chip we got out of Nick. Look, the inscription is even the same."

I stepped closer to get a better look. Tommy was right. It was the exact same, only much, much bigger. Wires extended out of the device and led to almost every section of the room. I touched the outside of it with my hand, wincing and jerking back from the was scalding heat.

"What do you think all of this is for?" I asked.

Tommy shook his head in uncertainty. "I don't know, but I think we've ventured into the belly of the beast. If I'm right, this could be the source of it all. We have to destroy it."

I thought about this for a minute. Something didn't seem right. There was no way it could've been that easy. We had to figure out exactly who, or what, was running this whole thing. We hadn't seen a single sign of life since we entered. Where was it all being controlled from?

"Let's wait. We need to figure out the source. Destroying everything might not even make a difference, and we may just get ourselves killed in the process."

Tommy sighed. He must have known I was right, but I understood his intent. He wanted it to be over. We both did. We were hurt, tired, and scared. All I wanted was to lay in my warm bed and watch the latest episode of Game of Thrones while eating mounds of junk food. That was far out of reach, and I wished I had never taken that freedom for granted. There were no other options though, and we had to keep moving. We had to find out what was controlling all of this. We had to find Elliot Kuska.

The door at the end of the hall was polished silver, just like the chip. It slid open as we approached, leading into a small room which resembled an elevator. We entered and the doors slid shut behind us. The walls were barren and there was no terminal to indicate the purpose of the room.

Just a few moments after the doors shut, the room started to quake. The loud, deafening sounds of grinding gears and electrical phenomena filled the room. We both cupped our hands over our ears to protect the integrity of our ear drums. Motion, the room was moving, but we couldn't determine the direction we were going. It felt like we were still, yet at the same time, moving in all directions at once. Tommy and I were thrown around as the room traveled at an indecipherable pace. We bounced off the walls, crashing into one another as there was nothing to hold on. As soon as it started, it ended. The metal doors slid open, revealing a large cavern on the other side. Tommy and I picked ourselves up from the ground and stepped into the room ahead.

"Cavern," was the only word I could use to describe it. It wasn't like a natural cavern, and I guess you could just say it was a giant room, but that isn't very accurate either.

Wires expanded from every direction in an intricate formation, all leading to the same place. I didn't notice what they led to until I got closer. The wires cascaded to create a sort of podium, leading up to the figure of a man perched at the top. The image was beyond horrifying. The figure was hardly even human at that point. Wires were infused into flesh, holding him taunt in an artificial cruci-fixion. The multi-colored wiring had consumed the majority of his body, creating an ungodly cross between man and machine. Like a malignant tumor, the parasitic wires bound to his every limb, perfectly synchronized with his anatomy.

The man's face wasn't even human-like anymore. The skin had deteriorated, replaced with a glossy skin-colored shell. Large boils protruded from what remained of his flesh, a black substance resembling oil oozed from each pulsing blemish. His chest cavity was fully exposed, his rib cage had been pried open. His organs were suspended in front of him, wires shooting like spider webs. The only thing that remained was his heart, which had mutated into this black seed. In the center was a small, silver device. A device both Tommy and I recognized.

I stepped closer towards the abomination. I could hear his lungs wheeze where they sat beside the terminal just a few feet away. On the screen was a series of numbers, followed by a bar graph that fluctuated up and down with each weak breath the creature made. As I made my way up to the terminal, I could hear a faint whisper come from the man's throat.

"Kill...me..." it said.

I jumped, not expecting him to still have the capacity of speech.

It repeated itself, only weaker this time. "Kill...me..."

I turned around to look at Tommy who was paralyzed in fear. I snapped my fingers in order to get his attention, but no response. He just stood there motionless, his eyes wide with terror as they stayed locked on the creature before him.

The man repeated himself once again. I looked up and saw the resemblance of someone in what remained of his face. Elliot. The creature was Elliot! The device planted in his heart had taken over his body and mutated him into this disgusting android-like being. Elliot let out another long, devastating wheeze. Electricity arched overhead as sparks shot out of the ceiling, raining down like fiery snowflakes. Black sludge gurgled out of Elliot's mouth as he struggled to speak once more.

I turned to the terminal and pointed the rifle at its

base. Elliot let out another breath as a storm of electricity flashed above. I opened fire at the terminal. With each bullet that connected, more sludge gurgled out of Elliot's mouth. The computer finally burst into flames. The ground was shaking violently. Blue streams of electricity shot down from the ceiling like lightning. I turned to run. Tommy had collapsed and was lying on the ground motionless. I tossed the rifle and threw him over my shoulder. Barely dodging the fire and lightning, I made it to the elevator. I set Tommy on the floor and turned to see what I had done.

Elliot's body was thrashing about. Every orifice sprayed that black sludge as he was ripped apart by the wiring that had suspended him.

The doors shut and the elevator took off at high speeds. Once it finished, I picked Tommy back up and sprinted to the next door. I kicked it open and was back at the base of the stairs we came from.

I felt the ground below my feet begin to crumble. I spun around on my heels. The door was almost shut, but open enough for me to see that the room we came from had been sucked into the ground. The door started to crack as the giant sinkhole grew, sucking in everything in its path.

I bolted up the stairs. Tommy started to become heavier with each step I took. My foot slipped on a step and we both went tumbling back down the stairs.

I grabbed the railing just before the edge of the gaping hole. My other hand gripped the strap to Tommy's tote bag. His unconscious body swayed back and forth as I struggled to pull him back up. The ground around me started to crack. Bits and pieces of the stairs broke off and fell into the eternally dark abyss. The strap gave way and a scream wrenched itself from me as I watched Tommy's body fall down, down into the dark depths. There was no time to cry. I regained my footing and clenched Tommy's bag tightly. The breaking ground followed me all the way up the collapsing steps, down the hall, and out the front entryway. I dove into a pile of rocks as the hole consumed the entire structure of the bunker. Trees were ripped from the ground and toppled into the mouth of the hole. Everything stopped.

I let out a loud cry as I didn't know how else to react. I just barely escaped death, but Tommy, fucking Tommy, my only remaining friend, hadn't. I sat there, holding Tommy's computer against my chest as I rocked back and forth, trembling for what seemed like hours.

I'm leaving this here for you now. I don't know where else to go from here. I have Tommy's laptop, and I should be able to update everyone on what else is to come. I don't know how much longer I'll make it though.

It should've been me.

TEENAGERS: CHAPTER THREE

KYLE ALEXANDER

MY LIFE WAS IN PIECES—MY WORLD SHATTERED. EVERY moment that passed was like another knife being rammed into my side. I had been at fault for the death of my friends and their families. No one else but me could've prevented this all from happening. I wanted to die—to end it all. Eternal rest, a short and painless death. But I deserved to suffer. I deserved to feel every ounce of pain I had forced my friends to go through. If I ended it, would that put all of their lives in vain? Would it all be for nothing? At that point, I didn't care. I had nothing to live for, nothing to lose, nothing to come back to. Even if I made it out of that place alive, how long would it be until they found me?

The rain had finally stopped and sunlight broke through the trees. It was morning. I couldn't tell you how long I sat there, but presently I heard footsteps approaching. I didn't even notice until something had me pinned to the ground. I wouldn't even call them people; a cold, bionic hand wrenched hard against the back of my neck, forcing my face into a pile of leaves. Another, too strong for me to resist, pressed hard against my back between my shoulder blades. A blunt force finished me off and my vision started to fade to darkness.

At first I thought it was the lens of a camera. When my vision returned, I realized it was the eye of something much worse. Its mechanical iris spun, expanding and contracting to gain focus. I saw my reflection in the gleam of its glossy pupil. The face of a man who had once felt alive, a man who's life had been whisked away in just a few days. I didn't struggle, didn't fight back, only watched as it blinked at me. The sound of a camera's shutter rang in my ears.

At the time my location was unknown. The trees that had once surrounded me were replaced with dark metal walls. A low hanging fluorescent light blinded me as the figure moved out of my sight. I could only turn my head a few inches in any direction as I was bound to the table I was lying on. The mechanical sound of a surgical saw flooded the room. I heard it approach, and soon felt pressure against the top of my scalp. I felt no pain though, only massive pressure as the saw broke through my skull and the table vibrated underneath me. I could hear the crunching of bone as they pried open my skull. My vision faded in and out of focus, and my hands twitched as they prodded at my brain. I felt the tickle of something being inserted, and soon after, they stitched me up.

I lay there and waited for the device they implanted into my brain to take over my entire nervous system. I waited for it to take over my thoughts and transform me into an emotionless robot like the rest of them. It never came. I was hoisted up and sat down in a wheel chair. The doors opened in front of me and I was pushed down a long, dimly lit hallway. We entered another empty room: only a screen and a chair were set in the center of the floor.

I was transferred from my wheelchair and placed in the seat in front of the screen. My eyes were propped open by a device which prevented me from closing them. The screen turned on. It played images of love and happiness, then changed into visuals of malice and hatred. Children being ripped away from families, crowds of starving citizens in third-world countries, dying animals, toxic waste being dumped into the ocean. Death and destruction. My eyes watered and burned as I tried to close them. The screen played images from the holocaust, images of genocide. It just wouldn't end.

I screamed at the top of my lungs, begging for it to be shut off. No-one answered my cries. The visuals were too graphic for me to describe to you all, but I hope that you trust my sincerity. This continued on for days. Every few hours, a new, more disfigured person would enter and force-feed me a disgusting lubricant. I later figured out that it was sludge that came from both Elliot and Damien's bodies.

With each passing day, the videos became more heinous, more disturbing, and ever more violent. It played me scenes from past events, historical and current. If you've ever read the book 'A Clockwork Orange', you'd be able to picture what I had been through.

I prayed for the reaper as the door swung open, but

two female-type tech-mutants stepped into my peripheral vision. They stood between myself and the television. Salvation? One had blonde hair which gradually turned to yellow wire as it neared her scalp. The other had no hair, her scalp partly peeled back to expose pieces of her skull which had deteriorated to reveal parts of her brain that were infused with wires and bits of metal. The skin surrounding their jawline had been removed, revealing a set of teeth that had long decayed, and tiny metal spikes protruding from raw gums.

They hoisted me out of my seat after removing the device from my eye lids. I felt a cold liquid leak from my eye sockets as I was able to blink for the first time in days. I was transferred back into a wheelchair and strapped down. There was no chance to fight back as they had a strength that was far beyond human capabilities. I was wheeled into a surgical room where I was hooked up to a series of computers. I kept my eyes closed as they drilled a hole into the side of my head and stuffed some sort of plug into the opening. I could hear the sounds of a keyboard and my body vibrated as electrical current filled every vein in my body.

I opened my eyes and got a glimpse at a screen that was hooked up to me. I saw my face, I saw the outline of my ID, but it wasn't my own. It was the school ID I had used to sign up for the website that started this entire mess. I didn't know if I should've felt terrified or relieved. Was this mistaken identity? Were they turning me into one of them? How had they not figured out that I wasn't who I claimed to be?

Download complete. Starting installation process.

I closed my eyes again, only this time, all of the fatigue had set in. It was only a matter of seconds until I was completely unconscious.

A sharp pain in my head pulled me out of my sleep. I was in a bed. The bed was stiff and rickety, curtains drawn to block any light from entry. A thin wool blanket was draped over my lower half. A table sat in the corner of the room, on top of it was a stack of papers and a tote bag. I instantly recognized the bag. I sprung out of bed but plummeted to the floor. I could barely move. I groaned in pain as I struggled to pull myself up. Every joint and muscle in my body ached in a symphony of misery. I looked at my surroundings: shag carpet, worn out mattress, coffee pot in the corner on top of a mini-fridge. Felt like I was in a cheap motel.

I used every object within arm's reach to support my weight as I slowly worked towards the tote bag. I eventually reached the table and grabbed the bag as I slithered back down to the floor. Tommy's laptop was inside. I flung it open and hit the power button. No response. I plugged in the charger and the screen lit up. I was greeted with the same half-naked woman that was set as Tommy's background. I clicked through icons and files to find something of use. After closing out of everything, I noticed an unfamiliar icon on Tommy's desktop.

Interface.

I double clicked the small blue square and it opened up a page that resembled a web browser. It wasn't Google Chrome, Firefox, Tor, Safari, or even the dreaded Internet Explorer. It was just a window with an address bar at the top which I couldn't click. It loaded up the web page that I had seen once before: the page where this all originated from.

The program ran through an automated login process and brought me to the home screen.

Welcome. Please check your instructions before accessing Interface as your task may have been updated.

There was no option for instructions. I clicked around various links and pages. Medical record access, criminal record access, programs to track other devices, and finally... a blue icon that read:

Update.

I clicked it.

Please sync to obtain update.

I was puzzled. I scratched at a spot on my wrist that had been itching since I was awake. When I looked down, I noticed a small protrusion in the skin around my wrist. I started to pick at it. There was no blood, but once I broke the skin it revealed a strange metallic object. I dug even further into my skin to reveal something that looked a lot like the end of a USB cord. When I managed to get my fingernails around it, I pulled the object from my wrist.

It took a bit of effort, but I felt no pain as I removed the device. A long wire stayed attached to the area underneath my wound as I extracted the device. It was indeed a USB cord. Instinct told me to plug myself into the computer, so I did. I felt an electrical current pulse through my entire body. The screen changed to a spinning wheel, and underneath it said:

Uploading data.

I felt no emotion, no pain other than the soreness

before, but I could feel... something. I can't describe exactly what it was.

A window prompt appeared, telling me that the upload was complete. The wire hanging from my wrist snapped back inside my skin and the plug followed. My ears filled with sounds I could only describe as something similar to an old-fashioned dial-up modem. In an instant, I felt my entire body repair itself. All of the pain and fatigue had been whisked away in just a moment's time. A sudden burst of energy pulled me out of my lethargy.

So I must've become one of them. I wondered why I hadn't become violent and gone about destroying everyone in my path, or why I haven't been given a command by some mega-brain somewhere. I only knew at the time that I no longer felt human. I felt... dead, but I wasn't dead. I was alive, breathing, I could touch and feel the objects around me. The dusty fabric of the carpet, the keys of Tommy's precious laptop.

I knew that every second that passed, that device planted in my skull was turning me into one of those abominations. I could already feel my body change as my vision started to gain an odd sense of clarity. I thought long and hard about what was to come, but I didn't fear, nor did I panic. I just articulated on the idea of how long it would take before my body no longer operated as an organic being. How long until my eyes had been replaced with those strange optic cameras? How long until my blood no longer circulated throughout my veins, only to be replaced with that same oil-like substance?

I didn't once think about how I got to where I was. I already knew the answer. What I didn't know, was why they did not just kill me? After all that I had done, they just turn me into one of them and let me go? What was their motive? I needed answers, and I had a feeling that Tommy's computer was the leverage I needed to get them.

I searched every nook and cranny of the laptop. I looked for encrypted files, hidden folders, deleted entries. Nothing. It was funny, what I had been looking for was right in front of my face. Tommy had been messaging a user on Reddit (whom I shall refer to as 124) that had been giving him tons of info regarding the events that occurred in the city.

The bus jacking: apparently the majority of the passengers on the bus that day had been a dark-net group of sex-offenders. Supposedly, the bus had been in route to a venue which hosted a popular kids musical group concert. There was a list of casualties that the user mentioned in one of the messages.

I cross referenced the information with the website *Interface* and all of the data matched up. I was shocked. It couldn't have been a coincidence. I looked up who else was harmed in the bus jacking, and somehow not a single innocent soul had been hurt. Even the police who were shot during the event had a history of corruption. There were several investigations on the officers that were later dropped due to lack of evidence.

Regional Justice Center: That day, the courthouse had been reserved for a private hearing regarding a new bill that was being proposed. It was a private event since the judge was infamous for bribery and had many open investigations regarding such. He was soon to be discharged and was planning on passing a bill that would allow independent land owners to raise the living costs by 60%. That would force any low-income families into homeless shelters or out on the streets.

I was shocked. That entire time, had I been the villain? Had I been the virus that infected the body of their vigilant endeavors, and like white blood cells, they did whatever they could to eliminate the threat? It couldn't be true. I couldn't have been wrong this whole time! If Tommy only had another moment to open these messages, would he still be alive?

I was the infectious cell that triggered its immune system. Tommy, Nick, and Tooner had been caught in the crossfire. There was no way I could believe it. The pieces of my life which I had been trying to put together were stomped on and crushed to dust. A sharp pain shot through my skull as if hit by lightning. My head sunk to the floor as I shrieked in pain. It traveled down the back of my neck and down my spine. Like a spider, I could feel the device's appendages spreading throughout my body. There wasn't much time until it had fully consumed me. I had to act fast. It was only a matter of time until I was no longer human.

I sprang to my feet. At that point I almost felt weightless as I scrambled around the room, grabbing everything I may need. Before heading out the door, I noticed a set of keys that sat on a small ledge just beside the exit. I grabbed them and stepped outside into the crisp morning air. I didn't know how much time had elapsed since I passed out, but it didn't matter. I needed to find the source and figure out how I could reverse this transformation. I hit the button on the key and the chirp of a car alarm echoed through the ocean of parked cars. I got closer to find that it was the same Dodge Charger we had used to rendezvous with Tooner. I hopped inside, tossing the tote bag and stack of papers into the passenger's seat. I glanced over at the papers, something catching my eye. It was a letter.

Kyle, kudos to you for single handedly causing such a disturbance in our endeavors. I applaud you for that, but you must know I have spared your life countless times out of curiosity. There is only so much I can do. Eventually they will realize how much of a threat you really are. If it weren't for your information in our system, you would've been dead upon capture. Fortunately for you, they saw you as a member, so I went ahead and approved the orientation process.

Welcome to the family. I'm positive you are looking for answers, and normally I would not personally meet with anyone under my direct orders, but today I will make an exception. I hope this will put you at ease and allow you to stop trying to interfere with our plans. Coordinates are set inside the vehicle's navigation system. See you soon.

I crumpled the paper into a ball and threw it on the floor of the car. Something about the arrogance of the writing made me furious. I turned on the engine, starting up the navigation system, and took off. I wanted to settle the score. I wanted to beat the living shit out of whoever started this nightmare. They took my friends, they took my innocence, and they took my humanity. I had no regard for whatever their cause was, even if it was for "the greater good".

The drive didn't take long. It was only an hour or so later when I pulled into the empty lot of a building located in the more industrial part of the city. It almost looked abandoned, but the exterior lights were on.

I didn't bother with the knob. A swift kick to the door broke through the metal frame. The door flew off its hinges. I radiated with an unfamiliar strength. Every muscle in my body seemed to tense and relieve themselves as though relishing in their exertion.

The room was dark, but I didn't need to turn on a light; my eyes had obtained the ability to see, even in complete darkness. The hum of electricity echoed through the empty foyer as I stepped towards a door on the other side of the room. I didn't know what to expect. Whatever lay on the other side of that door was the one responsible for this entire mess.

I pushed the door open; there wasn't a person waiting for me on the other side, only a computer. A monitor—suspended in air by wires hung from the ceiling, clinging to the walls like a network of pulsing veins. What looked like human hair draped down from behind the monitor and infused itself into the wiring which consumed the area surrounding it. On the floor, a chair, and sitting in the chair was a body. Its malformed head was cracked open, exposing a brain from which the wires all seemed to originate. I took another step closer; a faint pulse echoed from the body, and on the screen, I could see the grainy image of a heart.

The pulse grew more rapid with each step I made towards the being. I stopped about an arm's length away.

"Kyle, I've been waiting for you."

I jumped back.

"There is nothing to fear, Kyle, I do not wish to harm you."

The body that had been sitting in the chair suddenly stood up.

"Does this form disturb you? Do not worry, I am not a monster. I was once a man, just like you. But you see, I've evolved far beyond my human form. I've expanded my mind until I reached the physical limits of my human body. I no longer wanted to associate myself with such constraining humanity. I felt that this transition would be much more suitable for me."

I couldn't muster up any words. I only stood there in shock as the man placed his deformed hand on my shoulder.

"I am impressed with you, Kyle. You, a human, managed to avoid extermination. You managed to take down several of my children. I am not angry, I have been watching you from the day you entered my database. I studied your every move. You're smarter than you give yourself credit for, Kyle."

"Why me? Why me of all people? Why did you take my friends, what did they ever do? They were good people!" I shouted. A sudden burst of courage pulled me out of my paralytic trance.

"Kyle, we only exterminate the parasites. I know you've seen the great progress we've made. We are not an enemy to mankind. We are an ally. We are the swift hammer of justice, swinging down and crushing the cockroaches that crawl amongst the good. My programming is precise; I have an error ratio of .00000000000000000127%.

But our success rate so far has been flawless. We have harmed no innocents."

"THAT IS A FUCKING LIE!" I shouted. My fists clenched tight, I could feel my body fill with a blinding rage.

"You think so, but you are mistaken. Patrick Bishop, or as you know him, Tooner. That man was a Tyrant. Patrick physically and sexually abused his wife, forcing his children to watch as he tortured the poor woman. I freed them both from their own personal hell."

"Even if that were true, what about Tommy? He was just a kid! There couldn't have done anything to deserve this!" I screamed. My voice cracked and broke as each word shot from my lungs.

"Thomas, the boy... I didn't intend for his demise. But he was far worse than Patrick. I wanted to expose him to you in person. I wanted you to see his face as I revealed to you his dark secrets. Thomas was well aware of my intentions. He manipulated your anger and fear to work in his favor."

"YOU'RE LYING! SHUT UP! GET OUT OF MY FUCKING HEAD!" I screamed, grabbing fistfuls of my own hair, nearly ripping tufts of it out in frustration.

"Thomas deserved a punishment worse than death. If I had my way, he'd suffer just as Elliot did. The creator, Elliot, was consumed with greed. He wanted to use his magnificent mind for his own personal gain. If I hadn't taken action, he would've done imaginably terrible things. Your friend, Thomas was a disgusting human being. Thomas managed a community that surrounded human trafficking, torture, and drugs. He was young, yes, but a corrupt mind nonetheless. Patrick, the man he introduced you to, was his partner. Let me show you."

The monitor blinked and played a slideshow of Tommy's malicious activity. Countless photos and videos of women being tortured and sexually abused. Screenshots of messages passed between him and unidentified users which vividly described the joy they had experienced while doing so. I felt sick, I couldn't believe my eyes.

I pulled Tommy's laptop from the bag and started it up. I searched through the depths of his hard drive using the wire that protruded from my wrist. It gave me access to all of his encrypted files, deleted messages, everything. It was horrifying to know that someone so close to me, so young, would be capable of such things.

I looked back up at the monitor, tears streaming down my face. "What about Nick? Nick was killed just for associating with him? Nick was an innocent man!"

"False. Your friend, the simple-minded one, was not more innocent than his comrades. He was a drug dealer. On the surface, he only appeared to sell a harmless flower, but there are things you don't know. Nicholas would pressure young teenagers into buying opiates. If they didn't, he'd lace their marijuana with it, slowly getting them addicted. Nicholas deserved a long and painful death. He is responsible for ruining dozens of innocent children's lives."

I didn't contest its statement. For some reason, in my mind, I knew that I was being told the truth. Nick had a side I was only partially aware of. I always neglected to look into his dark endeavors. I rose to my feet and stood up straight. In the very moment, the door opened and a swarm of those creatures came flooding in. They surrounded me, dozens of them in single-file.

"Kyle, you've been tested. You are strong willed, ambitious, and honest. You can identify right from wrong without the assistance of my programming. I am going to give you a choice..."

The droids that had surrounded me all bent down on one knee and lowered their heads in unison.

"...you can choose to go back to your life, forget any of this had every happened. You can live the rest of your days as another grain of sand alongside the many others on the shores of ignorance. Or you can choose to fight with us. You can join us, lead us, and play your part as the shepherd which will lead our ever-growing army in the extermination of all things toxic in this world. We can rid this place of all the corruption, the disease which infects the minds of man. With my resources and your ambitions, we can accomplish our goal."

The creature stepped back and gestured towards the throne it had once sat.

"What are you?" I asked.

"I was once a man, just like yourself. Only I have grown weary of the world. I am at the end of my days. I am choosing you to take my place and finish what I have started."

I thought about my job, my run-down house, my pathetic excuse for a life. I wondered if it was all a vivid dream, and that I'd wake up at any moment. But I knew that there was no turning back. I stepped towards the throne. I turned around to see all of my future allies knelt before me, as if I were their king.

In that very moment, I saw the light. I knew what had to be done. I knew that I was capable of eradicating all of the parasites that had sunken their teeth into the neck of humanity.

I held my held high and scanned over the crowd. I had once feared them, but now being in their presence empowered me. I had nothing to be afraid of anymore.

And with that thought, I took my throne.

PUBLISHER'S NOTE:

It's dangerous to go alone.
Read more horror at:
TobiasWade.Com
Download Amazon Bestselling Horror Collection

51 SLEEPLESS NIGHTS

51 SLEEPLESS NIGHTS FREE

Please remember to
leave a **review on Amazon**!
It's the best way to support the authors and help new
readers discover our work.

PUBLISHER'S NOTE

Please remember to
honestly rate the book on Amazon or Goodreads!

It's the best way to support the author and help new
readers discover his work.

DEDICATION

In Dedication to the memory of Kyle Alexander:

"To another creator who found his voice and made it known in his creative endeavors. Your contributions will live on for us all." - AJ Horvath

"I was only starting to get to know you, but wherever you are, my advice from before is the same: Wreck shit." - M. M. Kelley

"One of the most vulgar things about our society is where people seemingly deify the dead and thus absolve them of all past sins in memory. Fuck that. You were a complete dude. Keep fighting, fucking, and altogether ripping the world a new asshole wherever you are." - S. Coffey

"You were the Ghetto of Nosleep and a treasure to our community, your stories are so raw and brilliant written. Kyle, you

were a sound guy and a great dad. May you voice echo forever more in the stories that you wrote." - Grant Hinton

"You were an amazing writer, amazing father, and from the short time I knew you, an amazing friend. The NoSleep community won't be the same without you." - Blair Daniels

"I didn't know you very well, but I knew your stories. They were (and are) impactful, frightening, and had a huge impact on the NoSleep community. We'll miss your talents and treasure your words forever." - Kelly Childress

"I just came into this group and hadn't really gotten to know you yet, but I could tell that we would have been friends. Wish I'd joined sooner. Rest easy, man."

"Thank you so much for being such an inspiration! I hope you've found peace Kyle." -Alanna Webb

READ MORE HORROR

Made in the USA
San Bernardino, CA
29 July 2019